COINCIDENTAL ENTANGLEMENT

Lillie Timmons

We have the power to alter the plasticity of our brains. And if you maintain an open mind to the evolution of humans, you may find when we can use our entire brain, the Impossible becomes Possible.

- Lillie M Timmons

TABLE OF CONTENTS

ACKNOWLEDGMENT

The character Dr. Wayne Riggert, D.D.S., is based on a real person. Though I have taken artistic license with his character the following is true.

My dentist, Dr. Riggert, is appreciated for the excellent care he extends to his patients. He participates in advanced courses for the latest, and greatest technology, and procedures. Traveling to third-world countries, he extends free care to impoverished people. In addition, he is an accomplished photographer exhibiting his exceptional talent in framed photos of his travels in his office.

Dr. Riggert retired from his practice early to pursue quality time with his family, travels, photography, and other interests. He is profoundly missed.

CHAPTER 1

Gabriella

I've been sitting on the edge of my bed, in the dark, waiting for the guard's shift change. I stand and tiptoe to the open window, looking out, making sure no one is in sight. I drop my suitcases out the window as they make a thud when they hit the thick grass below.

Holding my breath and looking out for the guards, I lower my cloth ladder made from my bed sheets. I carefully secure the ends of my sheet to the legs of my dresser and pull as hard as I can on the knots I tied, ensuring they won't come undone.

I lift my right leg out of the window straddling the ledge, placing my foot in the first loop. I apply my weight to test for strength, then bring my left leg out placing it in the second loop. I'm at the mercy of my own device as I let go of the window ledge and hold onto the sheet.

Carefully, I place one foot at a time in one loop after another, traveling down the length of the sheet. I feel unsteady as the cloth gives and folds under my weight, but still holds me.

I make it past the second floor when I come to the end of my sheet and jump the rest of the way. I successfully dropped without injury landing behind the shrubbery, but I'm still not clear. I've only just made it out of my room. I have a way to go yet.

Grabbing my suitcases, I connect the smallest to the larger suitcase with the telescoping handle. I make my way several feet across the yard to the gate hidden within an ivy-covered wall. I place my hand through the vegetation feeling my way until I grip the handle and pull with all my might. It's been years since this gate has been used, but it opens just enough for me and my suitcase to slip through.

Once I'm on the other side of the gate I make my way past the guard station by staying in the shadows and between the bushes and trees. Entering the forest at the back of the estate, I follow a path until I see the first white luminescent ribbon tied to a branch. It glistens as my flashlight passes over it. It is the first marker directing me through the dense woodland.

Walking for some distance, I continue to take the ribbons off the branches as I find them. It would mean death to anyone suspected of assisting me if it were discovered I had help escaping. I finally make my way to a clearing when I see a car parked on the dirt road.

I approach cautiously when I can see my cousin sitting in the driver's seat. When I look through the window, Julia turns, smiles at me, and tells me to get in. We hug with tears in our eyes careful not to get too excited at this point because we still have a way to go.

Julia turns the key in the ignition and the car comes to life with a slight humming sound. I can hardly hear the engine as this is an electric car. She drives slowly without headlights, and the car glides over the dirt road with barely a sound until we approach the main road. Turning on the headlights, Julia turns onto the highway, picks up speed, and heads toward the airport.

I climb into the back seat to give myself more room while I change clothes. Having nothing suitable to climb down a two-story mansion, I was forced to wear my pajamas and sock-slippers during my escape.

Once I turned 18, I was forced to wear clothing appropriate for a princess. For the last 3 years, the only clothing I've been permitted to wear is dresses, skirts and blouses, evening clothes, and heeled shoes.

Lots of uncomfortable heeled shoes. I can hardly wait to shop for clothes as a free person.

Changing into a pale blue sleeveless sheath dress with a matching jacket and thigh-high hosiery, my only choice for footwear is uncomfortable stilettos.

Brushing my hair to the side, I hold it in place with a pearl and diamond comb. Making use of the makeup Julia brought me, I apply mascara to my lashes, a mauve gloss to my lips, and a little blush to my cheeks. Excitedly, I think about the possibility of a new future. One free of my father and the mafia.

Julia hands me my new ID and passport. She includes a business card with a date and time for an interview with Holbrook and Sons. This will put my education to use for the first time, as an accountant. The new name selected for me is Ella. Pretty safe and clever because people who are close to me call me Ella, short for Gabriella. My last name is no longer Farina. From this day forward I'm Ella Wingate.

My father has made it impossible for me to feel anything but resentment and revulsion toward him. I never want to see him again. He sold me to a 75-year-old man to excuse a debt he owed. He used me as if I were a piece of property he could exchange for a debt. The wedding is set for next weekend.

How could my father do this to me? I've never been on a date or permitted to be with a boy ever. He expected me to remain a virgin for a fat disgusting old man. He, himself, won't date a woman over the age of 25. I'd love to see him chained to a wall with a hideous fat bald woman with yellow teeth and body odor forcing herself on him. But of course, that would never happen. Only in my dreams.

Driving an hour on the freeway, we finally reach the airport. Julia watches for cameras as she pulls past the passenger exit area making sure we're not captured by surveillance cameras. We hug each other when I tell her I'll call her when I get settled with our code, a wrong number call from a public phone. It would be dangerous for her if anyone finds out we have communicated with each other.

I'm going to New Orleans hoping I'm not discovered in an area where my father has no business, influence, or friends. He has often said, "I wouldn't be caught dead in that gawd-forsaken city." It's the only reason I have chosen to start my new life there.

"Julia, how do I look?"

"Ella, you look like a million bucks. You always have."

"Thank you so much for helping me. Wish me luck."

"It was my pleasure and I wish you all the very best. Be careful and stay safe."

Closing the car door behind me, I walk to the porter, handing him the luggage ticket for my flight. He tags my large suitcase and puts it on the carousel ensuring it will be loaded on my plane. I tip him and continue to the first-class lounge with my carry-on in tow. This is an early bird flight and I have only a half hour before boarding for New Orleans.

I take a quick look around the lounge seeking out any signs of my father's guards and anyone who looks familiar. Feeling like everything can come to a screeching halt at any time, I convince myself to just stay calm. Ordering and sipping on a cappuccino, I hope I can handle the caffeine once it takes hold of my already adrenalin-overloaded body.

My eyes gravitate to the entrance when three large men in expensive tailored suits enter the lounge. My heart skips a beat in fright, and I nearly drop my coffee as these men are positively mafia.

When you're raised in a crime family, you recognize the men a mile away.

The tall man in the middle, a gorgeous devil in disguise, is definitely the head honcho with his guards flanking him. He's a man of distinction who commands attention. He's beautiful with his dark hair and sky-blue eyes, but he reeks of danger. He exudes the confidence of a Mafia Don as all eyes turn to him.

Standing slowly, and looking down, I turn away from them, walking to the front of the lounge. Taking a seat with my back to them, I'm hoping against hope they don't notice me. Lifting my carry-on case, I place it on the seat next to me attempting to discourage others from sitting there.

Not recognizing these men, I wonder if they know my father. They must know him, he owns this part of Nuevo Laredo, Mexico, and beyond. Maybe they're here doing business with him. That's certainly a possibility. There aren't many in this area not doing business in one way or another with Leo Farina.

My nerves are at high alert causing me to jump at the sound of someone dropping their case. I look instantly and realize it is nothing to be concerned with. I must try to calm myself while waiting to board.

The wait isn't long when the door to the lounge is opened by a steward who steps to the side ready to receive our boarding passes. I'm the passenger closest to the door so I stand and step forward pulling my carry-on case behind me. Handing the steward my boarding pass he tears off his stub, returning the rest to me.

Continuing to walk down the passageway, I'm greeted by the flight attendant and the captain as I enter the plane. Looking at the number on my ticket I'm elated to discover I'm seated by the window.

As I attempt to place my carry-on in the overhead compartment, one of the large men I saw earlier steps behind me pushing my case into the compartment. I didn't realize these men were that close to me. Thanking him, trying not to show fear, I take my seat, noticing the soft leather I'm sitting on. I buckle my safety belt in preparation for takeoff and my four-hour trip as I look out the window.

CHAPTER 2

Anthony

My eyes immediately settled on this beautiful young kitten the minute I walked into the first-class lounge. This blond beauty isn't using her obvious good looks to her advantage. Instead of taking the center of attention, she tries to be inconspicuous, attempting to blend into the crowd, which is ridiculous. There isn't anyone in the crowd that can measure up to her.

She seems unsure of herself and doesn't project self-confidence, nor does she seem experienced. I'd like to get to know her. It interests me to think of the possibility of finally meeting a girl who isn't flirting with every man she sees. As I observe her, she acts indifferent and avoids looking at any men at all. At least in this lounge.

For some reason that draws my attention. I'm usually overwhelmed by the women who find me appealing. My friends are constantly joking about how the women are so attracted to me that I need to beat them off with a stick. They like hanging out with me because they know they'll eventually end the evening with women I have no interest in.

But this young beauty saw me come in and, incredibly, she stood and walked in the opposite direction. I know she got a good look at me because I got a good look at her. I'm intrigued. What's her name and what's her story? Does she have a boyfriend? She must, but I don't want to think about her with another man because I'll eliminate him for sure.

She sits purposely with her back to me so I can't make eye contact with her. There's no way I can get her attention and that irritates me.

She doesn't know who I am. But I'm wondering if that would even make a difference if she did. This one doesn't seem to impress easily.

As far as I can see she doesn't seem to be traveling with anyone. Reacting with alarm when someone dropped their briefcase, she looked to see what it was but didn't look back far enough to see me. She's nervous. Is she running or hiding from someone? That's a real possibility and makes me even more curious. That would explain why she's ignoring me.

I'm getting a call. Grabbing my cell out of my pocket, I answer, "Angelo, what is it? … What's the damage? … Did we lose any men? We won't be there for about four hours; we're waiting to board our flight now. Put them on ice till I get there."

I motion for Dominic and Giorgio to lean in, and I tell them there's been an attack at our port. "We've lost some of our products, but we didn't lose any men. They're holding two soldiers for us, so we'll be taking care of business when we get there." As I put my cell phone back in my pocket, I think.

I'll have to change my plans. I thought I might ask Pretty Kitty out for dinner when we land. I would have made it hard for her to say no, but I'll catch up with her later. I'll make her an offer she can't refuse.

The steward opens the door motioning for passengers to step forward to show their boarding passes. My kitten reaches the doorway first. I'll hold back a pace or two. I don't want to make her nervous. I'll take my time and act indifferent and uninterested. But she's added interest in what otherwise would have been a boring flight.

Gabriella

As people entered the plane, taking their seats, the large man who helped with my carry-on was about to sit next to me. His boss, Big, Bad, and Delicious, indicated with a nudge on his guard's arm he would be seated elsewhere. My heart is pumping erratically cautioning a clear and present danger. The man obviously in charge then took the seat next to mine. *Is this where it ends? Have I been found out?* Finding it hard to breathe, I try to calm myself.

Out of my peripheral vision, I see him looking at me. I quickly gaze out the window and stare aimlessly at the baggage being loaded onto the plane. This man's exquisite aftershave both attracts and overwhelms me emitting his wealth, power, and peril. I'm feeling queasy from the anxiety brought on by his presence.

I'm thankful these first-class seats are so large and comfy. Having room to slide across the luscious leather, I manage to leave a gap between us as I lean closer to the window. The beautiful man next to me, however, fills his seat with his large muscular body.

After the last passenger enters, the cabin door is shut and secured. The captain announces through the plane's PA system in a deep soft voice, "Ladies and Gentlemen welcome aboard, and please buckle your seat belts. We'll be taking off shortly. The sky is clear, and it should be a comfortable flight to New Orleans." As the plane's engine roars, I feel myself becoming nauseous.

I am not sure if it is a result of my fearful reaction to the man sitting next to me or if it is the plane starting to move on the runway, but I quickly grab for the puke bag and bend forward ready to lose the contents of my stomach.

The plane begins to move down the runway as the engines roar loudly, picking up speed. I feel like I'm riding on a missile about to explode when the man next to me tells me,

"Bend over place your head close to your knees and take deep breaths."

The plane lifts off and is in flight climbing higher and higher. My ears start popping, I am still clutching the puke bag in my right hand, as I grip the arm of my seat with my left. The man places his hand over my hand.

When the plane levels off, I sit upright without incident and lay back in my seat. Embarrassed and not looking in his direction, I softly say, "Thank you." He keeps his hand in place over mine a while longer then finally pats my hand before he removes his.

"Do you feel better?"

"Yes, thank you."

The captain is heard saying, "You may unbuckle your seat belts and are now free to walk about the cabin." The flight attendant approached us and asked what we would like to drink. They both look at me when I stutter, responding, I … I'll take a 7UP please."

How embarrassing. I know they saw my take-off moment, but it's not like I made a scene or anything. The man orders a bourbon as the flight attendant smiles coyly at him. Returning with our drinks, she's definitely interested in this handsome man, understandably, as her expressions and movements are rather obvious. There is nothing subtle about her.

After the flight attendant hands Tall Dark and Dangerous his bourbon, she bends over him to hand me the 7UP. She is just about to brush herself against him when he intercepts her by taking the 7UP from her and handing it to me. I can't help but notice the tell-tale tattoo of a wolf head on his hand. There's no doubt in my mind he's mafia.

Does he know about me? Is there a contract for my return? Is he working for my father or my betrothed? I need my heart to stop pounding so fast. *I'll learn if I've been recognized and my fate when we land.*

He looks at me and says, "My name is Anthony what's yours?"

When he speaks to me my heart starts up again, beating uncontrollably as I feel myself turn beet red. I find it hard to breathe as I say, "Hi, ah, my name is Ella … Ella Fa ..Wingate."

Oh my gosh, I almost said my real last name. Living with an assumed name is going to take some practice if I intend to live a free life. We finish our drinks, the plastic cups are disposed of, and we settle in for the flight.

However, I've been sitting here for a while with a full bladder and hesitate to make a move knowing I'll have to climb over Anthony. I fail to act for far too long, and my bladder is signaling an SOS. The situation is urgent now, and I can't hold it any longer.

Standing I apologize and excuse myself for disturbing him. As he moves his leg, I move too quickly in front of him not giving him time enough to move his other leg. I find myself between his legs. *Oh, my gawd, can it get any worse?*

My back is to him, and I'm holding onto the seat in front of him when he grabs me by the waist. I'm frozen, unable to move as he moves his left leg out from in front of him. Reaching down I push his left hand off my waist as I misstep into the aisle, but I quickly regain my footing. *These darn high-heeled shoes.* Feeling myself blush in embarrassment, never once looking directly at his face, I begin to walk quickly to the aircraft lavatory.

CHAPTER 3

Gabriella

Reaching my intended destination, and locking the door behind me, I relieve my bladder and wash and dry my hands, but now I dread returning to my seat. I stand at the sink looking in the mirror trying to decide what I should do. *There is nothing I can do. I'm in an airplane thousands of miles in the sky locked in a tiny lavatory.*

I was standing here for some time when someone knocked on the door. Immediately unlocking and opening the door, I find the flight attendant standing in front of me as she says,

"The gentleman sitting next to you is concerned. He asked me to check on you to see if you're all right. Do you need anything?"

"Oh no, I'm fine thank you for asking."

She stands there waiting for me to exit. *Crud, he asked her to check on me.* Now I must go back and sit next to Mr. Grabby Hands. Following the attendant to first class, noticing there are no empty seats in coach I can slip into, I dread crawling over him again.

To my surprise, he's standing in the aisle waiting for me. I can't avert my glance in time as I look into his absorbing blue eyes. Immediately looking down, thanking him I quickly return to my seat. I hope he doesn't talk to me. He makes me too tense wondering if he knows who I am. He turns and looks at me saying,

"Is New Orleans your home or are you just visiting?"

My heart skips a beat, as I turn my head in his direction careful not to look into his eyes. I respond,

"It's going to be my home. I just moved there."

"Do you have family there?"

Oh, my gawd stop asking me questions. I respond with a "Hmm."

"Was that a yes, or no?"

Crud! I'm panicking now and thinking about how I should answer. *Do I lie or tell the truth? A lie might come back to bite me.* "No, I ... I don't have family in New Orleans."

If he's waiting for me to ask questions about him, it's going to be a long wait. I don't want to know anything about him.

Anthony

My Ella is very shy. I think I like that in this kitten. She's not avoiding me; she just isn't comfortable talking to strange men. I have a feeling she's this way with all men. That makes her even more attractive to me. I feel aroused because her actions are submissive, never looking into my face. Has she been raised this way?

I would enjoy being Ella's teacher, instructing her, commanding her, and if she doesn't comply, even punishing her. This could be the girl and the relationship I've been looking for. This could be the queen I've been seeking.

"Ella, do you have a job?"

"Almost. I mean, I have an interview tomorrow morning."

"Who are you interviewing with?"

"Holbrook and Sons. For an accounting position."

"An accountant! That's impressive. I would not have guessed that as your occupation."

"I always liked numbers. Equations are like a puzzle that I enjoy solving. The harder the problem, the better I like it."

Very good, I found something that excites her to make her open up. She's finally showing interest in our conversation especially when talking about her expertise. This kitten is special. I wish I didn't have to take care of business when we land. I'm not letting her get away from me so easily though. I'll have Giorgio shadow her and keep an eye on her for me.

A girl like Ella alone in a city like New Orleans will need protection anyway. I have a feeling that she's running from something. It doesn't add up for a naïve pretty young woman like Ella deciding to move to a place like New Orleans for what – a fresh start. A fresh start from what?

"Do you have a boyfriend, Ella?"

"Um, …"

"You didn't answer my question. Do you have a boyfriend?"

"Um … Sort of …well … not in the conventional sense. I mean we are, were, friends, but we were never permitted, I mean we never went out … on a date."

"You said you weren't permitted. What did you mean?"

"Sorry, I misspoke. I meant to say we went to different colleges and a long-distance relationship was impossible."

"Did you like him, Ella?"

"He is a very nice boy. And yes, I like him a lot."

It sounds like she wasn't permitted to have boyfriends. There's only one family that has that much power in bringing up their daughters. And they're successful in ensuring their daughters remain innocent for one purpose – to align two families with an arranged marriage. That and her behavior make me feel she's been raised to be submissive. I could be wrong, but I don't think so.

"Do you write or talk to one another or ever see each other?"

She shakes her head and looks out the window. My cue to stop asking about him. I got my answer anyway. Their relationship was cut off before it began.

Ella could be running from an arranged marriage, if so, it won't take long for them to find her. Wingate must be an assumed name because there is no syndicate with the name Wingate. But in Laredo, the Farina mafia is named after Leo Farina. Is Ella his daughter? I didn't even know he had a daughter. If so, he has kept her existence hidden well.

This could be problematic for me. But I've made my decision. Whoever she is, she's mine.

"Where are you staying Ella?"

She looks at me with a strained look on her face, then turns her head away from me, looking out the window again.

"Ella, I know my question seems very personal but there are places in New Orleans where a young woman like yourself should not be staying. Please, tell me where you're staying."

Good, she's going to cooperate. Opening her purse, Ella pulls out a folded piece of paper. She looks at it and then hands it to me. Looking at the address, I realize she's staying at the short-term rental cottages. Not wonderful but not as bad as it could have been. It's close

17

to Holbrook and Sons. She didn't do this planning on her own. She most definitely had help.

"Ella, this area isn't as bad as some, but I wouldn't stay there too long. Use it as a transitional place only and move to an apartment as soon as you can."

She nods, thanking me, taking the paper from me, and returning it to her purse. She seems distressed and uncomfortable answering my questions. Maybe I should hold back on the questions for now. She just put on her earphones and turned the screen on in front of her to watch a movie.

About an hour into her movie, I notice she's not even watching her screen. She's gazing out the window. I think this girl is in trouble and worried I've recognized her. I don't know who she is yet, but I intend to know all about her soon.

Our plane lands and people stand gathering their carry-on luggage and personal items. Those of us in first class are exiting first, all except Ella. Presumably, Ella's lingering in place so she's far behind me and the last person off the plane. I'll give her the space she needs and a false sense of security for now. Giorgio will be watching over her until I'm able to return.

CHAPTER 4

Gabriella

Purposely lingering behind the crowd, I'm the last person off the plane. I would have hesitated longer, but the captain was waiting for me to exit. Removing my carry-on case from the compartment above, I head for the luggage reclaim area where passengers are waiting for our luggage to appear. Carefully looking around at the crowd, I realize Anthony and his guards are nowhere to be seen.

I'm relieved they're gone; he doesn't know who I am after all. All that fear for nothing. I could have enjoyed the attention of an exceptionally handsome man. He was nice to me. But I need to put that out of my mind he's mafia. Not just any mafioso but I think a Don. I reach for my suitcase, pull it out of the conveyor, and walk to the exit.

Continuing to look around, seeing if I recognize anyone, I walk toward the line of taxi cabs parked one behind the other. The porter opens the door of the first taxi for me. Thanking him I tip him just before entering as he lifts my suitcase and places it on the floor of the taxi. Tipping his hat he says,

"I hope you enjoy your stay in New Orleans, miss."

I respond, "Thank you, I intend to."

Opening my purse and looking at the paper, I repeat the address to the taxi driver. He nods and takes off. It's quite hot today so I slip off my jacket. That helps slightly with my comfort, but I need to buy some casual clothes before I do anything else.

I asked the taxi driver if there were any clothing stores nearby. He informs me there is a boutique a block from where I'm staying. That's wonderful news as I settle back and get comfortable.

When we stop in front of the cottages, I pay the driver as he gets out of the taxi and carries my suitcase to my door. I thank him as he nods and walks away. *Wow, that's some service! Having never ridden in a taxi before, I'm wondering if all taxi drivers are that polite and accommodating.*

I unlock the door to my cottage and look around. It's a little nicer than I expected. It has faux wood-covered floors adorned with throw rugs, acceptable furniture in the living room, a small table and chairs in the kitchen, a stocked kitchen with cooking and eating utensils, a small bathroom with a shower stall, a double bed and dresser, and a closet in the bedroom.

My bedroom at home is larger than this entire unit, yet I'm excited about being here as I wheel my suitcases to the bedroom. This cottage represents freedom in which I can come and go as I please. I place my suitcases on the upholstered bench at the foot of the bed and then I'm on my way to the boutique.

The boutique is about a city block from the cottage. When I enter the store, I'm grateful to see shoes and immediately gravitate to that area. I don't spend much time deciding. Anything would be more comfortable than the heels I'm wearing.

I select a pair of sandals, a pair of flats, and a pair of tennis shoes. Slipping on the sandals, I make my way to the clothing area. I complete my shopping spree with 2 sleeveless blouses, 2 tank tops with spaghetti straps, 2 pairs of shorts, and 2 pairs of jeans.

I make my way to the counter, and the sales associate perks up when she sees everything I've selected. After paying for my purchases, I change into my new jeans and a sleeveless blouse. When I step out of the dressing room, I stop to admire my reflection in the mirror. Continuing, I exit the store with my new clothes and walk back to the cottage.

After removing the tags from my new clothing, I put them away and then unpacked my suitcases. I hung up the dress I chose for my interview and set my alarm clock, placing it on the bedside table. It's hard to believe I'm here. I did it! I'm starting my new life.

Grabbing my purse, I head for a little grocery store I pass on my way from the boutique. Entering the store and nodding to the cashier, I pick up a basket and explore one aisle after another, making my selections.

I find my favorite magazine and place it in my basket. As I continue to shop, I observe a man staring at me. Concerned, I keep a watchful eye on the man who has made me uncomfortable. He seems to be following me into each aisle of the store. Cutting my shopping short, I choose just enough staples to start my day.

Stepping up to the cashier, I place my items on the counter. The man watching me stands back, pretending to be looking at a magazine, waiting until my groceries are bagged. When I leave the store, being ever watchful of my surroundings, I notice he leaves the store right after me.

Am I in trouble? I pick up my pace when I hear his footsteps getting closer. I pass an alleyway but don't look in that direction. I am concentrating too hard on the sounds of footsteps behind me. I'm thankful it's still daylight and I'm hoping the man following me doesn't try anything. I hear a shuffle and a loud grunt behind me, then nothing.

Hesitantly I stop and look back but find no one behind me. The man is gone! He must have turned into the alleyway and wasn't following me at all. *That man frightened me.* I thought I had been recognized. Making my way back to the cottage with no further concerns, I unload and put away the groceries, finally relaxing on the sofa with a soda and my magazine.

As the adrenaline in my body finally subsides, I feel exhausted. My body is telling me I need to sleep. Admiring my new sandals, I'm quite satisfied with how comfortable they are with all the walking I did. It's so nice to wear something other than heels. I slip them off my feet, undress, and prepare to take a shower.

I forget to bring in the body wash and just realize there aren't any towels. Padding barefoot to my closet I slip on my robe, continue to the kitchen, and grab the body wash I just purchased. Alarmed, I see a shadow out the kitchen window. Quickly stooping down in fright and crawling into the living room, I wait with my back next to the wall.

I guess I was spooked at the grocery store. Thinking someone is looking in, I am afraid to move too soon. After waiting a while, I finally peek around the wall at the window. Someone is probably just walking by on the path behind the cottage. Convinced there's no one there now, I pick up the phone and dial the office asking for towels. The manager responds,

"I'm so sorry Miss Wingate. It seems they weren't restocked after housekeeping left. I'll be right over."

Waiting by the door I can hear her footsteps when she nears so I open the door before she can knock. She apologizes for the inconvenience, handing me a stack of towels and washcloths. Thanking her she turns and leaves when I close and lock the door.

Returning to the bathroom I shower, dry off, and get into bed falling asleep almost immediately.

I'm well-rested and excited about my very first interview for potentially my very first job. I'm too excited to eat much, so a banana and a glass of orange juice is all I can manage. I'm dressed in a navy-blue cap-sleeve dress paired with my new flats and my hair is swept into a French twist. I'm already feeling confident and more comfortable in my new shoes than I can remember.

I've given myself twenty minutes to walk the distance of two city blocks to Holbrook and Sons. It's going to be another hot day but walking to work this early in the morning shouldn't cause me to have that melted look when I arrive.

I reach the front of the building with butterflies fluttering feverishly in my stomach. Pushing on the glass door, I step inside and walk to the counter. After announcing my name and my appointment with Mr. Holbrook, I'm told to take a seat; I'll be called when they're ready. Looking at my wristwatch, I confirm I'm five minutes early.

I wait and wait and when I check my watch again, I realize they'd kept me waiting thirty minutes. They must be interviewing others. I must have misunderstood; I thought the interview was just a formality. I was led to believe I was a shoo-in.

Disgusted and heartbroken I stand and walk to the door. The lady at the counter asks,

"Miss, where are you going?"

Answering I say, "Obviously I misunderstood. I thought you were interested in my mathematical skills. My mistake."

As I open the door and walk out, I can see the woman running toward the back somewhere, but I turn my head and keep walking. My eyes are misting, and I will myself not to shed a single tear. I should have been prepared. This is just another disappointment in a long line of disappointments. I just make it to the corner of the building when a man comes running after me.

"Miss Wingate, … Miss Wingate, please stop."

I stop and turn to look at the man standing before me but not looking directly into his eyes.

"Miss Wingate, I'm Bruce Holbrook and I deeply apologize for the delay. We had a bit of an emergency this morning that kept us from our schedule. Won't you please come back and go through with the interview."

I'm sure my face is flushed and reflects my disappointment. My eyes are lowered as I stand motionless when he reaches out and touches my arm to escort me back to the building. I nod and say, "Okay, yes sir, I would like to go through with the interview."

As I'm escorted back into the building, Mr. Holbrook explains,

"We had an electrical malfunction this morning and were in a panic to make sure our backup systems were handling the added stress to protect our digital data. I should have sent word to inform you, but all hands were occupied, so to speak."

We enter the elevator and ascend to the third floor. Upon exiting the elevator, Mr. Holbrook escorts me to his office. I'm seated in front of his desk; he sits in his chair and opens a manilla folder. He tells me how impressed he is with my college transcript and my SAT scores. He comments,

"It appears your 100% devotion to your studies left no time for extracurricular activities."

I respond, "True, there was no time for extracurricular activities. My goal was to obtain my bachelor's degree in applied mathematics by my 21st birthday."

"And you most assuredly succeeded. Congratulations on your commitment to your goal. Miss Wingate, you will be working in the capacity of a financial advisor as well as a stock analyst. Have you ever had experience with stocks and bonds?"

"No sir, I have not. But if you give me two uninterrupted weeks of research, I believe I can fill that position to your satisfaction."

"Miss Wingate, I have prepared a test tailored to meet the needs of this position. There will no doubt be a few questions of which you may have no working knowledge. Just take your best guess."

He takes the test in hand and leads me to his conference room, asks me to be seated, and tells me I have an hour to complete the test."

I ask him to provide me with 3 sharpened pencils and multiple sheets of paper before I begin. His lips curl at the corners of his mouth as he smiles. He leaves the room and returns with the items I requested. As he checks his watch, he tells me I may begin.

I start work on the first question and find it rather simple. I continue until I reach the last three questions. As suspected, he left the most difficult questions for the last. Taking my time, I'm challenged and determined to solve these problems. I'm working on the last and most difficult equation when Mr. Holbrook enters the room calling time.

He looks over my shoulder and tells me to finish. He quietly walks to the other side of the table, takes a seat, and watches me as I solve the problem. I place the test in order on top of my worksheets and slide it across the table to him. Only giving a glance at the first portion of the test, he concentrates intently on the last three problems. Looking at me with a broad smile he says,

"You're quite impressive, Miss Wingate. I was told you wouldn't disappoint me, and they were right. Congratulations, you're hired,"

I'm beaming and feeling so much better about this situation. My very first job and it wasn't a shoo-in. I had to prove myself and I did with flying colors. Just then a handsome man not much older than me enters the room with an arm full of folders. He sets them down and introduces himself as Jake Holbrook.

As Jake sits next to me, he explains I'll be working closely with him until I learn their procedures and familiarize myself with the laws that govern their business. Father, son, and I begin the workday with the business accounting portfolio. I'm in heaven.

It's noon when Mr. Holbrook orders lunch stating, "We normally go out for lunch but I'm saving time by ordering in. I want to complete this assignment by the end of the day."

Lunch was over long ago. The sun has set and darkness has crept over the city as Mr. Holbrook moves what is left of the pizza we shared for dinner. Happy we completed our project he says,

"Congratulations, Ella, you just completed and earned 3 hours of overtime at double your salary. Money well spent. Welcome aboard."

I smile with pride and satisfaction for my first day on the job. It was so rewarding and enjoyable. I'm thrilled that my future finally seems bright.

CHAPTER 5

Gabriella

Mr. Holbrook tells me Jake will be driving me home, apologizing for the late hour. He explains they wouldn't dream of allowing me to walk home after dark. Mr. Holbrook thanks me for sticking out the day so the project can be completed.

"Ella, we'll see you tomorrow at 9:00 a.m. Get some sleep."

I'm comforted by his words of appreciation and thoughtfulness. It was a long but satisfying day. I take my purse and walk with Jake to the elevator and to his car. I think he can't be too much older than me. He's very handsome and has a nice personality. I like him.

Jake parks in front of the cottages, gets out of the car, comes to my side, and opens my door. He walks me to my cottage and tells me,

"Ella, I enjoyed working with you today. You did a great job." Watching as I insert my key in the lock, Jake tells me, "Go inside and lock the door. I'll wait until I hear it latch."

I'm tired but it's a good tired, and I'm elated at my accomplishment and what I've achieved. It's fulfilling to know I can have exactly what I want in this life despite my family name. If I work hard enough, I can make my way on my own terms.

I had reservations, reflecting about walking out before the interview. But I rationalized that my actions revealed I'm a person to be respected and refuse to be manipulated or treated less than I am. My actions have a positive effect on getting my foot in the door, so to speak. Proving myself was the icing on the cake, giving me great satisfaction.

This morning when I step out of my cottage, I see Jake leaning against his car waiting for me. I smile as I approach him,

"This is a surprise. It most certainly isn't necessary for you to drive me to work. But thank you so much."

"I pass by this area every morning, so I thought I'd pick you up on the way. You're welcome."

It's a very short drive to the building from the cottages. Upon entering the building, we stop as Jake introduces me to Helen who works at the front counter. Helen welcomes me and hands me my employee badge.

Helen explains the badge has a computer chip embedded in it allowing access to certain areas that are otherwise off-limits to others. Thanking her, Jake and I continue to an office that has my nameplate attached to the door. Not only is this a surprise but it also gives me an odd feeling to see the name Ella Wingate. I have to keep reminding myself: I'm no longer Farina but Wingate.

"I have my own office. This is incredible. Thank you."

"Of course. Someone of your caliber should have her own office. And it's right next to mine, I might add. We're giving you a project of your own sooner than we originally planned. But that's why your office is next to mine. If you need help, I'm just an open door away,"

I enter my very own office with much excitement. It's a nice size with a beautiful desk and credenza. The chair is a plush luscious leather and there's a framed floral oil painting hanging on the wall. The beautiful pale and muted colors of the art are perfect. As I admire it Jake says,

"We have an assortment of paintings we use for our offices. I suggested that one just for you. It seemed to mirror your personality."

"Oh, thank you, Jake. It's beautiful."

The rest of the day flew by. It seems I have a personal assistant, but I question if I need one. Jake explains I'll need to keep everyone updated with emails, memos, reports, spreadsheets, etc. something my PA will take care of and distribute to the right people, leaving me time to do the important part of my job.

The week has flown by and it's the end of another long day as Jake comes to my door asking if I'm ready to go.

"I just have one more computation."

"Stop! Put down the pencil, and back away from your desk." He's smiling as he says, "Come on, you can finish it tomorrow."

I hate to stop but I stand and grab my purse. Reaching the doorway I turn, looking back at the spreadsheet on my desk that's calling to me. As I take a step toward my desk, Jake grabs my hand and pulls me out of the office. Reluctantly, I accompany Jake to the car. With a blink of an eye, we're in front of the cottages.

Jake gets out of the car, walks to my side, and opens the door for me. He walks me to my cottage and tells me,

"I'll be waiting for you in the morning at the same time and the same spot."

I laugh at the silly expression on his face as I open the door just enough to step through. Turning and peeking around the door I say, "Thank you, Jake. I'll see you tomorrow."

As I turn to set my purse on the coffee table, shock and fear take hold of my entire body. I'm frozen in place when my eyes lock on Anthony's eyes as he's sitting on the chair in the corner of the room. Fear has gripped me with such force I can't say anything or move.

I'm finally able to lower my eyes so as not to look at Anthony's face, "W…What are you doing here? H…How did you get in?"

"Sit down … Gabriella … We have much to discuss."

Oh, my gawd, he knows who I am. My heart jumps into my throat, causing me to feel lightheaded and nauseated. My knees begin to weaken when Anthony says,

"Sit down Gabriella."

"I can't go back. Please don't take me back."

I sit on the sofa burying my face in my hands and I ask, "How did you find out?"

"I suspected you were running from something or someone when I spent time with you on the plane, but I didn't find out your true identity until three days ago."

"What are you going to do?"

"I'm here to offer you a choice. I know your father, Leo Farina, sold you to a 75-year-old man named Vincent Amato for a debt he owes. You won't survive him."

I can feel the tears forming in my eyes as I listen to Anthony.

"I can protect you if you marry me. Once we marry your father will no longer have control over you. I will pay what your father owes Vincent Amato so there will be no debt, and he will no longer have a claim to you. But I have conditions."

"Conditions! What, are your conditions?"

"First for my protection, you will look me in the face and into my eyes when I speak to you and when you speak to me. Next, you will come to live with me. When we wed you will share my bed. You will be submissive in our bedroom only. During the day you will be my equal. You may work as my accountant in our business when I feel you are ready. You will be treated well and have anything you desire."

"Everything except love and my freedom."

"Love and freedom are overrated. My last condition is you need to ask me to protect you, knowing the full depth of what you are asking for."

"You want me to ask you to protect me as I'm giving up my life to marry you?"

"Yes. Or you can greet your father's men when they come to take you to Vincent Amato. It's your choice."

"Why are you doing this?"

"When we are married it will align the Vitale and Farina families in an alliance that will guarantee our strength and dominance for generations to come."

"Anthony, I just made a new life for myself. A free life. One where I'm my own person. I have a job, my own office, and my own apartment. I've made friends and I come and go as I please far away from the mafia life."

"I want your answer in 24 hours. If I walk away from this, you are on your own. No one will come to your defense. It's up to you."

"So, you are considering walking away from this situation?"

Anthony stands without a response and walks out my door. Devastated and shattered beyond belief, I think of how far I've come to gain my freedom and to have a normal life. I don't know if I'll ever be able to accomplish this again. I like my new job, I like Jake, and I even like this tiny cottage. *Was it all an illusion? Was I only setting myself up for the ultimate disappointment?*

I'm too upset to eat, and sleep is nonexistent. I'm considering an alternative plan to marrying a man I just met. I'll look for another place to stay. I'll change my name again, dye my hair, and get horn-rimmed glasses. I'll dress a little more hip or funky, whatever they call it. I can make myself unrecognizable. It might work. I've got 24 hours before I give my answer either way.

The adrenalin running through my body is allowing me to meet the day. I see Jake in front of the cottage exactly where he said he would be. I rush to greet him as he opens the car door for me.

"Ella, is everything all right? You have a rather serious frown on your face."

"Oh, yes Jake, I'm fine. I didn't sleep well last night."

"I hope you're not thinking about the work I made you leave uncompleted last night."

"No, I love work and my job. It was just an off night."

I've been deep in thought all morning. I can't seem to come up with an idea that keeps my father's men from finding me. It's affecting my work because I've been working on the same equation for an hour now. Jake is at the doorway and says,

"Come on, I'm taking you to lunch. I think you need a break."

We're seated in a restaurant and are given menus when I decide to tell Jake everything. Turning toward him, I begin, "Jake … I need to talk to you!"

Jake turns to me while I prepare to tell him my story when I notice Anthony entering the restaurant and walking towards us flanked by his guards. Anthony stops in front of our table and says,

"Gabriella, come. It's time to go."

My shock is evident. My eyes are like saucers and my mouth is wide open. I shrink into my seat clutching the edge of the table with both hands. I close my mouth swallowing hard, looking at Anthony with fear.

Jake looks at Anthony and then at me when he says, "Ella do you know this man?"

I look at Anthony telling him, "I've decided against your proposal."

Jake starts to stand as he says, "She's just given you an answer, and judging from her reaction it's evident she doesn't want to go with you."

Anthony responds, "Sit down Jake. If you know what's good for you, you'll stay out of this."

Anthony slowly opens his suit jacket to reveal the gun holstered under his arm. *Oh, my gawd.* I place my hand over my mouth to keep from screaming. Looking at Anthony I plead,

"Please don't hurt Jake. I'll come with you, just don't hurt him."

Anthony releases the side of his jacket, hiding his gun once more as he holds out his hand to me. I hesitantly reach out as he quickly grips my hand and pulls me to my feet. Looking at Jake, I tell him "I'm so sorry." Anthony gives Jake a silent threat not to intervene. He slowly shakes his head as we turn and leave.

Anthony escorts me to the entrance of the restaurant with his hand resting on my waist, his guards following close behind us. I try to turn back to look at Jake, but Anthony keeps me from turning as we continue walking out of the restaurant.

CHAPTER 6

Anthony

Once Gabriella is in my car, she looks at me asking, "You said I had 24 hours to give you an answer and I just told you I decided against your proposal. You also said you would walk away from my situation, so why have you kidnapped me?"

"I changed my mind on 24 hours for an answer and I said 'If' I walk away. I haven't kidnapped you. You came willingly without making a scene I might add."

"After you threatened me and Jake when you revealed your gun."

"I didn't threaten you at all. I was merely showing you my new gun." *Concealing my humor.*

"Anthony, why didn't you wait until the 24 hours were up like you said?"

"Things changed and you were getting too cozy with your boss. I didn't want you to lead him on." *Again, I attempt to hide my smile.*

"What! He's, my boss. I wasn't leading him on, and you know it. Where are we going? My cottage is back there."

"I like you when you're annoyed. You've been looking at my face during this entire conversation."

Gabriella blinks a couple of times, takes a breath, and then looks down. I grab her by the chin and say,

"Ask me!"

She tries to pull away when my grip tightens on her chin and I repeat,

"Ask me!"

"I've decided against your proposal. I don't want to marry anyone. I'll take my chances.

"Gabriella, ask me!"

"I'll be leaving everything I've accomplished and want."

"Holding her chin firmly I repeat, "Ask Me."

With tears forming in her eyes, knowing there is no other choice, she says,

"Anthony, ... will... you please ... protect me?"

"Do you agree to my conditions?"

"Yes ... but I have a condition of my own."

"What is it?"

"I never want to see or communicate with my father again."

I nod and respond, "Agreed." Leaning toward her, looking into her deep blue luminescent eyes, I place my hands on her cheeks bringing my face close to her mouth and I kiss her sensually on the lips.

She isn't expecting me to kiss her, but she doesn't pull away. Instead, she innocently puckers her inexperienced lips for me. Pulling back, I look into her eyes. She seems dazed with half-closed eyelids.

"Gabriella, I'll make it good for you. I'll make you happy, and you'll experience love, pleasure, and freedom."

Kissing her again I suck her bottom lip into my mouth. Then gently forcing her mouth open with my tongue, I taste her, and explore her, swirling my tongue dancing sensually with hers, leading her into her first significant kiss. She attempts to regain her composure trying to conceal her embarrassment. Touching her lips with her fingers she looks thoughtfully into my eyes and asks in a soft voice,

"Where are you taking me?"

"To the airport."

"But my things are at the cottage."

"My men packed all your things when you left for work this morning. They're in the back."

"Anthony, I loved my job. It was challenging and satisfying. They even gave me my own office with a personal assistant. They treated me like I was somebody special. It was my very first job and they made me feel good about myself."

Taking her hand and bringing it to my lips I tell her,

"I promise you; you'll have another job just as rewarding with a bigger office and two personal assistants. You are a very special person, always remember that."

When we arrive at the airport, the guards pull the suitcases out of the vehicle and line them up for the porter to load on the luggage truck. Walking to the first-class lounge Gabriella says,

"It feels like Déjà vu. I escaped my father and was driven to an airport then waited in a first-class lounge to board a flight to freedom less than a week ago. My life has taken an unexpected detour in a different direction. I don't even know our destination."

"Where are we going."

"We're headed for Los Angeles."

Gabriella looks exhausted. I'm sure my visit last night caused her sleepless concern and my appearance at the restaurant shocked her with additional distress. Once we board the plane she sits in her seat and is asleep almost immediately. She is so fatigued she even sleeps through take-off. A blessing in disguise.

The air conditioner in the plane's cabin is slightly cooler than expected so I motion to the flight attendant asking for a blanket. Gabriella's arms are cold to the touch as I cover her. She doesn't move as I study her delicate hand and short-manicured nails before I kiss it and tuck it under the blanket.

I stare at my pretty kitten, placing a strand of her golden hair behind her ear. Thinking to myself, I had to move sooner than I planned. It seemed her boss Jake was showing her more attention than he should be, driving her home and picking her up daily. I was concerned that my impressionable Gabriella would fall for him, making it more difficult to lead her in my direction.

I regret frightening her when revealing I was carrying a gun, but I thought it was the quickest way to gain her compliance. It did the trick but at what cost? Does she fear me now? I'm drawn to this woman. I care for her enough to pay her father's debt and make her mine legally. My attraction for her makes me believe we were made for each other.

I'll think about telling her one day that I had already paid her father's debt to Vincent when I offered her a choice last night. No one was trying to find her; she was free and clear. But I had already invested in our future together, deciding she would be mine, so I tricked her into accepting my proposal. I'm sure we'll laugh about it one day, … maybe when we're old.

I won't tell her I tipped the airport cab driver to take her luggage to her door when she first arrived in New Orleans. And Giorgio took care of a man up to no good when he followed her out of the grocery store. He also scared some boys away who were peeking into the windows of the cottages. Giorgio did a good job keeping me informed and protecting her. He also felt Jake's attention toward Gabriella appeared more than professional. A reason I acted sooner than planned.

I'm not sure how long it will take Gabriella to settle into her new life. I'm hoping she can transition into her place by my side without disruption or resentment. Eventually, she will find the same happiness under my employment that she felt when hired at such an impressive level for Holbrook & Son. I admit that was quite an accomplishment for her first job.

I'll need to make arrangements to assign her something challenging. I'm not sure I want her to know too much about my business too soon. Too much knowledge will be dangerous for her. I'll have her verify the completed work looking for errors in the final computations of my accountant first.

I'll start her off with managing the accounting for the ranch and horses. That should keep her busy for a while, working with the vets, trainers, handlers, and jockeys. She'll need to learn the industry, history, races, and the different breeds.

The attack at our port resulted in minimal losses, and the information gained from the men captured revealed it was the work of a gang rather than the brotherhood. They won't be bothering me again. There have been no further problems at our port, everything is quiet, and running smoothly as business continues as usual.

We've landed in LA, and it feels good to be home. Giorgio and Dominic retrieve our luggage while I escort Gabriella to the curbside when Angelo pulls up in the limo. I'm encouraged as this turned out to be a good time to make Gabriella mine.

Gabriella enters the limo and looks through the window quietly watching people coming and going. Her solemn expression worries me.

I take her hand in mine and bring it to my lips. "Gabriella, everything will work out I promise." She looks at me with a forced smile, but she doesn't utter a single word.

Arriving at my ranch high in the hills, Gabriella's eyes are wide as we pass my impressive main entrance with iron gates attached to miles of fencing stretching as far as the eye can see. When we approach the pasture with my horses in full view, she says,

"You have horses. They're beautiful."

We pass the stable and training pen, continuing to the pathway to my sprawling ranch. She looks at me and says,

"Is all this yours?"

"It will be yours also once we're married. Do you like it?"

She replies in a soft expressionless voice, "It's beautiful."

I'm disappointed in her reaction. I expect more enthusiasm from her while she observes my kingdom. I need to be patient. She is still adjusting to the change I've made to her life.

The limo parks in front of the mansion. Giorgio and Dominic retrieve our luggage as my housekeeper opens the door. "Gabriella, meet Jenna our housekeeper."

Jenna extends her hand and says, "It's a pleasure to meet you, Gabriella."

"Thank you. It's nice meeting you also."

"Please follow me. Mr. Vitale asked me to prepare your room which is next to his. Once you're married, you'll be sharing Mr. Vitale's room."

My kitten seems overwhelmed as she takes in the foyer furnishings and art on the walls with Giorgio close behind carrying her luggage. They ascend the staircase when I say,

"Gabriella, Jenna will help you unpack. When you are settled, please come down for dinner."

CHAPTER 7

Gabriella

I would be looking at my current circumstances differently if I didn't feel like my dream of freedom was ending. I need time to accept this turn in my life. Looking around I realize my father's mansion can't begin to compare to Anthony's ranch. The expanse of his property and this mansion is far more than I could ever imagine.

This guest room is larger than my room in my father's mansion if that's even possible. The furnishings must have been imported. I don't believe you can find this exquisite furniture for sale in local furniture stores.

Giorgio lifts my suitcase, setting it on the king-sized bed, nodding as he walks out. Jenna unbuckles and unzips the cases, opens them, and begins to help me unload, fold, and hang my clothing. It doesn't take long to place my clothes in a dresser and walk-in closet. There is so much extra space that the closet looks bare, the dresser is less than half full, and the armoire is empty. Jenna says,

"You'll have to go shopping soon so you'll have multiple choices and changes of clothing."

I look around this beautiful room. The windows are adorned with floor-to-ceiling sheer curtains with tie-back drapery framing the window. The soft muted colors of the fabric match the wallpaper that accents one wall. It is beautiful, but is it a prison like my father's house?

Jenna asks if I'm ready to go down to meet Anthony. I nod following close behind her. It would be very easy to get lost in this mansion until I'm familiar with the layout. I'm led to the dining room set for dinner. Remembering I didn't have lunch, I acknowledge my stomach growling with hunger as I breathe in the aroma of the food.

Anthony, standing at the head of the table, motions for me to sit next to him while he pulls out my chair. Thanking him I sit down when he scoots my chair closer to the table. The meal is being served when Anthony introduces me to Michelle and Angie, the cooks. As Anthony fills my plate he asks,

"Are you settled in? Do you have enough room? Are you comfortable?"

"Thank you, Anthony. Yes, everything is very nice." Taking a mouthful of food, I savor the deliciousness of the meal. Swallowing I say,

"You need to tell me my boundaries, so I don't wander mistakenly into forbidden territory."

Anthony looks at me as he says, "Are you serious Gabriella?" He shakes his head stating, "What a horrible life you must have been forced to live. He takes me by the chin to face him. "There are no boundaries on this entire ranch. You may go anywhere you desire."

"Even to look at the horses?"

"Yes. We have motorized utility carts to make the trip faster and easier to get to the stable. But until the horses recognize you, I would like you to be accompanied by one of the staff when you indulge in your tour. Okay"

"Yes, thank you."

I'm astonished that I'm not a prisoner at all. I'm trusted to go anywhere I please. My life is starting to look promising. I realize I've just been told I'm an unrestricted member of the household. Remarkable.

Continuing with our meal, Anthony asks,

"Would you like our wedding ceremony here at the ranch or do you prefer we marry at the courthouse by the Justice of the Peace?"

He's asking for my preference! But I'm not sure I'm ready to answer, "Anthony, I think having the ceremony here would be more special. Besides, it's so beautiful here and the courthouse would be so cold and impersonal.

"Wonderful, I was hoping you would choose the ranch. Is there anyone you would like to attend the ceremony?"

"The only person I have in my life is my cousin Julia. But since she's the one who helped me escape, I don't dare communicate with her, fearing I would bring attention to her. My father would kill her if he found out."

"Well, in time the people who live at this ranch will become your family. You will learn to depend on them and hopefully appreciate their friendship."

"Now, have you thought about choosing your bridal gown for the wedding? I'll schedule a bridal boutique to come tomorrow with multiple gowns for you to choose from."

"Anthony, are you telling me the choice is mine?" That causes a flutter of excitement when I ask, "Do you mind if I don't wear high-heeled shoes? It's just that heeled shoes are uncomfortable, and it would be wonderful if I didn't have to wear them on my wedding day."

"Gabriella, anything you want. I don't mind if you go barefoot. Tell me what you would like, and I'll have the wedding boutique bring everything here for you to choose from. They'll be here tomorrow morning. Is that acceptable?"

I'm trying to adjust to my new life and wish I could answer him with more enthusiasm. I look into my future husband's eyes when I find a soft-spoken man who is considerate of my feelings. He is quite handsome, and he appears to care about my comfort. I reply,

"Thank you, Anthony, I don't know what to say." *Yes, I do, please take me back to the life I started for myself.*

I'm awakened by a knock on my door when Jenna excitedly enters my bedroom announcing,

"Gabriella, wake up. The wedding boutique is here. They're bringing up the dresses for you to try on for your wedding. Hurry, get ready."

Not able to see clearly just yet, I blink trying to clear the haze from my eyes as I jump out of bed and put on my robe. I barely have on my slippers when a large full-length mirror is wheeled into the room. Two large rolling clothes racks follow and are placed against the wall.

"Jenna, why didn't you wake me earlier?"

"I didn't know they would be here this early."

Sitting at the foot of the bed I watch as the curator pulls different styles of dresses off the rack for me to view. I shake my head in disapproval until she shows me a long very simple off-the-shoulder satin and lace fitted dress. It has a removable satin train that ties at the waist and trails at the back just enough to add to its elegance.

I'm overjoyed as she holds up a pair of white satin flats and a short veil. I slip off my robe as the curator helps me on with the perfect dress. She places the shoes on the floor in front of me. Slipping my

45

feet into them, I'm delighted and wiggle my toes admiring them. They're wonderful!

She sets the veil on my head to complete the look. Jenna claps her hands with a broad smile as she says,

"Oh, Gabriella, you are simply the most beautiful bride."

I'm awe-struck that this couldn't be more perfect for me. I'm elated and look flawless. The curator shows me beautiful matching panties, bras, and negligees. I selected almost everything she brought with her. All except the thongs. I have never liked those things, so I shake my head making a disapproving face. I eye Jenna as she picks up one of the thongs with the tips of her thumb and finger, examining it in silent disgust.

I asked the curator if Anthony should know what I've chosen before it is charged to his account. She responds,

"Mr. Vitale gave you Carte Blanche saying you were to have anything and everything you wanted."

"He did? Thank you."

"I understand the wedding is this afternoon. You're the very first person I've worked with who selected her entire wedding ensemble the morning of the wedding. Congratulations!

"I'm also surprised. Remarkably, you had just the perfect dress and shoes for me."

This day starts with a bang, even though I'm somewhat reluctant. The butterflies in my stomach seem to get more active as the day continues. Jenna tells me the chairs have been set up and the florist has come to arrange the flowers ordered for the occasion.

I ask her if I can have breakfast in my bedroom, so I don't ruin the surprise. *I'm starting to experience the excitement of this day.* Shortly after Jenna leaves, Anthony enters asking,

"Gabriella, why haven't you come down for breakfast?"

"Anthony, I asked to have breakfast in my bedroom, so I don't ruin the surprise of things being prepared for the ceremony."

Looking relieved, he kisses me and responds, "Good idea. I'll have breakfast with you. It's our wedding day after all. Did you get everything you wanted?"

"Yes, Anthony, thank you so much. It's all so perfect. I hope you like what I chose."

"I'm positive you'll be perfect, and I'm glad you're looking forward to the ceremony. I promise it will be as memorable as any wedding should be."

I shower and dress in my bridal gown with Jenna's help. My hair is up in a French twist and the veil is set in place with two white hair pins. Taking one last look at my reflection I feel more beautiful than I've ever been. The timing of my wedding though isn't my original plan for myself.

Jenna lifts the lid off a box, pulls back the tissue paper, and hands the bridal bouquet to me. It's gorgeous! Anthony has made sure our wedding is perfect. I don't know how he did it. Jenna follows me down the stairs holding up the satin train, so it doesn't snag on the steps as we descend.

This is it! My wedding! Butterflies are taking flight in my stomach. Anthony has made sure nothing is lacking for our ceremony. Giorgio, dressed in a tux, is standing at the doorway to the great hall that's been transformed into a Chapel adorned with flowers. The entire ranch personnel are dressed in their best to help celebrate this day with us. Conflicted, I try to come to grips with what is about to happen.

As I stand at the doorway with Giorgio and look in at the altar, I see my handsome husband-to-be, dressed in his tuxedo with Dominic standing at his side. He looks at me with adoration and pride in his eyes. The music begins as everyone stands. Giorgio extends his arm to me as he escorts me down the aisle to Anthony.

As I stand next to Anthony listening to the minister, I think about how all of this came to be. My escape from my father's clutches and an arranged marriage to a 75-year-old man. I think about how a coincidence leads to meeting the man who comes to my aid, and who I'm about to marry.

We pledge our vows of love and devotion. Dominic hands Anthony my ring as he, in turn, places a beautiful diamond ring on my finger. Then Dominic hands me Anthony's ring. Taking Anthony's hand in mine, I slid the gold band on his finger.

After the minister pronounces us husband and wife, Anthony takes me in his arms and kisses me like I've never experienced. I feel weightless and intoxicated as we turn to the applauding crowd. I will never forget the thrill of this day. I believe that in time Anthony will become the love of my life. I hope my thoughts aren't wishful thinking. It would be easier to believe if this day wasn't the result of a condition for my freedom.

CHAPTER 8

Anthony

I admire my bride as she is a vision to behold. It was such a coincidence that I was on the same flight as she was that fateful day. It wouldn't have been possible to meet her otherwise. We were meant to be, and I will treat her like she so richly deserves. I'm a lucky man.

I've decided not to tell Gabriella her father requested to be present at our wedding. He thought he would be invited to walk Gabriella down the aisle. I recognized his plan to intimidate her with his presence and his silent threat that he still controls her regardless of her age or marital status. I know men like Leo Farina. In his eyes, Gabriella is his. He doesn't care about her, only that someone else has what's his.

I don't trust Leo. My guards are aware of the circumstances leading to this distrust between him and me. He was not in favor of my paying his debt to Vincent Amato. It seems Leo had very specific reasons to marry his daughter off to Vincent. But Vincent is at an age where he chooses the money rather than a young virgin bride. He didn't hesitate to accept my payment relinquishing his claim to Gabriella.

My entire organization is ever watchful for the slightest sign that Leo might move against Gabriella. Though both our syndicates are aligned, Leo is a menace to be watchful of, and I must be vigilant.

Dancing with my bride, I look around and think how well our wedding turned out. The last-minute preparations for a full-scale formal wedding were handled efficiently as everything was ordered, delivered, and set up with no problems.

Gabriella looks like a dream in her wedding gown. The 5-star chef and staff I hired created an excellent meal and an exceptional wedding cake. The band is playing a mix of music, and everyone is enjoying themselves. All those who work on the ranch are in attendance bringing their wives, husbands, girlfriends, and boyfriends. All in all, our last-minute wedding was a success with all the trimmings.

Gabriella hasn't stopped smiling since she walked down the aisle to me. I can't get enough of her. I don't think I've let go of her since I kissed her at the altar. I still can't believe that this woman is mine. I'm looking forward to a lifetime with her and I'm prepared to protect her with my life.

The celebration is winding down and we see people out as our guests start to leave. I notice that Giorgio and Dominic have relaxed somewhat and seem to be enjoying themselves. They both relaxed their serious façade and managed to smile several times during the evening, except when they caught me glancing in their direction. I chuckle to myself at their reaction. I realize how fortunate I am to have two personal guards who would take a bullet for me.

It's been a while since I have enjoyed myself to this extent. Being the head of a syndicate doesn't offer many joyous occasions or celebrations. Business is the driving factor in our existence and strength is the major priority for our success. When an occasion arises to celebrate like this, we try to let ourselves relax and enjoy the event.

I'm looking forward to consummating our marriage tonight. I've tried to make everything perfect for Gabriella because this will be a momentous occasion for her. Now it's time to see the last of our guests out, turn off the lights, and step hand in hand up the stairs.

Reaching the top of the stairs, I pick Gabriella up in my arms and carry her into our bedroom. Setting her down by the bed, I loosen my tie and slip off my jacket. I didn't realize part of Gabriella's dress is removable as she unties the train portion of her wedding gown laying it across the chair. Stepping closer to her, I take hold of her zipper, unzipping the length of it down the back of her dress. Bending down, I kiss her shoulder and the back of her neck.

Gabriella walks to the closet to hang her dress. I continue undressing until I'm left with only my jocks remaining. She slowly returns to me looking nervous, wearing only her white satin and lace undergarments. My gawd what a vision!

Gabriella is stunning as she turns allowing me to unhook her lace corset. When it's dropped to the floor, Gabriella reacts and pulls her hands up to her chest covering her breasts. Taking her slightly shaking hands in mine, I bring them to my lips, and I kiss her fingers.

Continuing, I unhook her satin garter belt adorned with pink rosettes and blue bows from her stockings, rolling the stockings down her legs. She steadies herself holding onto my shoulders as I pull them off one leg at a time. Standing before me, my blushing bride, is wearing only her bridal panties. She is a wondrous sight to behold.

I slide Gabriella's panties down her legs. As she steps out of them, I bring them to my nose to inhale her scent deeply into my lungs. Gabriella's expression shows how truly naïve she is as she blushes in shock, attempting to avert her eyes from the panties I'm holding. When I remove my jocks setting my erection free, Gabriella's eyes fall to my heavily endowed genitals. Try as she might, my engorged erection seems to be the only thing her shockingly wide eyes can focus on.

Taking her in my arms, I lift her onto the bed. Climbing on the bed after her, I nestle next to her slipping my arms around her, kissing her with passion while gliding my hand over her beautiful body. Bringing my mouth to her breast, I kiss and then suck her nipple, skimming my teeth lightly across her pink nub. Cupping her other breast and gently rubbing my thumb over her nipple, I can feel Gabriella tremble under my touch as she holds onto my shoulders.

My hand slides to her mound where I brush my finger gently across her folds, lightly massaging the tip of her sexual region between my fingers. She responds to my foreplay with soft sighs and moans as if she's afraid of making noises. Her movements tell me I'm successful in seducing my bride and I insert my finger into her sex, feeling the moisture swell within her as her body readies to accept me.

As I slowly insert my swollen shaft into her, I'm met with a slight resistance, but I push through into her channel. Advancing, I penetrate through her maidenhead and stay motionless deep within her, allowing her to adjust to me. I feel a slight fog take over my consciousness. Continuing, I inch further into her extremely tight sexual region.

Hesitating, I begin to feel a warm glow in my mind and body. I feel as if we are levitating, and my weight is being lifted as we seem to be rising from the bed. My arms that were holding my weight off her are now holding onto her. I should be reacting to what is happening, but it seems so unreal and more of a dream state.

My overwhelming desire for my bride is something I've never felt as I begin to move my body out and then in, out and in, kissing her, encouraging her, and worshiping her in a way I've never experienced before. Our movements are in sync as one, climbing to reach that climactic conclusion. Though my eyes are closed, I can see a warm glow behind my eyelids emanating from her, tying us together as we cling to each other in ecstasy.

I dissolve into a feeling that we've melted into each other, merging and entangling, becoming one person. It is so real, the feeling, the climax, the euphoria. I've never experienced anything like this in my life. I seem to be caught in an uncontrollable high and Gabriella seems to be glowing with light radiating from her entire body. *Am I hallucinating or is this real?*

It takes a moment, but reality becomes normal again as the perceived levitation, our becoming one, and glowing lights become but a memory. I must have been hallucinating; that's the only explanation acceptable for our coincidental entanglement. I hold Gabriella close as we rest.

Leaving our bed, I walk to the en suite. After rinsing Gabriella's blood from me, I wet a washcloth, wringing out the extra water, and take it to the bed where I clean the blood from Gabriella's core and between her thighs.

Her eyes are half closed, and she appears to be in the afterglow of our lovemaking, looking as if she's in a trance. She smiles at me, bringing her hands to my face, and pulling me close as she kisses me tenderly. I immediately experienced the unmistakable feelings that we just bonded … for life. It's an odd feeling but it's as if Gabriella has become part of me.

Gabriella turns to her side as I wrap my arm around her pulling her next to me. Lying next to her soft warm body, I sense well-being and tranquility, rare feelings for me. It isn't long before I drift off into an unusually deep sleep.

I wake up feeling better than I have in years. Kissing my bride and bringing her close to me, I explain,

"Our breakfast will be served to us while we linger in bed. Then we'll get ready for our honeymoon."

I no sooner finish speaking when there's a knock on the door. When I say "Enter" The door opens and the most mouthwatering aroma fills the room. Breakfast is served and I have an appetite this morning.

We finish a delicious breakfast, share our first shower together, and then get dressed ready to begin our honeymoon. Our luggage is packed in the SUV, we say goodbye to the staff, then begin the drive to the airport.

It only takes us an hour to reach the airport. I didn't tell Gabriella our destination until we reached the steps of the airplane. She reacts excitedly to our Hawaiian honeymoon squealing with delight and slightly bounces on her toes. Her response amuses me when she gives me a hug and a kiss.

We board the airplane and make ourselves comfortable in first class seats. Gabriella is seated next to the window for her comfort and pleasure. The only difficulty she'll experience is take-off. I hope the mild sedative I put in her drink this morning will help her through the moment. We buckle up and wait for the roar of the plane's engines.

Our plane cruises through the clouds while we settle back in our seats looking forward to a romantic honeymoon. Gabriella looks slightly dazed; as the sedative has done its job. Take off for Gabriella is nothing more than an irritation that she handles well.

I hand Gabriella the pamphlets of the islands we'll be touring. She'll enjoy reviewing them when the sedative wears off. Dominic and Giorgio, sitting directly behind us, are discussing who stays on the beach and who goes in the water when we go snorkeling. I smile when I overhear their conversation. Dominic doesn't like swimming in the ocean.

Gabriella

I feel completely relaxed as the plane takes off with engines roaring, lifting us into the sky. Anthony hands me some pamphlets but my thoughts drift to my first sexual experience. I'm re-living last night while looking out at the clouds.

I think about Anthony's gentle kisses, his soft touch exploring my body, and his encouraging words to follow his lead. I reminisce about my excitement, how safe I feel in his arms, and how I trust him to guide me into passionate love making.

I am overcome with the sexual desire he brings out in me. I'm reliving the moment when I begin to drift into weightlessness, a new experience for me: A remarkable floating sensation takes over during our passion. My husband is everything I ever imagined and more, and I'm deeply in love with him.

It's been a long flight when our plane lands. The cabin door opens when a mobile passenger staircase is rolled to the door. When we descend the stairs, we're greeted by women wearing bikini tops and grass skirts who present us with beautiful leis of fresh flowers.

Entering the airport, we see our guide holding a sign with the Vitale name. He explains that our luggage is being sent to our hotel rooms while he leads us to a limousine. Our twelve-hour flight finally reaches paradise and we're here at long last to make memories.

This all seems so magical. Our wedding, our wedding night, this tropical island. I didn't foresee any of this when I first met Anthony. I was too frightened of being recognized. I'm looking at our destiny now and see a promising life.

CHAPTER 9

Anthony

When we enter our hotel suite Gabriella walks toward the glass doors. I follow her as we step onto the balcony overlooking the ocean. Holding her snugly against me, I kiss her shoulder and her neck with the ocean breeze blowing against our faces. We linger there and admire the afternoon sun while I hold her tight against me.

"Anthony, this is heaven. Everything is so beautiful. Even the air is fresher."

"Yes, it is beautiful here. Would you like to rest before dinner?"

"Yes. Sitting in the plane for twelve hours was tiring. I think a short nap before dinner is a good idea. Do you want to join me?"

"You nap. I'm meeting up with Dominic and Giorgio to go over a few things and reading through messages that need a response. I'll be back soon."

Later in the evening, we enjoy a delicious meal. After dinner we watch Hawaiian entertainers showing off their talent with fire eating, twirling fire batons, and walking across hot stones. After the show, I encourage Gabriella to join the other women in a Hawaiian dance-off. She causes my body to react, shifting uncomfortably in my chair, as I watch her sway her hips to the music. She won a lei and a photograph for her participation.

We enter our suite, undress, and step into the shower. Nestling close to each other, I wrap my arms around Gabriella kissing her tenderly while letting the water flow over our bodies. I ask,

"How are you feeling, kitten? Are you tender or are you okay to make love to me tonight?"

She smiles and stands on her toes so she can reach my mouth and kisses me sensually.

Gently fondling her with my finger I suck her nipple. Bringing my erection to her sex, I rub the head of my shaft between her thighs and across her folds until her knees give out. I lift her and tell her to wrap her legs around me. As she does, I slowly insert myself into her. Her hands are wrapped around my neck when I insert my tongue into her mouth dancing, tasting, and swirling with hers.

I rest her back against the tiled wall as I steady myself and she closes her eyes. With the water flowing over us, that feeling of light, warmth, and euphoria captures me as strongly as it did last night. I hold onto Gabriella with one hand and grasp the shower head with the other as that feeling that we're levitating takes hold and both my feet leave the floor.

I'm not hallucinating, this is happening! Do I feel alarm or amazement? I'm in such a state I let myself be pulled into her trance. I decided to be amazed.

That same fog takes over my mind as I push my body in and pull out, over and over until we reach our climactic sexual orgasm. This feeling I have for Gabriella is so new and so foreign, so overwhelming it makes me weak. As I again touch the floor, I carefully let Gabriella down feeling like I've just left the twilight zone.

We lather ourselves over every inch of our bodies and rinse off. I accept that what's happening during intimacy isn't normal, realizing this is something extraordinary that needs to be protected. I don't plan to bring it up for discussion just yet. Climbing onto the bed with my magical bride, we cuddle in each other's arms and fall into a deep sleep.

For four days, we island hop from the main island to Maui, Oahu, and Kauai. We stroll on stunning white sand beaches, snorkel in the clearest blue waters, hike to waterfalls, and fly above volcanoes in a helicopter. Checking out other things to see we explore a coffee farm, a pineapple plantation, and a chocolate factory.

We venture into a gift shop where Gabriella finds handmade leather key chains with charms of intricately carved wooden marine animals that match ballpoint pens. She asks,

"Anthony, can we buy enough of these as souvenirs for the staff? These are so beautiful and truly represent our magical honeymoon. They even have matching gift bags for them."

I examine the unique key chains and the assortment of Hawaiian sea animal charms. Each one is different, indicating monk seals, sea turtles, manta rays, dolphins, whales, and a Hawaiian octopus. The matching ballpoint pens have a picture of the corresponding animal. I respond,

"Yes, Gabriella, these are very nice, and I believe everyone at the ranch will appreciate that we thought of them."

Our last day is spent on the beach basking in the sun sipping with a straw from a freshly cut coconut. I want to take Gabriella in my arms and make love to her, but I can't take a chance that someone might see a levitating couple having sex. I smile to myself as I think it might cause alarm.

"Anthony, this is the very best time of my life. I will never forget how wonderful it has been. I can't thank you enough for bringing me."

"I'm glad you're enjoying our honeymoon. I'm having as much fun as you are and I'm looking forward to many more fun-filled days in our life together."

We both feel the letdown as we pack our things for the flight back. Neither of us is looking forward to the long voyage home. We've spent quality time with each other getting to know each other intimately. This paradise has offered a relaxing atmosphere free from the stress of everyday responsibility as head of the syndicate.

Fortunately, there have been no disturbances at home requiring my attention or concern. Our treaties are holding strong, and the other families are content with our business dealings.

The drive to the airport is a solemn one as Gabriella looks sadly out the window. She's trying to remember every little hill and mountain, taking last-minute pictures of the scenery as we pass by. She catches sight of a little grass shack and begs to stop so she can get close enough to take a picture. Giorgio doesn't wait for my command. He pulls to the side of the road and parks. He and Dominic escort us to the shack, allowing a grateful Gabriella to take her picture.

We arrive at the airport sporting a healthy glow from our sun tans. We're wearing Hawaiian shirts Gabriella bought us. We couldn't refuse her as she would have been hurt if we didn't wear them home.

Gabriella is wearing a colorful fitted dress that matches my shirt. She insists on going native so everyone who sees us will recognize where we've been. No one would ever believe that I have given in to the whims of my wife. But we'll soon be back to reality and the mafia don will reappear again.

It's evening when we land in Los Angeles. Exiting the plane I take a deep disappointing breath. The sky is hazy, and the air is thick with traffic emissions. It's amazing to me how we have become so accustomed to our surroundings. We fail to recognize what we breathe in daily until we visit a tropical paradise.

We arrive at the ranch where the staff greet us enthusiastically with smiles and hugs. Our colorful shirts are the center of attention and cause quite a stir. Exhaustion affects us all when I excuse Giorgio and Dominic from their duties. Gabriella and I say good night to the staff and retire to our room. It was an enjoyable trip, one I'll remember.

CHAPTER 10

Gabriella

It's morning and Anthony is starting his workday. I begin to unpack and then lay out our souvenirs. Emptying the bags full of pens and key chains, I place each matching set in a matching gift bag. I write on each bag personalizing them with the following:

In Celebration of our Honeymoon.
From Anthony and Gabriella.

Placing all the gift bags into a larger colorful Hawaiian bag, I head downstairs to Anthony's office.

Finding Anthony hard at work, I knock on his open door. As he looks up, giving me his undivided attention, I tell him I'm going to give everyone their souvenir. I approach his desk, kiss him, and show him the gift bags with the note I added. He smiles, kisses me, and says, "Be sure and have someone go with you until the horses recognize you."

In the kitchen, I find Jenna, Michelle, and Angie hard at work. I hand each one a gift bag telling them,

"I had such a wonderful time on my honeymoon that I felt compelled to share my experience with these souvenirs."

They show their delight while enthusiastically opening their gift bags. They remark with excitement as each examines her gift with words of appreciation. I'm given hugs and kisses by each of them. I ask,

"Is anyone available to take me to the stable?"

A man leans around the corner to say, "Hi, I will." Jenna reintroduces Matteo, our stable manager. Holding out my hand I say,

"It's nice to meet you again, Matteo," while I hand him a gift bag. "Thank you for sharing our wedding celebration with us and thank you for accompanying me to the stable."

He takes the bag with a smile, thanking me, and motions for me to follow him. We exit the house and are on our way to the utility cart when Matteo motions to the gardeners. As they approach us, I'm again introduced to Danti, Luca, and Marco. Shaking hands with each man, I hand them their gift bags. They smile, nodding, as they thank me.

I'm a little taken aback, however, when I notice Matteo is armed, but I'm even more surprised when I notice the gardeners are also armed. I ask Matteo about the guns, and he explains,

"Everyone on the ranch is armed, even the house staff. The only difference is the women hide their weapons from view." I shake my head in disbelief and try not to worry about all the guns. It's easy to forget this is mafia territory after all.

We walk to the motorized utility cart and climb in; Matteo shows me how to turn it on. He drives us to the stable as he explains where to park.

"While the horses are familiar with these carts, they are always parked in an area so as not to be a hazard to them."

We exit the cart and walk toward the training pen. Standing by the fence we watch as Matteo explains that Carlo, our trainer, and Angelo, the handler, are putting an Arabian Stallion named Quicksilver through his paces. Matteo cuts into an apple and hands me a slice. He tells me,

"When Quicksilver is brought to us, hold your hand flat with the apple in the center of your palm," I ask,

"Won't he bite me?"

"Not if you hold your hand outstretched and flat."

We don't wait long until Carlo leads Quicksilver close to me. Matteo nods for me to feed Quicksilver the apple slice. Excitedly I stretch out my arm and Quicksilver takes the apple. He allows my touch as I reach up to pet him behind his ear telling him,

"Quicksilver, you are so beautiful and I'm very glad to meet you." The horse nods his head and scrapes the ground with his hoof. Matteo and Carlo reveal their surprise as Matteo says,

"Mrs. Vitale, he's never responded to anyone like this before. He's responding to you like he truly likes you."

"I'm honored because I truly like him."

I'm shown the other horses while touring the stable. I offer a slice of apple to each horse as I'm introduced to: Sweet Georga Brown, Prancing Beauty, and American Queen. Each greets me with a nod of the head and a scrape of the hoof. I'm honored by their response to me. I have an odd feeling there's a sense of history between us. It's as if our souls recognize each other.

I continue to hand out the rest of the gift bags, except for two for Giorgio and Dominic. Returning to the house, I rush to Anthony's office. Excited by my news, I explain how I am introduced to the horses while feeding each of them a slice of apple.

"Anthony, do you think I could ride them someday?"

"That's a bit ambitious, Gabriella. Maybe someday. You need to be a trained rider to handle them. Quicksilver and the others are highly revered and respected. They're only ridden by experienced professionals."

I feel a twinge of disappointment but try to hide my reaction. I'm deciding that someday is better than never. I ask,

"If I leave the souvenirs here for Giorgio and Dominic, will you see that they get them?"

"Of course, Gabriella, I'll make sure they get them. I'll see you later at dinner."

The morning passes quickly and after lunch, I'm not sure what to do with myself as I tour the mansion. Feeling a little bored, I'm anxious to take the utility cart and drive around the ranch. I want to look at the wooded area that begins at the edge of the property. *I wonder how far back the woods will go.*

I peek into Anthony's office finding him already lost in work. As he invites me in, I enter, and ask him if I can drive around and tour the ranch. He responds,

"Gabriella, do you have a gun?"

"What! Of course not."

"Do you know how to use a gun?"

"No, why."

"Until you learn how to shoot a gun, you'll need to take someone with you. There are mountain lions, an occasional bear, and wolves who come down the foothills and make their appearance from time to time. Being in one of those open utility carts is simply not safe. That's why we take measures to protect ourselves."

"Is there someone who can go with me?"

"Drive to the stable. I'll call down and have one of my men go with you."

Leaving the house, I drive to the stable and park the cart. When Gianni approaches carrying a rifle, my concerned expression must have given me away. As he steps closer to the cart, he places the rifle behind the seat. Smiling he says,

"So, you're sightseeing today. Don't worry Mrs. Vitale, we rarely ever need a gun. It's for precautionary measures only. You won't even know it's there."

As he climbs into the cart, I notice he has the keychain clipped to his belt loop. Looking closer I can see the pen is in his shirt pocket. I smile at him when he notices I've seen the keychain and the top of the pen. He nods smiling back, and I feel delighted that a man like Gianni is using my gifts with pride and appreciation.

Gianni points to the road I should take on our tour of the lay of the property. I drive in the direction he points out. The ranch is vast with blooming fruit trees and an impressive vegetable garden. There are native plants everywhere. There's a fenced pasture, a racetrack, a building that serves as a repair or workshop, and a large two-story ranch house for those who work and live on the ranch.

Additionally, a rather large guardhouse is equipped with the latest technology. They even send drones out to monitor and protect every inch of the ranch. There is one hovering over us now, so we wave acknowledging its presence. I can see the drone is equipped with firepower. It dips in recognition of us and goes on its way.

"Gianni, are guns attached to that drone?"

"Yes, Mrs. Vitale. It's better to be prepared and not need it than to need it and not have it."

Ominous but very impressive. I'd hate to be an uninvited guest caught on the grounds here.

"Dare I ask? Gianni, what happens to trespassers?"

"They are dealt with accordingly."

On that note, I'm not going to ask for more information regarding trespassers. I don't think I'm prepared to hear the answer. As we continue touring the ranch, I see other drones flying through different areas. I'm not sure if I feel safe or threatened. Every inch of the ranch is monitored and seemingly recorded. I'm feeling troubled about the threat that causes such serious security.

We tour the grounds for a couple of hours and finally head in the direction of the wooded area when Gianni's cell phone rings. Upon answering the phone, he hands it to me telling me it's the Boss. I stop the cart and place the phone to my ear, I say,

"Hi, can you see us?" I look around for the drone. Anthony answers "yes," and then says he wants me back now. Something has come up and he needs me to get ready to receive guests.

"I'm on my way right after I drop Gianni off at the stable," Anthony says he wants me on my way to the house now. "Okay, I'll be right there."

I start the cart, turn around, and drive toward the house apologizing to Gianni for not being able to drop him back at the stable.

"Don't worry about me Mrs. Vitale, I'll take the cart back myself. We can finish your tour another time."

Arriving at the house I waste no time as I rush in to ask what Anthony wants me to do. It seems we're having an unexpected meeting with ten men, members of the mafia I haven't met yet. He tells me my clothes have been laid out on the bed for the occasion. I nod, responding,

"Yes, Anthony I'll get ready right away," As I turn to go up the stairs Anthony asks,

"How many gift bags do we have left?" I answer, "We have twelve more gift bags, remember? You purchased an extra dozen."

"Great, bring them down when you're ready. Gabriella, you have forty-five minutes."

CHAPTER 11

Gabriella

I rush to my room, undress, and cover my long hair with a shower cap before entering the shower. I won't have enough time to shampoo and then dry my hair. Turning off the water, I dry off and use my curling iron in a few strategic places styling my hair to the side and holding it in place with a decorative comb.

I pad barefoot to the bed to find a beautiful silk lavender knee-length dress, lingerie, hosiery, and a matching pair of lavender heels that are not stilettos. They have a shorter hill which thrills me to no end. Slipping them on, I find they are luscious soft leather with enough room to wiggle my toes. Anthony makes sure the shoes I wear are comfortable.

Coming down the stairs carrying the bag with the souvenirs, I rush to find my handsome husband already dressed in his dark suit. I turn around slowly so he can see me in my new clothes from all angles. He looks at me smiling adoringly telling me how beautiful I am. I lift the souvenir bag accompanied by a questioning expression. When Anthony explains,

"We have extra souvenirs to accommodate this evening's meeting. These men are mafia and cold-blooded killers, but they expect to be treated the same as everyone else in my organization. If my men are given a piece of bubble gum, the men coming tonight expect to get their piece of bubble gum. It doesn't matter if they don't chew bubble gum or even like bubble gum, they still expect to receive the bubble gum. Understand?"

Laughing at this impressive man's bubble gum example I answer, "Yes Anthony, I think I do understand. I presume the bubble gum scenario is for my sole benefit."

"Word got out about you gifting souvenirs honoring our honeymoon. These men expect to receive their souvenirs from the wife of the Don who originally gave them out. They weren't at our wedding so you will be meeting them for the first time."

"What should I say?"

"Just tell them the same thing you told our staff when you handed them their gifts."

Giorgio and Dominic stand slightly behind and flanking us when Anthony and I are at the door greeting our guests. The men are served cocktails as they gather to socialize until all the men have arrived and are introduced. When they are all accounted for, the staff escort the men to the dining table as dinner is served. After the meal Anthony stands announcing,

"My lovely wife Gabriella has something she wishes to present to you."

Anthony picks up and rings the small dinner bell as Jenna brings in the souvenir bag, handing it to me. Standing at Anthony's side, I begin with,

"It's been a pleasure meeting all of you this evening. I'd like to tell you that Don Vitale, this great man, this leader of men, surprised me by taking me to Hawaii for our honeymoon. It is a tropical paradise and a thrilling experience I will never forget. It is the most fun I've ever had in my life. Because of that, I want to share that happiness with others with these souvenirs of our honeymoon."

I walk to each man at the table. As each large frightening man stands, I present him with a gift bag, and I try not to think about bubble gum. They accept the gifts as if they are receiving gold coins.

After the last man receives his bag, they all stand and applaud me. Returning to Anthony, I curtsy to him. He smiles, holding my hand and motioning to me as he presents me to our guests. I nod to the men and excuse myself.

I feel foolish and get carried away with the curtsy. We hadn't rehearsed any of it and I hope I didn't embarrass Anthony. He seemed delighted with my speech and the men's reaction to me. Knowing women are not permitted to attend business meetings, I take leave when I think the time is right.

When Jenna opens the door to the kitchen, I enter as she congratulates me. The staff was listening at the door. She tells me I had done very well, showing extraordinary respect to Anthony and the other men. She says I should be a politician.

I smile with relief that it is over. You never know what's going to happen at events like this. Proceeding to the library, I relax reading a book until Anthony calls me back.

The meeting lasts an hour when Jenna informs me, I am to return and accompany Anthony to see the men out. Dominic and Giorgio stand committed at our sides. Each man nods and shakes my hand, showing their respect before exiting the house. I finally feel less tense when the last man leaves. Something about these men has me on edge.

Jenna leaves to return to the dining room to clear the table with Michelle and Angie when she rushes back waving an envelope. She hands Anthony the envelope addressed to me saying,

"Mr. Vitale, this was left in the middle of the table."

Anthony looks at me telling me, "I didn't want to worry you, but those men were part of the Farina mafia. We had business to discuss since we are now aligned. It's been agreed your father never comes to this property since this is your home. Your father and I will meet on neutral ground when it's necessary to meet in person."

"I want nothing to do with what's inside that envelope, Anthony. Please burn it."

"Gabriella, it wouldn't be prudent not to read it first. This is the first time he's tried to contact you, but I doubt it will be the last. I won't upset you with its content. But I need to know what he's planning."

"I'm going to change Anthony. Thank you for this beautiful dress and these wonderful shoes."

"You're welcome, they suit you well. I plan to thank you personally later to show you my gratitude for your excellent performance this evening. I especially liked the curtsy."

I blush red with embarrassment as Anthony chuckles giving me a hug and a kiss, swatting my backside as I turn to leave.

Anthony

I expected Leo to attempt to contact Gabriella. Walking to my office, I pour a drink, sit in my chair, bring the liquid to my lips, and swallow. Tearing open the envelope and removing the paper within, I find there is no term of endearment, such as Dear. The letter simply begins with Gabriella. Why am I not surprised?

Gabriella

Your responsibility to me is not being fulfilled. You are still my daughter and as such you owe me a certain level of respect. You have cost me a fortune that would have been ours if you had married Vincent Amato as I set in motion. He had a bad heart and died leaving his fortune to a stepson instead of you. You were not meant to marry Anthony Vitale. You were meant to marry Vincent Amato. In time I will call upon you to collect what you owe me.

He didn't even sign it; that says a lot. So that is his plan. He wanted Gabriella to marry a 75-year-old man with a bad heart so he could take what she would have inherited as his widow. Leo would have succeeded if he had been able to reclaim control over Gabriella. He isn't giving up easily and still has plans for her.

Gabriella is beautiful, young, and desirable. Any man would take her in a hot second no matter the cost. She's not only beautiful but also intelligent and accomplished. The men's reactions to her tonight prove their attraction to her. This is proof I cannot trust Leo Farina. I can't allow Gabriella to go off the ranch without heavy protection. She's in danger and I must protect her.

I make a few calls, wrap up some business, and head toward our bedroom. As I stop in the doorway, I find Gabriella sitting on the edge of the bed wearing a rather sensual negligee. She stands greeting me with her arms outstretched, turning slowly so I can view her lovely body. When she has turned full circle, she blushes. She's unsure if she has pleased me when I tell her,

"Gabriella you are the loveliest woman I've ever seen. Did you choose that gown just for me?"

She nods and smiles showing pride in her choice to please me. As I approach her, I'm unbuttoning my shirt and dropping it to the floor. She unhooks and unzips my pants letting them slide down my legs and I push them aside with my foot. She pulls down my jocks freeing my full erection.

Pulling her to me I kiss her mouth, neck, and shoulders. I slip the thin straps of her gown past her shoulders and down her arms. The rest of the gown follows gliding down her body to the floor. Picking her up I gently lay her in the bed, vowing to myself I'll never let her go.

After another mind-boggling love-making session, I'm becoming addicted to the levitation and the feelings that rush through my body when I'm in her. There is something magical about the act that can only be experienced with Gabriella. It completely encompasses my mind, my senses, as well as my physical being. The feeling completely envelopes my whole body, lingering well after we experience intimacy with each other. I can count on the deep restful sleep that comes after.

Waking feeling energetic, I'm ready to start the day as I walk to the en suite to shower. Having shaved and dressed, I walk to the bed, and bend down to kiss Gabriella telling her,

"I'm on my way to my office. I'm preparing for Quicksilver's upcoming race and the last-minute business that still needs to be addressed." Gabriella sits up and responds,

"I'll see you in a bit. I'll come down as soon as I shower and dress."

On her way to my office, Gabriella meets Jenna in the hall with the breakfast tray she requested and brings it to my office. Setting it down on my desk she says,

"Since you're hard at work, I thought we could share breakfast here together this morning."

Smiling, moving things off the top of my desk, I make room for our breakfast. Gabriella asks if she can go to the stable. She tells me that Matteo plans to introduce her to the bookkeeping procedures for the horses, trainers, and vets. And possibly continue the ranch tour.

"Anthony, I want to get started as soon as possible with my new job as one of your accountants. I have a lot to learn and want to contribute my expertise. I'm eager to prove myself to you."

"Gabriella, you have absolutely nothing to prove to me. I know about your exemplary qualifications and how you're considered a mathematical genius. You'll probably be bored quickly when you take over the horses and racing accounting."

"Well, if I get bored, I can always get a second job with another company."

I hate to burst her bubble, but she'll be working for my company only. I don't want to tell her that her father has become a threat to her. Therefore, going off the ranch will be dangerous until the threat no longer exists. It's already going to be difficult to take her to Quicksilver's race.

Gabriella kisses me then places our empty plates on the tray, taking it with her as she says,

"I'm dropping these off in the kitchen. Then I'm on my way to the stable to begin my adventure."

"Gabriella, I'll check with you in a while to see how you're doing. Enjoy yourself."

CHAPTER 12

Gabriella

Sliding onto the seat of the utility cart, I start it and drive toward the stable. Quicksilver is in the training pen alone. *That's strange I don't see anyone else; there should be someone with him.* I park and approach the fence as Quicksilver gallops toward me.

"What are you doing out here all alone boy? Where's Matteo and Angelo?"

Quicksilver tries to warn me as he rears up on his hind legs, then scratches at the ground with his hoof. I turn around just in time to see the man dressed in black grab my arm. Turning me so my back is to his chest, he covers my mouth with his other hand and drags me toward the stable.

As I'm pulled into the stable, I see Matteo and Angelo lying on their stomachs with their hands tied behind their backs and tape covering their mouths. When Matteo sees me, he starts struggling against the ropes, but another man, also dressed in black, hits him on the head with his gun.

Struggling with the man holding me, I bring my leg up and kick my heel back onto the man's knee sliding my foot down his shin, stomping on his foot as hard as I can. A trick a girl at boarding school showed me for a quick getaway.

The kick does its job, however, it's not as effective when one is wearing tennis shoes. The one time I wished I were wearing heels! He bends over in pain but retains his hold on me. He is angry, turning me to face him, showing fury in his distorted expression, reminding me of a bull about to attack. He slaps me full force across my face.

The slap is so brutal it might as well have been a punch. I see stars and it feels like I am out for a second. He throws me over his shoulder, knocking the breath out of me momentarily. I can feel my tooth throb and my cheek and eye start to swell. I kick and twist my body trying to free myself from his grasp, but he has a forceful hold on me.

Anthony

I end my phone call when Jenna and Michelle rush into my office informing me that no one from the stable is responding to their calls. Just then it felt like someone struck me, leaving a sharp pain on my cheek. Looking at Michelle and Jenna in a daze, I realize neither one of them could have hit me; they're too far away. I'm disoriented for a second but then I feel Gabriella's fear and pain. I shout, "Sound the alarm now!"

Reaching for my gun, I run toward the front door where I'm met by Dominic and Giorgio. Rushing to a utility cart, looking toward the stalls, we can see our men, reacting to the alarm, running toward whatever awaits them. I see Quicksilver in the training pen galloping in agitation his handlers are nowhere to be seen. Suddenly, I feel pressure on my stomach, losing my breath for a second. *My gawd! I think I'm feeling whatever is happening to Gabriella. Is that possible?*

I'm going to cause significant agony to whoever is hurting Gabriella. A shot rings out from the stable as my men take their positions. I yell, "Hold your fire!" motioning not to shoot anywhere near Gabriella.

Taking my position by the stable entrance, I direct some of my men to go around to the other end of the stable to cover both exits. I shout at whoever is inside, "You're surrounded and there is no possibility of escape. Let my wife go and come out with your hands up."

Gabriella screams out "There are three of them. Mmph mmm." Her voice becomes muffled. I feel the impact when he must have punched her in the stomach. I just about fell to the ground from the shock of it. *When I get my hands on the man hurting her, he'll be begging to die before I'm done.*

Creating a diversion, the intruders let the horses out of their stalls waving their arms, directing the horses to leave the stable. That action gave two of my men a chance to sneak into a small side door built specifically for shoveling hay into the stall. One guard is able to cut Angelo loose, but Matteo is still unconscious bleeding from his wound.

My men point their guns and fire at the intruders. One armed man is brought down with a hit to the thigh. The second man gives up quickly dropping his gun and holding his arms up in surrender. The third man holding his knife at Gabriella's neck, ducks anticipating an attack from one of my men behind him. As he is distracted and his eyes are turned from me, I quickly rush in and grab my whip. I'm now standing face-to-face with a dead man holding my wife.

Gabriella looks into my eyes as she silently communicates her intent to drop to the ground out of her captor's hold. As she brings up both her legs, her unexpected shift in weight causes her captor's grip to loosen as she falls to the ground. I feel the knife, as it pierces her neck, and I witness the resulting bead of blood from her wound. I am enraged looking at Gabriella's swollen face and now the cut on her neck.

Holding the whip, I lift my hand and flick my wrist hitting my target. The whip rips the knife from the man's hand hurling it out of his reach. My guards pull my stunned Gabriella to safety away from the fight they know is about to begin.

I give him three lashes of my whip, throw the whip aside, and then commence a full-on face-to-face knock-down drag-out fight with the man who caused Gabriella such pain. He lands only one good punch to my gut when I take my eyes off him to glance quickly at Gabriella who limps to sit at Matteo's side.

I purposely don't use my gun on the man who I mercilessly beat. A gun would end him too quickly. I want him to feel everything he has coming. I glance at Gabriella as she tries to care for Matteo, freeing his hands and keeping her head turned from the fight. My guards stand protectively behind her back.

Gabriella is aware I'm administering punishment for this man's egregious act against her. She is not ready to personally witness such savagery. Gabriella did not interfere even knowing the man I was beating would not survive.

I use a rag to wipe the blood from my hands and I instruct my men, "Bring the horses into their stalls, and interrogate the two remaining intruders. Bring me the results."

Addressing Angelo, I tell him, "Bring Matteo to the mansion. It will be easier if both the doctor's patients are centrally located. Let the doctor know if anyone else requires medical attention. And call the cleaners when your interrogation is done."

I walk to Gabriella and pick her up in my arms. She places her arms around my neck, closes her eyes, and rests her head on my shoulder, as I carry her to the utility cart. Speaking in almost a whisper she says,

"Thank you, Anthony, for saving us. Do you think Matteo will be okay?"

She winces as I set her in the cart. I put my arm around her and kiss her forehead as she lays her head on my shoulder.

"I think he'll be just fine, but he'll have one heck of a headache when he comes to."

"Anthony, how did they expect to take me off the ranch?"

"We'll have that information after they're interrogated."

This was one hell of a way to start the day. Angelo, Dominic, and Giorgio are busy getting information from the two men we captured. With their motivation, it shouldn't take long to get the information we want.

I'm getting Gabriella settled and ready to see the doctor. The side of her face is bruising, turning blue, her eye is swollen, and she has a sizeable welt on her stomach. She touches her tooth with her finger testing its strength. The small cut on her neck is mostly superficial. The knife only pierced the skin at the curved tip of the knife. I want to kill the S.O.B. again for what he did to her.

Gabriella insists the doctor tend to Matteo first. When Matteo finally comes to, he is diagnosed with a concussion and is ordered bed rest for at least two days. Because of his concussion, the doctor orders someone to be with him to wake him during the night.

The doctor completes his examination and gives Gabriella a clean bill of health. She asks if she can look in on Matteo. Helping her to her feet, and holding her hand, I escort her to Matteo's room.

Matteo, objecting to bed rest, sits up until I tell him he will not leave the guestroom until I say he can. He isn't happy, laying back and grumbling under his breath, but he makes sure I can't hear him. Smart. Matteo thanks Gabriella for her thoughtfulness in looking in on him and tells her he is happy to see she's okay.

Satisfied that Matteo will be fine, Gabriella reluctantly decides to go back to our room to rest a while.

About an hour later Dominic, Giorgio, and Angelo return with the information I'm expecting. Sitting in my office, Dominic begins when he is interrupted by a knock on my office door.

I respond "Enter." Gabriella opens the door and asks to be present during our meeting. We look at each other as she says, "Please Anthony, I have a right to know why this happened."

I motion for her to come in as Angelo places one of the chairs next to me for Gabriella. When she takes her seat, I nod for Dominic to begin again. He continues,

"The three men were sent by Leo Farina to bring Gabriella to him. They were passengers in one of the SUVs driven by one of your guests last night. The three men jumped out of the moving vehicle they were in to avoid drawing attention to themselves. They made their way to the stable waiting all night until morning."

"Why didn't the cameras pick them up?"

"When the SUVs entered the ranch, they were in continual motion with no break between them and no slowing or stopping at any time. The three men were in black clothing with masked faces. Once they jumped out of the moving vehicle and hit the ground, they remained motionless until the SUVs passed them by. The men were not detected, then they crawled slowly on their stomachs to the stable."

"How did they know Gabriella would be at the stable this morning?"

"They said their boss told them, 'He had a feeling the odds were good she would be there.' They said they didn't receive further explanation."

"And how did they expect to leave the grounds with Gabriella?"

"They had a helicopter circling high above. We all heard it a couple of times. But it never came close and disappeared as soon as we surrounded the stable."

"Yes, I also heard it, but it didn't register to me at the time that it was part of the plan. If they had succeeded and she was placed on that helicopter I would never have found her."

Gabriella looks devastated as the color leaves her face. "I'm a married woman and 21 years of age. My father has no right to me, legal or otherwise. He betrayed me and then sold me to a 75-year-old man. There is no love between us, and I owe him nothing."

"Gabriella, your father arranged your marriage to Vincent Amato because of his age and the fact he had a bad heart. He was planning on his untimely and early death so you would inherit his estate. Then he planned to take it from you. He didn't consider your escape and someone like me stepping into the picture."

"Anthony, how are we going to stop him? I'm no longer ..." Gabriella looks at the men in the room. "... An underaged, innocent girl."

CHAPTER 13

Gabriella

Having heard my father's plans for kidnapping me, Anthony excuses the men but asks me to stay.

"Gabriella, you don't realize your beauty, grace, and worth. Any man on this planet would jump at the opportunity to have you at his side, regardless of your marital status."

Reaching for my hand, he lifts it to his lips, then rests my hand on his thigh as he continues,

"It's evident your father isn't giving up on regaining control over you. You'll be heavily guarded until I can take care of your father. Gabriella, I will do whatever is necessary to neutralize this situation. That would include a permanent solution where he's concerned. Do you understand my meaning?"

"Yes, Anthony I understand perfectly."

I can't believe my father's plan and the way he carries it out. The harshness of my treatment was executed by such aggressive behavior. No one ever hit me before, no one ever dared to treat me in such a manner. Did my father give my abductor permission to do whatever he deems necessary to make me comply?

How did he know I would be at the stable? Can he read my emotions or thoughts now that I've become a woman? I can't be

connected to him; I just can't be. I don't feel love toward him. Is he even my real father?

Mother states their marriage is an arrangement between two families with no introductions between them beforehand. Try as I might, I have no memory of seeing any form of affection between my parents.

Mom explains our race did not originate on this planet and our heritage is much older than the Earth itself. We come from a long line of beings that can connect with others both emotionally and physically. We have the power to access a much larger portion of our brains than a normal human does.

She says that my love for a man will bond me to him and him to me once I reach adulthood. She warns me not to reveal to anyone that I'm different in any way. History has proven that humans are fearful of things they can't explain, and we are thought of as a threat to their society. We become guinea pigs to their scientists who dissect us or are imprisoned and hidden away by the governments who rule us.

She claims our power is diminished over time by procreating with humans, which eventually strips us of the extraordinary traits that make us special. Our life on earth takes a toll transforming us into humans. To keep us safe our remaining gifts should be utilized silently communicating through our minds only.

Trying to calm myself after such a frightful morning, I aimlessly tour the mansion slowly walking through areas I haven't seen yet. I familiarize myself with the layout of this beautiful mansion. Opening a door on the main level and looking in, I find this large room is being used primarily for storage.

"Anthony, I notice the room down the hall is being used for storage. The room would be perfect for my office. Because our offices won't be next to each other, your meetings will remain confidential. Additionally, any meeting I might have would not disrupt or disturb you. Will you think about it?"

Anthony smiles, shaking his head. "I'll have the staff empty the room and bring in the office furniture today."

"Really! Thank you, Anthony." Standing, I grab him around the waist giving him a bear hug.

Santino and Marcello have the room cleaned out in a jiffy and it takes 25 minutes to clean with Jenna, Michelle, and Angie's help. I only changed my mind once about where to place my desk, two upholstered chairs, and an exquisite bookcase with glass doors. *Perfect to exhibit books, figurines, or other special items.*

Jenna brings down framed photos of our wedding and honeymoon. They are placed on a floating shelf Marcello installed on the wall. *Perfect! Absolutely perfect.*

While standing in the middle of the room, I admire my new office. I'm visualizing how framed photographs of the horses will look on the bare wall above the credenza. I'm deep in creative thought when Anthony appears in the doorway.

"You did a good job setting up your office, Gabriella. It's very nice."

"Thank you, Anthony. This day didn't start well, but it's much better now than it began. And I have you to thank for it."

"I'm thankful it's better than it began also. I've enhanced our security. From now on no one gets on this ranch without a thorough search of all vehicles and people in it. Now we need to discuss the logistics of the upcoming race."

"Will I be going to the race also?"

"Yes. I can't leave you behind with minimum security. Next weekend's race is at the Santa Anita Park. It will be crowded with people so you must agree you will not absent-mindedly wander away from your security. You must remain with them at all times. You must be aware of your surroundings and cannot let your guard down for an instant."

"How exciting! I've never been to a horserace before."

"Gabriella, this isn't an amusement park with families in attendance. It's a racetrack with heavy gambling and a few very bad people. There will be some people losing more than they can afford. How they react to a loss can't be predetermined. Always be vigilant about who's around you."

"I'll be watchful of my surroundings, I promise. How should I dress for the occasion?"

"Wear your blue dress. As Quicksilver's owner, you should always be dressed like the socialite you are. You will be sought out to be photographed regardless of the outcome of the race."

"Anthony, will I really attract that much attention? I'm … I'm not sure I'm ready for that kind of scrutiny. Can't I stay in the background somewhere?"

"There is no background for you. As my wife, you will always be at my side, front and center. Don't worry just be yourself, you'll do just fine."

The next morning as I'm drying off, I notice that my cheek is no longer discolored, my eye is no longer swollen, and the welt on my stomach is gone. The spot on my neck is nothing more than a scratch. I look and feel normal again, except for the occasional ache in my tooth. I'm energized and decide to look in on Matteo before going down for breakfast. There is no response when I knock on his door. As I open the door and peek in, I discover he's still asleep.

I'm not sure of the last time anyone checked on him. Upon entering his room, I call out his name. He doesn't respond. He appears to be in a deep sleep and still doesn't respond when I shake him on the shoulder. Concerned about his condition with the concussion, I shake him harder.

Anthony enters the room as I'm shaking Matteo and questions me in a harsh tone.

"Gabriella, what are doing in Matteo's room?"

"Anthony, he won't wake up. Help me. When was the last time anyone checked on him?"

Anthony walks to the bed, pulls me away, and starts to shake Matteo. When Anthony's shaking doesn't effectively wake Matteo, Anthony slaps him a couple of times on his face. I breathe a sigh of relief when Matteo finally opens his eyes looking startled and disoriented. Anthony says,

"Hey, Matteo, you scared us. How do you feel."

"I feel like I've been kicked in the head by a mule. What's going on?"

"We were checking on you and couldn't wake you. Remember the doctor told us to wake you periodically because of your concussion? Do you think you can eat something?"

"Yes, boss, I think I could."

"I'll have Michelle send something up. Why don't you sit up until your food arrives to help keep you awake for a while?"

As Matteo sits up, I start to reach for his pillows to fluff them when Anthony blocks me, hitting the pillows and placing them behind Matteo's back. I'm silently questioning why Anthony is acting this way. He tells Matteo he'll check on him later, grabs hold of my hand, and leads me out of the room.

I can't keep up with his long stride as he pulls me along the hallway. I trip on my own feet and lose my footing before Anthony seems to calm down and stop. He looks at me as if I've done something unforgivable, pushing me into our bedroom and closing the door behind us.

"Anthony, why are you treating me like I've committed a crime?"

"What were you doing in Matteo's room? You can't go into another man's bedroom, at least not without a chaperone."

"A chaperone! Anthony, I was checking on him like the doctor instructed. I tried to wake him when thankfully you came in. You woke him when I couldn't. Why are you acting this way?"

"It is not appropriate for the wife of a Don to go into another man's bedroom and touch him. You will not do that again. Jenna, Michelle, or Angie will take care of Matteo's needs. Not you. Do you understand? … Gabriella, … have I made myself clear?"

Looking at him with such hurt, I answer, "Yes Anthony, I understand. I don't know what to say other than I meant no harm. I'm … I'm sorry my actions upset you."

I have no idea why Anthony's acting this way. I didn't realize I broke a cardinal rule when I touched Matteo's shoulder attempting to wake him. How am I supposed to work with Matteo after this? I'll have to be very careful from now on not to look like I'm fraternizing with the male staff.

Yesterday started so horribly that I was looking forward to a better morning today. But it seems my decision to look in on Matteo was a terrible mistake. Anthony showed me another side of himself that is concerning and a little frightening.

How quickly I forget Anthony Vitale is the mafia and the head of this family. He gave me a sense of false security until now. I need to be very careful how I communicate with the male staff from now on.

There is no such thing as relaxing when around these men. I must always be on guard of my surroundings. Even at home, it would seem. I turn to leave so he can't see the tears begin to swell in my eyes, when he says, "Where are you going? I didn't excuse you."

I stop with my back to him, refusing to turn around to let him see the tears sliding down my cheeks. I put my head down and asked,

"May I be excused?"

Anthony takes a deep breath before he finally says, "Yes, … you're excused."

CHAPTER 14

Gabriella

As I rush down the stairs, Jenna greets me with a big smile. Holding my head down partially, I force a smile on my lips, wishing her a good morning with the most pleasant voice I'm capable of making. Dashing out the front door, I'm hoping against hope she didn't see the tears streaming from my eyes.

I get in one of the carts and drive toward the back of the ranch. I forgot for a moment there is no place to go without being seen by cameras. There is no privacy to shed my tears without being seen by everyone.

It isn't long before a drone is overhead following me. I stop, get out, and lean against the cart keeping my back to the drone. It buzzes behind me and then comes over my head to face me. I turn away wiping the tears from my face so it can't see I'm crying.

The drone flies over my head to face me again. I smile and wave it away, turning around with my back to it once again. The operator of the drone is determined; he flies it over me to face me yet again. I give up. I look at it and say,

"Hi! What can I do for you?"

A voice comes through the drone announcing, "Mrs. Vitale, if you head back to the stable someone will accompany you while you tour the ranch. You can't be on your own unless you're armed."

I smile, nod, and get back in the cart looking at the drone. "Okay, thank you, I'm on my way." The drone follows me protectively until

I reach the stable. I'm sure it would have fired on a wild animal if I had been threatened. I appreciate their protection, keeping me safe. But now everyone knows there was a problem that caused me to cry. There is no privacy and no secrets here.

I can see the horses grazing in the pasture as I park the cart and walk into the stable. The stalls are being cleaned and new hay is being spread on the floor. I nod and smile at the men working as I walk casually toward the end of the stable to a stall I know is not in use.

Since the stall is unoccupied there is no camera. I shyly look back at the men making sure they're not looking at me before nonchalantly entering the stall. Hay is stored in this stall so I sit on a bale resting in a corner, deciding this can be my private place until I must find a new one.

Making myself as comfortable as I can be sitting on a bale of hay, I contemplate why Anthony acted so harshly toward me. Did he think I was acting inappropriately? Did he think I was in Matteo's room for something other than concern for his wellbeing? He did, and that troubles me the most.

He acts as if I betrayed him somehow. It most certainly would never occur to me to ever do anything that involves being an unfaithful wife. Maybe he thinks my kindness and friendship aren't acceptable regarding his men. Bringing my knees to my chest and clasping my arms around my legs, I rest my forehead on my knees trying to think of a solution to resolve Anthony's misgivings about me.

Suddenly, I realize it has become relatively silent. Just moments ago, the men were actively conversing with one another as they were working sweeping and cleaning the equipment. *Maybe they're done and finished for the day.* Anthony surprises me when he suddenly appears on the other side of the stall gate door looking in at me. He asks,

"Can I come in?"

Quickly standing I nod, and say, "Yes, Anthony, of course; it's your stable after all."

"Gabriella, please sit back down. We need to talk." I do as he says and sit back on the bale of hay giving him my undivided attention. Anthony comes into the stall and sits on the bale next to me. He looks at me and says,

"Gabriella, I want to apologize for treating you so harshly. When I couldn't find you, I thought to look for you in Matteo's room, knowing your concern for him. And there you were. I became so angry when I saw you bending over him, touching him that I fell into a blind rage. Do you have any idea how it looked to me?"

"Anthony, I'm so sorry. You have to know that I would never do anything to dishonor or disrespect you. I am and will always be a faithful wife. I would never break our bond. That couldn't have been further from my mind when I tried to wake Matteo."

"I admit I knew that in my heart, but I became jealous when you were offering your concern and attention to another man. Your youth and innocence haven't quite caught up to how you should properly conduct yourself with my men. You need to take this lesson seriously to avoid future misunderstandings."

"I do take this as a lesson not to be repeated. But now I'm not sure how to act or speak to your men at all. I most certainly don't ever want you or anyone to ever get the wrong impression of my actions ever again."

"Gabriella, I understand your eagerness to be accepted, but it would be best to remember you should never put yourself in a situation where you are in a room alone when talking to any of my men."

"Anthony, should I even talk to Matteo again? What will he think? Will he be uncomfortable to train me with the bookkeeping and the horses?"

"He doesn't know you were in his room alone and not aware I took issue with your presence. For all he knows we were both in the room together from the start. Your thoughtfulness and friendly gestures can easily be misunderstood to mean something more than you intend. Just be aware and maintain a certain decorum when communicating with my men."

Anthony takes my chin in his hand, looks into my eyes, and says,

"It's necessary you understand the seriousness of the situation to keep you and my men safe. I wouldn't hesitate to shoot one of my men, or any man, who would take advantage of a misunderstanding. I'm sorry I hurt you and caused so many tears."

Anthony puts his hand on the back of my head with his fingers entwined in my hair, pulling me to him as he kisses me on the lips exploring my mouth with his tongue. After a rather lengthy sensual kiss, he says,

"I love you, Gabriella. Do you forgive me?"

"Yes, Anthony, I'm sorry I upset you. I love you too."

"Let's get back to the house. You missed breakfast and it's time for lunch."

"Anthony, I'm embarrassed that the staff saw me … crying. I don't think I can face them just yet."

"No one saw you and if they did, they would never let you know they did. This is a family and families occasionally have disagreements. That's all. Come on, there is no need for you to be embarrassed."

Anthony drives us back to the mansion. We make our way to the dining room and there's a wrapped gift sitting on my plate. Anthony pulls back my chair for me. As I sit, he pushes my chair forward and sits at the head of the table. I look at the gift and then at Anthony as I ask,

"Is this for me?"

"Well … since it's sitting on your plate, I would guess that it is for you. Are you going to open it?"

"What's the occasion? It's not my birthday or Christmas and too soon for our anniversary."

"Let's call it … A Just Because I Love You Gift."

Smiling, I detach the bow from the package and carefully fold back the wrapping paper. There's another box with a latch attached to its lid. Removing the box, I find it's heavier than I expected. Setting the box on the table, I raise the latch and lift the lid.

It's a gun. A silver revolver with a pearl handle. I look at Anthony and the expression on my face must show my question. Why have I been given a gun? I have never held a gun let alone used one.

"Gabriella, it has come to my attention that it's time for you to learn to shoot a gun. You need a gun of your own to build your confidence. This one is small for your hand but is powerful enough to take down an animal or human."

"It's beautiful Anthony, thank you."

"You'll have lessons to learn to shoot, reload, clean, take apart, and reassemble. Once you learn, you'll take it with you while you tour the ranch on your own."

I start to close the lid of the box, but Anthony shakes his head and tells me,

"Take it out of the box."

"Now?"

"Yes now. I want to see you hold it."

"I reach my right hand over the gun and nervously touch the pearl handle with my fingers."

Anthony shows his impatience when he stands, steps toward me, and lifts the gun out of the box. He motions for me to take the gun from him. I hesitate but he says,

"Your fear is unacceptable. He takes my hand and places the gun in my palm.

"Hold your gun, Gabriella. Feel the weight of it. The gun is not loaded but always check for yourself. Pull this lever back to check the chamber for a bullet."

Anthony points to the area where I should pull back. He watches me as I follow his instructions. My hands are shaking slightly but I accomplish the task. There is no bullet in the chamber. The gun is indeed empty.

"Very good. See, there is nothing to fear. Once you learn how to handle your gun, it will be second nature to you."

Still looking at the gun I'm holding I gently return it to its box and ask to be excused. I'm thinking about where I should store it. Entering my office, I look around and finally set the box on the credenza. I open the box and stare at the gun when I notice for the first time that my initials are intricately etched into the pearl handle.

I gently lift the gun for a closer look at the beautiful lettering GV. Holding the gun with my outstretched arm, I aim as I pretend to take the shot. I didn't notice Anthony standing in the doorway watching me. He enters my office closing the door behind him. He steps toward me, wraps his arms around me, and kisses my shoulder and neck.

"Gabriella, you're lovely and look so confident holding that gun in your hand. It makes you feel powerful, doesn't it?"

I nod as he takes the gun from me and places it in its box. He says,

"I hope you know you mean the world to me, Gabriella."

I can feel his erection against my back while he holds me snugly against him. Grabbing hold of the hem of my shirt he pulls it over my head. He unhooks my bra and unzips my jeans; he slides them and my panties down to my ankles together in one action. He bends me over the credenza and unzips his pants.

I'm not sure what he's going to do when I look back at him and attempt to stand up. He places his hand on my back and gently pushes me back down over the credenza.

"Gabriella, I'm not going to hurt you, trust me, I'm taking you from behind. Spread your legs."

That caused me to panic thinking he meant he was going to take me where it's forbidden as he spread my legs apart with his foot.

He begins to fondle me with one hand, gliding his fingers across my folds and manipulating the tip of my sex. He cups my breast with his other hand working my nipple between his thumb and fingers. He leans into me inserting his shaft into my sex. My legs become weak, losing their strength, and are no longer able to support me.

Anthony's mouth clamps onto my shoulder, biting and sucking as he penetrates me deeply, withdrawing and plunging in and out of me with a wild passion. I'm in a fog as my body feels weightless and I have a sensation I'm floating. My arms no longer brace against Anthony's weight as we seem to rise together, connected as one, embracing as we climax together.

Our feet appear to return to the floor, and we find ourselves bent over the credenza, breathless coming out of our sex-induced haze. Lovemaking leaves me with an astonishing feeling. Anthony rests his head on my shoulder, holding me tightly against his body.

It takes a moment to come back to reality. Anthony lays me on the credenza resting next to me. We lay together as Anthony smothers me with kisses. We remain entwined in each other's arms until our breathing becomes normal again.

My day begins with my shooting lessons. Bales of hay are set up with paper targets lined side by side. A table is set up with ammunition and ear and eye protection. I am introduced to Monte who is an ex-military sniper and marksman and is the syndicate shooting instructor.

Monte nods his head as I approach. He instructs me to put on my protective earmuffs and goggles, remove my gun from its box, and load it. He briefly instructs me how to load the gun. I have Monte's complete attention while I follow his instructions. I don't want to disappoint him. He's so intimidating and powerful I desperately want his approval.

He stands close behind me showing me the correct stance. He helps me raise my arms and instructs me how to hold my gun in both hands. He tells me to expect a recoil then tells me to pull the trigger. When I do, the recoil surprises me but isn't something to worry about now that I've experienced it.

I missed the target with my first shot but hit the side of the head of the target with the second shot. My third shot is a bull's eye. I'm so proud of myself I do a little bounce. Every shot after that is dead center. Continuing, I gleefully destroy all the paper targets. Monte gives me a smile of approval, which is like receiving a badge of honor. After several rounds of practice, Monte says,

"Congratulations Mrs. Vitale, you're a natural."

After shooting all the bullets I make sure the chamber is empty, replace my gun in its box, and confirm the time for my next lesson. I shake hands with Monte and thank him for his time. I'm ecstatic that my lesson was so enjoyable. I can hardly wait to tell Anthony all about it.

CHAPTER 15

Anthony

It's the day of the big race and Quicksilver and Sweet Georga Brown are being loaded into the trailer while we get ready to leave for Santa Anita. I'm bringing eight heavily armed guards with me today. I nod to my entourage while overseeing preparations for the journey. I can't guarantee Gabriella's and the horse's safety with anything less.

My SUV will take the lead in front of the horse trailer then two SUVs will bring up the rear. We're always aware and ready for any possibility of being attacked on the way to the race. Quicksilver is the horse to beat, and everyone knows it.

This premier race of the year is the Santa Anita Derby, which has produced no less than 15 Kentucky Derby winners. Additionally, Santa Anita occasionally hosts the Breeders' Cup World Championships, the year's most-attended race after the Kentucky Derby.

We pull into our space and unload Quicksilver and Sweet Georga as Gabriella watches intently. She looks lovely as always. She planned to wear her stilettos, but I convinced her not to. I appreciate her thoughtfulness to make me happy, explaining I'm happiest when she's comfortable and able to enjoy herself.

We're racing against Greased Lightening today and the crowd is anticipating the outcome. I'm told the betting has reached frenzied heights. Pete, our jockey, saddles up after he is hoisted onto Quicksilver with his riding crop in hand.

Pete rechecks his stirrups and then leads Quicksilver with Sweet Georgia Brown at their side. Gabriella tells Quicksilver "Good luck boy. We'll be cheering for you. Have fun out there. And Georgia, keep our boy calm."

It's the strangest feeling but it's as if Quicksilver understands Gabriella and responds with a nod of his head and a neigh. *I take a second look at my horse, and I swear he winked at me. I think I'll keep that to myself.*

We make our way to my box seats front and center with binoculars hanging from our necks. Gabriella attentively watches every action, determined not to miss anything. The Carltons are seated in the box seats beside us.

Ed Carlton is the CEO of Carlton Motors and builds the most sought-after racing cars in the world. The Carlton Z2 rivals Audi's R8 hands down. Ed extends his hand when I introduce Gabriella to Ed and his wife Mackenzie. Ed responds,

"Congratulations Anthony and Gabriella on your recent marriage. Mackenzie and I are planning a get-together next weekend to celebrate our third wedding anniversary. I'd like to extend you our invitation to attend our gathering on Saturday at 7:00 pm."

Nodding, and thanking him, I accept his invitation to their anniversary party telling him we'll be there.

I accepted Ed's invitation for Gabreilla's benefit. Mackenzie is only a few years older than Gabriella. It will be easy for both women to relate to one another and find common ground to build a friendship. I want Gabriella to make friends and feel accepted in her new life.

The horses for the upcoming race arrive. The buglers, dressed in their red-and-gold uniforms, play "Call to the Post" dictated by tradition.

The jockeys ride the horses onto the track, entering through a tunnel that goes beneath the grandstands. A non-racing horse accompanies each racehorse to keep them calm as they make their way to the starting gate on the opposite side of the field. Sweet Georga Brown accompanies Quicksilver.

Once the horses are set up in the starting stalls, the bell rings, the gates open, and the race is on. Excitement and noise levels build, as the horses race around the end of the track and come into view. We're on our feet as the crowd goes wild amidst loud shouting, cheering, and general racket. Someone's ringing a cowbell, and another is blowing a horn.

The excitement mounts and peaks when the horses approach the finish line, finally crossing with Quicksilver leading the pack. Gabriella screams so loud I think she will lose her voice. Watching her reaction is almost as much fun as winning the race.

Grabbing Gabriella, I twirl her inhaling her essence in with a kiss. She is so excited she can barely stand still. We're escorted to the winner's circle with people congratulating me by shaking my hand and patting my back on the way. Quicksilver is adorned with a blanket of yellow roses across his neck when Gabriella and I are presented with a Breeders Cup World Championship Horse Trophy made of bronze.

We pose for photos and while the flashbulbs go off, we're presented with a check for six million dollars. That doesn't include my winnings from the off-the-track bets. My bookie will settle up later. All in all, a very exciting day and one for a celebration.

It didn't go unnoticed that Ed and Mackenzie were also rejoicing in celebrating their win. Ed bet on Quicksilver and is happy he did. Sometimes these races are a toss-up, and you have a 50-50 chance of selecting the winner. Those who bet on Greased Lightening are, unfortunately, not so happy.

We wait until Quicksilver is cooled off, rubbed down, and loaded into the trailer with Sweet Georga. I send four guards home with the horses, while my remaining four guards accompany us on a night out on the town.

I haven't told Gabriella that I own a club. I guess tonight is as good a time as any to mention that to her. It's the club's accounting that runs into difficulties and doesn't add up occasionally. I want Gabriella to take over the accounting soon.

As we're on our way to the club, Gabriella asks,

"Anthony, I want to learn to ride a horse. I would like to tour the ranch on horseback. If I can't ride one of our horses, can we rent one for me to ride?"

Smiling at her suggestion, I find it humorous and hold in a chuckle that would have led to a full-on laugh.

"Gabriella, if you're serious about learning to ride, we can search for a horse that you can call your own. How does that sound? I've been thinking of buying another horse and this would fit into my plans well."

"Are you serious? Will it really be mine, to name and take care of and ride anytime I want?"

"Yes, it will be purchased especially for you. Your name can go on the bill of sale as well as a photograph of you and the horse included in the Horse Breeders catalog."

"Oh my gosh, thank you, Anthony I can hardly believe this is happening to me."

"Did you enjoy the horse races, Gabriella?"

"It's something I'll never forget. I love the buglers in those beautiful red and gold uniforms, blowing their horns. I love how the horses are brought out with the jockeys leading both horses to the gate. It's magnificent. These races are steeped in tradition, adding elegance I didn't expect. As the horses finally approached the finish line, with all of us standing on our feet screaming, I thought my heart would explode watching our Quicksilver, the winner, cross the finish line. Anthony, I loved every exciting minute."

Taking her hand in mine I tell her, "I'm glad you enjoyed it. You'll have many more opportunities to see numerous races in the future."

We arrive at the club and Gabriella is awe-struck looking out the window at the extravagant marquee as 'Club Vitale' proclaims this is the club you want to be seen in. My doorman, dressed in an elegant uniform, is securing the entrance as the usual large line of people are waiting to enter. Deirdre Dupre, a popular singer, is headlining this week.

"Anthony, is this your nightclub?"

"Yes! And it's our club now."

Gabriella

We enter the club and are seated by the maître d', who hands us menus. I've only seen dinner clubs in old movies. This is right out of the elegant days of the past and I feel we should be dressed more appropriately for the occasion. This is Los Angeles and next to Hollywood after all, where businesses are always in competition with each other. This is undoubtedly a unique club. When we finish our meal, the table is cleared leaving only the centerpiece, a lit brass lantern. The waiter asks for our beverage of choice.

Once all the customers are served their drinks, the waiters disappear. The lighting is dimmed, the curtain on the stage is pulled back, and the band begins to play. The beautiful Deirdre Dupre is introduced and then bows as the audience applauds her. She begins her medley of songs as her backup singers join in.

She takes her microphone off its stand, carrying it in her hand as she walks on the stage opposite our table and sings directly to Anthony. As she serenades Anthony, acknowledging his presence in the audience, I must admit I feel a twinge of jealousy. I don't care for it one bit. As Deirdre strokes Anthony with her song, I place my hand on his leg stroking his thigh, rubbing my hand slowly up and down then squeezing his knee.

Anthony smiles as he places his hand over mine, entwining our fingers together and bringing my hand up to his mouth to kiss it. Somehow his gesture makes me feel safe and secure. I'm not sure if kissing my hand is a signal to Deirdre to move on or not. But I find myself relaxing when she finally turns away offering her attention to others in the audience. I don't know what came over me.

The show is fantastic. Deirdre's backup singers are also top-notch. Each singer exhibits a semi-solo to show off their voice, keeping the audience captivated the entire time they are on stage. I half expected a choir to join in, they are so thrilling. It is exciting and a treat to be entertained by such popular professionals. They receive a standing ovation from the crowd.

After the show, the entire stage slowly rolls back as a rock band is introduced and begins to play. People get up and fill the dance floor that was previously hidden by the stage. I'm impressed. This is a unique club. No wonder people are standing in line to get in.

Anthony stands holding out his hand and I jump to my feet to join him on the dance floor. I had no idea my handsome husband had such seductive dance moves. He's always so reserved, commanding respect, dominating any room he enters. He's the same on the dance floor yet he lets his reserved persona relax and shows off his talent.

Anthony is an influencer, a mover, and a shaker in the business world as well as on the dance floor. There isn't a woman in the room who doesn't have eyes for Anthony. Some of them are persistent in doing everything they can to make him notice them. I can't say I blame them. He is quite stunning. I can't believe he wants me.

The tempo of the music slows down to a hypnotic melody. Anthony pulls me to him with an unmistakable gleam in his eyes. I'm surprised the fabric of our clothing hasn't melted from the intense heat building between our bodies as we rub seductively against each other.

My gawd, Anthony is the sexiest man on this planet and my body is reacting to him. I close my eyes and start to feel like my body is floating, hypnotized by the beat of the music.

"Gabriella! Open your eyes! Now!"

I'm being held tightly in Anthony's arms as he almost hugs the breath out of me. My eyes are hazed over, and I can't see clearly yet.

"What's the matter? Did I miss a step?"

Anthony

I'm able to wake her from her trance just in the nick of time. I'm not so sure I could have held her down as she had lifted me to the tips of my toes with her feet hovering over mine. The dance floor is so crowded that I'm sure no one noticed. I'm sure it appeared she was standing on my feet.

I've put this off long enough. This could have been a catastrophe had I not been able to bring her out of it. It's time for us to discuss the elephant in the room. I kiss her on the forehead and brush a strand of hair away from her face, as her feet are again planted on the floor and she seems coherent.

"No, you didn't miss a step. But it's been a long day and I think it's time to call it a night."

My lovely kitten looks a bit bewildered as she looks around at the people dancing. I'm not sure she fully comprehends what almost happened. She does, however, seem a little unsteady on her feet, indicating that her trance requires some time to recover.

CHAPTER 16

Anthony

After a full day, we're set for the evening, snuggled and comfortable in bed, wrapped in each other's arms as I begin,

"Gabriella, are you aware we levitate when we're in the thralls of our lovemaking?"

"What do you mean, like ... we float?"

"That's exactly what I mean. You levitate and take me with you about four feet off the bed or floor. I put off discussing this with you because it hasn't been a problem until tonight."

"What happened tonight?"

"While we were dancing that last song, rubbing sensually against each other, you closed your eyes and laid your head on my shoulder. Then you drifted into what I assume is a dream state and started lifting us right off the dance floor. I was forcefully holding on to you, afraid you might float right out of my arms. Your feet were hovering over mine and I was being lifted to my toes while holding onto you. I couldn't allow anyone to see what was happening, so I needed to wake you."

"Anthony is that when I thought I missed a step."

"Yes. It took a few minutes for you to get back to normal. You almost gave me a heart attack."

"I remember I was feeling tired when you were rubbing against me and then that weightless feeling took over. I wasn't even aware where I was for a while."

"Have you always been able to experience that floating sensation?"

"No. The first time I remember feeling weightless was on our wedding night. It feels like I'm soaring, lifting as if I'm dreaming and in a hypersexual state. That's the first time I ever felt that way. But I continue to have that same experience every time we make love. I can't seem to control it."

"Well, it seems you were lost in that feeling while we were dancing. This is so extraordinary that we must keep this to ourselves. No one else can know about your capability."

"I don't know what to say, Anthony."

"This seems like a good time to add that I felt everything that was happening to you when you were being hurt by your would-be abductor. I felt the strike on your cheek, your loss of breath with pressure on your stomach, the punch to your stomach. And finally, I felt the instant the knife pierced your neck. How can that be?"

Gabriella looks at me with excitement in her eyes and a smile on her lips. "Anthony, that means I've bonded with you. I'm not only a part of you but you are a part of me."

"What exactly does that mean?"

"My mother told me when I came of age and met my true love that we would be bonded as one for life. I wasn't sure about what she was telling me … until now. It's true, what she told me, it's all true."

"Gabriella, have you any other abilities that other people don't have? And does your father know of your … uncommon capabilities?"

"I haven't experienced anything else, but my mother told me we can communicate with our minds as well as physically as you just stated you felt. I'm not sure if my father can read my thoughts. But he sent those men telling them I would be at the stable that morning. He knew I would be there."

"Or Gabriella, he might have guessed. He may not have necessarily known. It's a concern, but let's not worry until we know for sure if he can or cannot read your thoughts."

Gabriella frowns with concern as she also shows signs of fatigue.

"This has been a long and exciting day for you, Gabriella. I know you're tired. Let's not worry about any of this tonight. We'll just take each day as it comes and face any problems as they present themselves together. Okay?"

"Okay Anthony, I love you."

"And I love you, Kitten."

This is so unbelievable but here I am experiencing it firsthand. If anyone had told me, what I know now to be true, I would have called them crazy. I think I'm beginning to understand Leo's obsession and effort to get his daughter back. I wonder how far her abilities go.

Gabriella may be in for a surprise as she matures. I'll just have to stand by her, plan for the unexpected, and help her through it. I might begin by doing a little research on gravity and see if I can find anything on levitation.

My mind is wandering as I think about what's happened. Then it comes to me. I'm remembering what I thought was Quicksilver's wink. Did Quicksilver understand what Gabriella said to him? Can she communicate with horses … animals? My mind is on overdrive as I consider the possibility that she can.

There is no way I can sleep just yet. I get out of bed carefully, trying not to disturb Gabriella. I enter my office and shut the door behind me. Pouring myself a drink, I walk to my chair and sit at my desk. It suddenly hits me how serious and even dangerous all of this could be for Gabriella.

I haven't put in enough thought to consider the obvious consequences connected with her abilities. Not with just the human factor of being newsworthy but what if the government caught wind of her capabilities? That's a horrendous thought. Pouring another drink, I contemplate the caution we'll have to take from now on. Guzzling my drink, I linger to think about the precautions we'll have to take. I return to our bedroom with my amazing kitten.

As I get into bed, Gabriella turns to me. She puts her arm around my neck, kisses me softly, puts her head back, and looks into my eyes, saying,

"Anthony, make love to me."

"Kitten, you never have to ask me to make love to you ever."

I place my arms around her as my passion for her takes over. I don't know how I ever found such a wonder.

Gabriella

During breakfast, I ask Anthony if I can go to the craft store, the liquor store, and the make-up counter at Le Paré. I want to put together a gift basket for Ed and Mackenzie Carlton. I'm planning to present it to them for their wedding anniversary we're attending this weekend.

"Does Ed smoke cigars? And you'll need to tell me what we should get, champagne, wine, or something else, and where to get it."

"Um … yes Ed smokes Cuban cigars, but you can't get those just anywhere. I suggest both a fine white and a red wine. Tell me about your idea."

"I want to create a special gift basket with gold paper as a basket filler, topped with 2 crystal glasses with their names painted in gold, with your white and red bottles of wine, a basket of chocolate laced strawberries, two Cuban cigars in a gold lamé pouch for Ed, and smokey eye makeup in a gold lamé pouch for Mackenzie. What do you think?"

"It sounds like a fine gift basket. But how are you going to have their names painted on crystal glasses in less than a week?"

"I am going to paint their names in gold glass paint, but if I can't get the cigars for Ed then I won't get the eye makeup for Mackenzie. It's just something I think would be fun. I'm going to paint 'Smoke' on the pouch for the cigars and 'Gets in Your Eyes!' on Mackenzie's pouch, then add a CD with Romantic music."

"That would make your gift basket unique and special, especially since you created it. But it's too dangerous for you to go. You'll have to make a list and I'll send Jenna."

"No, please Anthony I need to pick things out. Please, I don't care if everyone on the ranch goes with me. It won't be the same if I can't choose the items I need. Please just let me go so I can shop for the things I want."

Anthony sighs, shakes his head, then says, "We'll take five men with us. You don't take a step without us, understand."

"Yes, Anthony, understood. Thank you." Throwing my arms appreciatively around Anthony's neck, I kiss him enthusiastically.

Anthony takes two SUVs. Dominic and Giorgio rode with Anthony and me in our SUV. Matteo, Angelo, and Santino are in the second SUV. I feel completely safe with all these people, but I can't help but notice, these men are on guard one hundred percent of the time. They're never relaxed when they're on duty.

We stop at a store dedicated to alcoholic beverages and beverage accessories. Anthony sends Santino in to purchase the wine. He comes back with the two bottles of wine in special bags with the wine maker's logo. Those look expensive. Our next stop is at a rather fancy tobacco store. Anthony and Dominic go in. They come back with Dominic carrying a small bag with the store's emblem. I ask,

"Anthony, what did you get?"

He replies, "I have a special friend who sold me a rather rare box of cigars."

I clap my hands and smile, "Does this mean we can go to Le Paré to get Mackenzie's eye makeup?"

Anthony nods his head with a big smile and says, "That's exactly what it means, Kitten."

Our next stop is at a French pastry shop. I start to open the door, but Anthony shakes his head holding a picture in his hand of the special strawberries I want.

Holding the picture up for me to view he says, "A dozen of these strawberries in a see-through box, correct?"

"Yes, Anthony." I am disappointed I'm not able to go in and look around at the shop, but at least we're getting everything I need so far."

The next stop is the craft store. Much to my surprise we all get out of the SUVs and enter the store. Anthony and Dominic are by my side when Matteo, Angelo, and Santino head for the entrances to stand guard.

Anthony gets a wheeled cart, and we head to the basket display. I chose a lovely basket that Mackenzie will be able to use in her decor later. I find the crystal glasses I want, the paint, paintbrushes, shredded paper basket filler, gold ribbon, and gold lamé pouches. Anthony and I selected an anniversary card and a Romantic CD titled, 'Smoke Gets in Your Eyes.' Perfect I was thrilled!

Our last stop is Le Paré. We pull in front of the busy store and as I get out, the men look anxiously at the crowd and a decision is made that I stay in the SUV. I get back in the SUV telling the men,

"Once someone helps you, please hand the sales associate the phone so I can tell her the products and colors I want. It'll be quicker that way."

When the men enter the store, they disappear into the crowd. It's concerning to think anything could happen with so many people that I start to get nervous. Finally, I get the call and ask the clerk for the eyeshadow, eyeliner, and mascara I want. They have all three in stock, the purchase is made, and the men come out unscathed, looking happy to leave the store.

I thank Anthony and the men for doing this today. Dominic drives the SUV from the curb and into traffic but there is so much traffic that Matteo is unable to get directly behind us. The men are on high alert when a second car squeezes in front of Matteo. Matteo is now two car lengths behind us. Dominic calls Matteo telling him he's getting out of traffic and is headed for the freeway.

Matteo finally finds an opening and can pass one of the cars in front of him. He's narrowed the gap between us by one car. When he passes the car, he reports that he recognizes one of the passengers, and it's not good. He's one of my father's men. Anthony tells me to get on the floor. Quickly unbuckling my seat belt, doing as I'm told, I lay flat on the floor.

It seems the car that is directly behind us is now traveling beside us on the right side. The car that Matteo passes is traveling beside us on the left side. Matteo is directly behind us now. Fearing the worst, I'm deep in a defensive state, visualizing an invisible protective shield around both our SUVs hoping I have the strength to protect us. I don't know why I think I can do this, but I must try.

I feel Anthony's hands on my back holding me down. *Am I rising?* I can't let go of my thoughts. I must continue to protect us. It isn't long before Anthony comments that the two cars causing concern are driving in the direction of the offramp as if they no longer recognize they are on each side of us. Anthony stops pushing on me and helps me back onto my seat. He gives me a questioning look and whispers,

"Did you do that? Did you lead them away?"

Responding in a whispered voice I say, "I don't know. I tried to protect us with a shield, but I don't know if I was successful in influencing their inability to recognize us."

"It's possible they were trying to see if you were in the vehicle before they acted. With our tinted windows and you on the floor, they couldn't know for sure. Anyway, we're safe, and on our way home."

Anthony puts his arm around me, kisses me on the cheek, and pulls me close to him. I place my hand on his thigh and thank him for our shopping spree. Though we had a scare, everything ended well, making this a successful day.

CHAPTER 17

Gabriella

The men bring everything for the gift basket to the dining room table. I fill the basket with the gold curly filler and nestle both wine bottles in their fancy bags in the basket. I lay out a brown paper bag to protect the table while I open the gold paint, remove the paintbrush from its wrapping, and begin to paint Ed's name in calligraphy style on one of the glasses. Then I paint connecting gold rings under Ed's name.

Taking the other glass, I paint Mackenzie's name in the same calligraphy style with the same connecting gold rings. I place both glasses on the side buffet table to dry with instructions for no one to touch either glass for an hour. Anthony, admiring the names I painted on the glasses, compliments me on my artwork and asks that I make a pair for us. I feel proud that Anthony likes them so much he wants a pair for himself.

I paint *Smoke* in black paint on the pouch that will hold the cigars and paint *Gets in Your Eyes* on the pouch that will hold the eye makeup. I lay them next to the glasses to dry. The CD is snuggled into the front of the basket while the strawberries go in the refrigerator until Saturday evening when the basket will be presented to Ed and Mackenzie.

I announce to everyone not to let us leave the house without the strawberries. I even stick a post-it note on the basket, so we don't forget and leave the strawberries behind.

An hour later I check to ensure the paint is dry as I place the glasses into the basket next to the wine. I fill Ed's pouch with two Cuban cigars and Mackenzie's pouch with eye makeup. I lay both pouches in front of the glasses behind the 'Smoke Gets in Your Eyes' CD. The only thing missing is the strawberries.

Once Anthony signs the card, I sign my name next to his then place the card between the bottles of wine. I tie a gold organza loop bow with a wire edge to the handle as a finishing touch. I wrap the basket in clear cellophane with a gold vein throughout to complete the look. Anthony looks at my gift, smiling and nodding as he says,

"You should go into the gift basket business, Gabriella. You created a fine gift."

"Do you think they'll like it?"

"I'm sure they will."

Saturday Night ...

Anthony is dressed in his white dinner jacket. I'm wearing a new gold lamé dress with strappy gold heels, a surprise from Anthony. Jenna places the strawberries carefully within the cellophane opening, setting them in the front of the basket. Anthony takes a picture of the completed basket with his cell phone. I feel like floating, I'm so proud.

Anthony told Ed he is bringing a plus two to his party, Giorgio, and Dominic. He lightens the explanation with a little humor by telling Ed the four of us are a package deal. Ed agrees with a chuckle, accepting Anthony's precautionary measures.

Ed and Mackenzie greet us at the door with enthusiasm. Dominic, who is carrying the basket, steps in after us and turns to me as I take the basket, handing it to Ed.

"This is a little gift from Anthony and me to help celebrate your anniversary. May you have a long and happy life together."

Ed shakes Anthony's hand as Mackenzie hugs me. Dominic and Giorgio stand as inconspicuously as possible trying to blend in. Ed carries the basket to the bar, setting it down as Mackenzie takes off the cellophane to look at the goodies inside. She lifts out the CD reading the songs it contains telling us she loves every song listed. She raises the strawberries out saying,

"Ahh Ed, look at these delicious strawberries. One guess at what they're paired with."

She lifts a bottle of wine out of the basket, slipping the cover off saying, "This is perfect!" She sets it back in the basket and takes out the other bottle. She slips the cover off it and Ed says,

"Wonderful, that one's mine!"

Mackenzie hands Ed the pouch that says "Smoke" and she takes the one that says, "Gets in Your Eyes." When Ed opens his pouch and takes out one of the Cuban cigars, his eyes light up and he turns to Anthony and pats him on his back.

"Thank you, Anthony there's nothing like a Cuban cigar."

Mackenzie opens her pouch and squeals in delight, giving me a big hug. She lifts the glasses out of the basket, handing Ed his. She asks her server to open one of the wines and pour some in each glass. They admire their names in gold, clink their glasses, intertwine their arms, and take a sip of wine. Then take a bite out of one of the

119

strawberries. Mackenzie reaches for the card, takes it out of its envelope, and reads the congratulatory sentiments to Ed.

Ed says, "Anthony and Gabriella, thank you so much for this splendid gift. Where on earth did you get this?"

Anthony says, "This is all Gabriella's creation. She thought it up and put it together."

I respond, "Anthony gets the credit. He chose the wine, was responsible for the cigars, and did most of the shopping. He went above and beyond helping me to accomplish this."

Ed shakes Anthony's hand and kisses my hand in appreciation as Mackenzie gives me and Anthony hugs. I'm happy they enjoy the gift basket, and Anthony seems rather satisfied with the results as well. We weren't the only ones who brought gifts for Ed and Mackenzie, but our gift takes center stage and stands out like a shining star.

Ed introduces us to the guests in attendance as we enjoy hors d'oeuvres and drinks while mixing and visiting with everyone. Anthony is especially attentive this evening. I don't think he takes his hand away from me for even a minute. We walk out on the balcony admiring the city lights in the distance when he turns and kisses me with passion.

"I'm so proud of you, Gabriella. I'm the luckiest man alive."

"I love you, Anthony, and I consider myself the luckiest woman alive."

We're called to the dining room as dinner is being served. I feel honored as we are invited to sit with Ed and Mackenzie at the head of their huge dining table. A prestigious honor considering the important people here tonight. The discussion drifts to Ed's famous racing car, the Carlton Z2, and the races it has won. Its performance never fails to amaze people.

Then someone brought up the Derby and Quicksilver's win. Everyone here tonight is a winner after betting on Quicksilver. They are boisterously reliving the moment Quicksilver crosses over the line with a glorious win, remembering the thrill of the moment.

After dinner, Ed invites the men to go out on the balcony to visit and indulge in manly conversation and smoke their cigars. Mackenzie invites the women on a tour of their mansion to show off her collection of paintings.

I get the distinct feeling that Anthony isn't comfortable with our separation because he sends Giorgio with me. He reluctantly joins the men as he watches me disappear with the women.

Mackenzie collects paintings from one artist who paints children and animals with unusually large eyes full of expression and character. They are uniquely charming, and I can see the resemblance between Mackenzie and me and what we find appealing. I think of her as a kindred spirit.

As we near the end of our tour, I feel familiar arms sliding around my waist as Anthony catches up with us kissing me on my neck. He implies he just came from the men's room, but I think that is an excuse to see what we're doing. He stays with us enjoying the last bit of the tour as the women join the men once again.

The evening comes to an end all too soon as we say goodnight and thank our hosts. We're shaking hands and hugging new friends goodbye as Ed says,

"We'll have to get together again soon. I'll call to set a time." Anthony responds,

"Anytime. I'm looking forward to it."

As I enter the SUV, I see a folded sheet of paper on the seat. I stop and turn back to look at Anthony. He looks over my shoulder and sees what concerns me. He reaches for the paper, unfolds it, and reads,

Gabriella,

The time has come for us to meet face-to-face and discuss your responsibility to the Farina family.

Anthony motions for me to get in. He climbs in after me and puts his arms around me protectively.

"Anthony, is it from my father?" Anthony nods and says, "Yes."

"How did he know we were here if he can't read my thoughts? This must mean he's here in Los Angeles. He must be living here. He left that note to let me know he can get to me anytime he wishes."

"We don't know that yet. He could have had one of his men deliver it. I don't think anyone at the party is responsible since the note was left in the car, not somewhere in the house."

"Anthony, I don't want to see or speak to him. I don't trust him. He just wants to use me for his own gain. He'll hurt me, Anthony, I know he will."

"I'm not letting him near you. You're just going to have to call the ranch your world until I can end this. It's too dangerous for you to be anywhere else for now."

"Can we have Ed and Mackenzie to the ranch for our get-together?"

"Yes, most definitely. Don't worry I'll try to make things as normal as they can be under the circumstances."

"Why is he doing this? He doesn't even like me Anthony. I just want him out of my life forever."

"Gabriella, I truly believe it has something to do with your extraordinary capabilities. Your mother prepared you for this when you reached adulthood. I believe you're not done growing as far as your special capabilities go. I think there may be more for you to discover, and I think your father knows that."

CHAPTER 18

Gabriella

I'm in my office reading about the different races and breeds of horses. The different Horse Races include,

Flat racing: Maiden, Allowance, Claiming, Stake, Triple Crown, and English classic.

Jump racing: Steeplechase, Hurdle, Timber, and Grand National.

Endurance racing: Mongol Derby.

The different Breeds of horses include Arabians, Quarter Horses, and Standard Brands.

Needing to take notes I search through my purse for a pen when I find my employee badge in the hidden side pocket. I'd forgotten all about it. When Anthony led me out of the restaurant that day, I couldn't return it.

Taking a break from my research I sit back and write a note to Jake, fold the paper, and place it accompanied by the badge in an envelope. I address the envelope and seal it; all I need now is a stamp.

Walking to Anthony's office I find him working on his computer. His door is open, and I knock to get his attention. As he looks up, I ask,

"Anthony, I need a stamp. Do you have one I can use?"

"Come in, Gabriella. What are you going to mail?"

"I found my employee badge. It has a computer chip in it, so I thought it was important enough that I should return it. I included a note and now I need a stamp."

"You wrote a note? May I see it?

"I've already sealed it. Do you have a stamp?"

Anthony holds out his hand asking, "May I see it please."

I hesitate when he motions me to come forward. I walk toward his side of the desk frowning with concern about why he wants to see my sealed envelope. Taking the envelope from my hand, he looks at the front, shakes his head, and then tears the envelope open removing the badge and the note.

I'm shocked at his action as it is the very last thing I expect of him. Feeling insulted, I look intently at his face as he unfolds the note and reads it. He crumples the note, drops it in his wastebasket with the envelope, and tells me to sit down.

I look at my crumpled note in the wastebasket and then look back at him with a stunned and questioning expression. He says, "Please, sit down Gabriella, and write what I say."

Annoyed, I pick-up the pen nearest me, tear a sheet of paper off the notepad on his desk, and sit down, waiting for Anthony to continue.

"Gabriella, please write the following: Mr. Holbrook (comma), I apologize for not returning your badge sooner (period). I assume you would want it back (period). Sign it, Ella Vitale."

Anthony reaches for a new envelope and slides it to me asking me to address it to Holbrook and Son. I ask, "What is wrong with what I wrote?"

"I'm glad you ask. First, you addressed the envelope to 'Jake Holbrook.' Too personal and not professional. Second, you use our physical address. Always use our Post Office Box as our return address in all correspondence. Third, you begin with, 'Dear Jake,' when you should have written, 'Mr. Holbrook.' Fourth, your note becomes a letter including far too much unnecessary information. Then you sign your letter, 'Gabriella.' They know you as 'Ella,' not 'Gabriella.' If they are curious, by putting in a little effort, they very well can connect you to the name Farina."

Becoming offended and irritated I ask, "Do you have a red ink pen?"

"Why do you need a red ink pen?"

"So, I can draw a red heart by my name. Or would that be considered too personal?"

Anthony has a scowl on his face as he tells me he has no red ink pens. I respond,

"That's okay. I'll just use this pen." I smile as I place the pen on the note.

"Gabriella, you'll do no such thing." Anthony reaches over the desk and grabs the pen out of my hand.

I start giggling at his response and can't seem to stop. He has the expression of a man on the edge as my giggle turns into a burst of full-body laughter.

"Gabriella, there is no need for your disrespect, and I advise you to stop laughing."

I can't stop laughing and I must sound hysterical because this whole thing is so laughable. Anthony stands, grabs my arm, and pulls me around the desk to him as he sits back in his chair, flipping me over his lap. He says that I need to be put in my place.

"Anthony, what are you doing? Stop that! Let me get up NOW! If you dare strike me in anger our bond will be broken. Please, don't hit me."

I wasn't sure if it was 'breaking our bond' or the word 'please' that was the deciding factor that brought him to his senses. He stopped what he was about to do but continued to hold me over his lap as he said,

"Gabriella, apologize to me."

"What! Anthony, it's you who should be apologizing to me."

"Gabriella, apologize or I'll punish you."

"You'll punish me! Are you serious?"

Humiliated beyond belief, still lying across his lap, I demand,

"Anthony, let me up!"

My lip quivers in anger, and my eyes fill with tears as I again demand to be let up from his lap. Once I'm on my feet I turn and attempt to leave. Anthony grabs my wrist, turning me toward him, and dares to say,

"Apologize to me!"

"And just what am I apologizing for, Anthony? Am I apologizing for being insulted by you, or is it because you belittle me when you crumple my note and throw it in the waste basket? How about when you offend me and then humiliate me by throwing me over your lap and threatening to hit me? Or should I apologize because I become so outraged by your condescending attitude toward me that I just responded accordingly?"

I'm dumbfounded when he demands,

"Yes, that last one. Gabriella, apologize to me."

My eyes are wide, my mouth is open, and I'm completely stunned. I am so angry I pull my hand from his hold and walk to my office closing the door behind me. Not wanting to add more conflict to whatever this is, I need a chance to calm down.

He was going to punish me for threatening to draw a red heart by my name and laughing at the situation. After what he did to me, I do not for one minute believe I am out of line and it's he who should be apologizing to me.

Wait ... is he jealous? Was this entire thing because he's jealous? Of Jake! Yes, he's jealous!

Sitting at my desk I'm stunned that this entire incident occurred because I wrote a note to Jake. I didn't know we had a Post Office Box and I used Jake's first name, that's true, but my letter didn't seem personal to me.

I thank Jake for the job opportunity and apologize for my abrupt departure. Mistakenly I signed it Gabriella, not Ella. So, I made a few mistakes. I can accept that he corrects me, but he is so condescending. I don't see it as constructive criticism. ... Did he mean it to be?

It shocked me that he was going to spank me. I can't allow him to hit me. It would have broken our bond. Looking around my office at the framed photos of our wedding day and Quicksilver, and us after winning the Derby. Realizing everything Anthony has provided to make me happy, I make a decision.

I guess I should apologize for threatening to draw a red heart by my name on a letter to another man. He became angry and didn't take it well. He reacted like I knew he would. But he made me so angry. I guess I should say I'm sorry.

I go to my door, open it, and walk toward Anthony's office. I walk past his doorway, to the other side, turn, and walk back, stop at his doorway, and look in at Anthony. He looks at me, then back at his computer. I stand in his doorway fidgeting with my hands and looking at my feet when he says,

"Are you going to stand there all night or are you coming in?"

"Do you want me to come in?"

"Do you want to come in?

"I'm just making sure I'm still invited to come in."

"Gabriella, please come in."

I step inside and fidget some more, taking a big breath not knowing how to start or what to say. On the edge of the desk, I see the envelope has a stamp on it and notice the note and badge slightly sticking out of the envelope waiting to be sealed.

I run my finger on the edge of the desktop as I slowly make my way to the other side where Anthony's sitting. He is leaning back in his chair with his arms folded across his chest watching me as I inch closer to him. Finally, my leg is touching his knee as I say,

"I'm sorry. I wasn't going to draw a heart by my name. I said it to make you angry."

"Thank you, Gabriella, I accept your apology."

I stand there waiting for Anthony to apologize to me, but when he doesn't, I respond,

"Don't you have anything to say to me?"

"I already thanked you. What else would you have me say?"

I'm so hurt and angry that I turn with a huff and storm out of his office. Going upstairs I take two steps at a time until I reach the top of the staircase. Entering our room, I grab a nightgown and underwear then walk directly to the nearest guest room locking the door behind me.

I take a shower hoping it will calm me down, dry off, and climb into bed. After tossing and turning a few times and hugging a pillow, I finally drifted into a tearful sleep.

CHAPTER 19

Anthony

I linger in my office for a while to finish some business. I text Giorgio to bring one of the gifts I have stored in the ranch house and to set it on our dining table. It's my apology to Gabriella and will be waiting for her at breakfast.

I know I made Gabriella angry. I should have reciprocated with an apology of my own, but I am still angry she felt the need to write a note to Jake. Then she had the nerve to tell me she was going to draw a heart next to her name. She knew exactly how I would respond to that.

I didn't intend to offend her. It just sort of got away from me, ending in a more sarcastic tone than necessary when she started laughing at me. I stopped her when I threw her over my lap threatening to spank her. I wasn't going to hit her. But I wonder if it's true that I would have broken our bond if I had spanked her. I don't think she would lie about something like that. I don't think Gabriella is capable of lying.

I guess I'll swallow my pride and see if my kitten has settled down and forgiven me so we can enjoy makeup sex. I open the door to our dark bedroom, take off my shirt, toss it on the chair, and remove my shoes. I can tell Gabriella is not in the room. I take a deep breath and sigh as I leave our bedroom and pad barefoot down the hall to the first guest room. *We will not sleep in separate beds. Not tonight or any night.*

The door is closed. I turn the handle and discover it's locked. *Does she think I don't have keys to every lock in my domain?* I smile as I pull out my Hawaiian key chain with the master key attached and unlock the door. The light from the hall shines in the room just enough for me to see, taking my breath away.

My magical kitten is hovering over the bed on her side with her arms wrapped around a pillow. This is new. Up until this moment, she's only levitated with me. I quietly approach her. Not wanting to startle her, I carefully climb onto the bed and settle into a sitting position, as I softly speak to her.

"Gabriella, won't you come to me please." She stirs slightly.

"Gabriella, please come down to me, my love."

She starts to descend until she is lying on the bed. She still appears to be asleep as I brush the hair from her face and kiss her forehead. I speak to her as if she's awake and can hear me.

"Gabriella, I'm sorry I upset you tonight. I love you with all my heart. Will you forgive me?"

Taking the pillow from her, I pull her into my arms and plant gentle kisses all over her face. She takes a deep breath, opens her eyes, and kisses me back, wrapping her arms around my neck. Unzipping my slacks and pushing them past my hips and down my legs, I throw them on the floor.

I pull Gabriella's gown over her head and toss it at the foot of the bed. I pull her lace panties down her legs and lay them aside. More than ready with my full hard erection, I anticipate what will most definitely be an over-the-top expression of our love.

Gabriella's scent is a sweet aroma that fills my senses with her erotic warmth. She's a walking contradiction. She has an innocence about her as well as sexually arousing heat that radiates from her spirit. She is a marvel.

My instinct is to breathe every bit of her into my lungs until my body is full of her. Her sweet lips are plump and soft and taste like a special exotic blend of berries, uniquely hers alone. Her beautiful body calls to me as I touch her perfect skin, which seems to glow with the touch of my hand. Her core invites me, and only me, to enjoy the exclusive intoxicating pleasures that only she can provide.

As I penetrate her, I feel a strong pulsating vibration pulling me deep inside her as we levitate and soar into weightlessness. Gabriella wraps her legs around me, crossing her ankles together as we drift above the bed. We assume a rhythm that causes our bodies and minds to react as one entity.

I'm lost in the most extraordinary miracle of lovemaking that two people can ever experience in a lifetime. My body feels every sensation possible from the top of my head to the bottom of my feet. It's as if I'm adrift in a sea of clouds.

We slowly descend back to the bed, still in a haze from our magical coupling. Returning to a natural sense of well-being, we have the knowledge that our love is stronger than any bonded pair on earth. We drift into our deep sleep wrapped in each other's arms.

CHAPTER 20

Gabriella

The sun is shining through the sheer curtains. I struggle to keep my eyes closed, bringing the covers over my face. As I turn my back to the window, I find myself face-to-face with Anthony. How long has he been here? Oh, now I remember through the haze that seems to be my mind. He climbed into bed with me last night. I believe he apologized … in a most seductive manner.

I look at his face, admiring his eyelashes that fan out on his cheek. I brush a clump of dark hair from his forehead. He has a perfectly shaped nose and kissable lips. How can such a beautiful specimen of a man make me so angry at times? I wish my mother were alive so I could talk to her about how he invokes such emotion in me.

He opens his beautiful eyes and smiles that lustful smile at me as he says,

"Good morning. Did you sleep well?"

"I did. Did you sleep well?"

"Yes, I most certainly did. Would you like to get dressed? I've arranged for Matteo to work with you on the accounting for the horses today.

I'm excited with the knowledge that at last I'm going to be shown the books and can finally offer my expertise. I kiss Anthony and bounce out of the bed.

"Hold on, wait for me. I think we should take our shared shower in our room. We don't want to waste our water now, do we?' He smiles that sarcastic innocent boyish smile.

I'm the only one who sees this side of my scary mafia Don. He's like two sides of a coin. On one side he's dominating, formidable, and threatening; on the other, he's playful, easygoing, and affectionate.

Not wanting to surprise the staff catching us nude, Anthony puts on his pants and hands me my gown. He looks out the door and down the hall, making sure no one is in sight so we can get to our room without surprising the staff. We take our shower, engage in a lustful round of morning sex, dress, and make our way downstairs to the dining room.

Approaching the dining room doorway, I see a brightly wrapped gift on the table. Anthony has that innocent smile on his face as we make our way to our chairs. He pulls my chair out, waits for me to be seated, then pushes me forward. He sits in his chair, crosses his arms on the table, and waits for me to open the box.

I grasp the box bringing it closer and ask, "Is this a special occasion that I'm not aware of? A holiday? Bastille Day?"

Anthony responds, "Just open it."

I take the bow off the package folding back the gift wrap. I entwine my fingers together looking at Anthony savoring the moment. Excitedly I take a deep breath, take the lid off the box, and push back the tissue paper. It's a leather holster for my gun. I hold it up admiring my initials burned into the leather.

"Anthony, it's perfect, thank you so much."

Anthony motions for me to hand it to him. He wraps the holster around my hips buckling it then takes the dangling leather straps and ties it around my thigh. He says,

"Your gun is small enough to put in your purse. But you need to carry it on you when you're outside and when you tour the ranch. You'll soon forget you're wearing it."

Finishing my breakfast, I leave the table still wearing my holster, making my way to my office. I open the box and remove my gun. Slipping my gun in the holster I snap the closure over the gun keeping it secure and in place."

I start to look for Anthony when he appears in the doorway. Holding out my arms I turn slowly modeling my holster and gun. Anthony steps forward, holds me firmly in his arms and says,

"You look like you belong on the ranch." He kisses me and asks, "Are you ready for Matteo to bring the books?"

"Yes, I'm ready to go to work."

"We'll need to use my laptop in my office today. Your new laptop hasn't arrived yet."

As we enter Anthony's office he goes directly to his desk. Sitting in his chair he begins to tidy his desktop and bring out paper and pencils in preparation for written calculations. He moves his computer closer to one side preparing for the space that will be needed when Matteo brings in the ledgers. I make myself comfortable in one of the chairs in front of the desk,

Matteo arrives, sets the ledgers down on Anthony's desk, and takes the chair next to me. After we greet each other, Matteo opens one of the ledgers and starts explaining how they are set up and how they are maintained. I ask,

"Are these ledgers backed up with a digital copy?" He responds,

"Not completely. We just recently started inputting the information into a program but haven't gotten very far yet."

"Will you open the program for me, please? I wish to evaluate if it's the best process for our use."

Anthony turns on his computer, opens the program, and turns the screen toward us. As I review the program and the information already recorded, I compare what is noted in the ledgers. I find areas that have not been recorded under the proper heading and other problems. Pointing out my discovery, I explain,

"Anthony there is a better program available for keeping your books. I would like to start the process of recording a digital copy of the new program from the beginning. I'm sure you'll be pleased with the outcome."

After downloading and demonstrating the new program to Anthony and Matteo with little explanation, they both agree to use the superior program.

Until I've been given my computer, I must remain in Anthony's office to begin inputting the information from the ledger into the new program. Changing places with Anthony, I sit in his chair behind his desk as he sits in my chair beside Matteo.

I've been inputting transactions for over an hour when Anthony excuses himself to take a break. Matteo is reciting figures to me from the ledger while I key the numbers into the program. I've just broken the tip of the pencil I've been using to double-check calculations.

Aggravated about needing another pencil, I avoid losing my place by reaching across the desk to get another. I was concentrating so hard that I didn't realize Anthony had returned. I look up just in time to see Anthony lean over the desk and grab the pencil as it hovers precariously in the air within my reach.

My eyes are like saucers, my mouth flies open, and I'm shocked to realize I absent-mindedly levitated the pencil. Anthony quickly places the pencil in his shirt pocket. We're certain Matteo did not witness the floating pencil as his attention is focused on the ledger and oblivious to what has just happened. Anthony pats Matteo's shoulder telling him to take a break.

I start to say something when Anthony shakes his head, ensuring Matteo is far enough away that he doesn't overhear what I'm about to say,

"Anthony, what am I going to do about this? How am I going to control this?"

"Don't panic. You're going to practice until you have it under control. For now, I'll finish reciting the figures while you input the information. Let's take a break and have lunch, then we'll finish up."

Anthony

Gabriella and I continue working after lunch. I excuse Matteo, feeling it was too dangerous to have anyone near Gabriella while she is experiencing her newfound abilities. She seems overwhelmed, as she should be. This is a lot for anyone to comprehend and accept. If anyone were to discover the power she possesses at this point, it would put her life in jeopardy.

She needs my support and love and I'm determined to help her accept and control her powers. I'm using the word "power" because that is exactly what she possesses: The power to act in a way that no other human on this planet can. And therein lies the danger she'll face from those who would use her powers against others.

We complete inputting the bookkeeping computations into the new program. This will be much easier to update and maintain, eliminating the human errors we've been plagued with in the past. Gabriella has not only improved my life but also improved the accounting process of one of my businesses.

I can't help but believe that I've also improved Gabriella's life as well. She now has a home that is equally hers, with the ability to go anywhere without restriction within her dwelling.

The same stands for the vast property that encompasses the ranch. She is free to take advantage of the property her estate sits on. She can explore, enjoy, and make changes for improvement as she sees fit. I am devoted to Gabriella, as she is loved, respected, and protected by me.

CHAPTER 21

Anthony

I am in deep thought trying to come to grips with all of this. I'm not sure I fully understand or have a handle on the metamorphosis Gabriella is exhibiting. I'm searching on the internet and looking up telekinesis to educate myself. It says,

"Tel·e·ki·ne·sis, the supposed ability to move objects at a distance by mental power or other nonphysical means: *'she possesses the power of telekinesis.'*"

It was sheer luck I returned to my office just in time to pluck the pencil out of the air before Matteo was aware of it hovering over my desk. She wasn't aware that she mindlessly brought the pencil within her grasp, with no physical contact, with nothing more than her mind. Her abilities are becoming an automatic phenomenon for her. Gabriella's extra-sensory powers are as natural for her as it is for us to use our physical abilities.

I research Gabriella's capabilities and look up "levitate." Wikipedia says,

"Lev· I ·tate, to rise or cause to rise and hover in the air, especially in seeming defiance of gravitation. Especially by means of supernatural or magical power:"

Hmmm. I search for the definition of gravity.

"Grav·i·ty, the force that attracts a body toward the center of the earth, or toward any other physical body having mass."

That doesn't tell me much, so I looked up "What is Gravity?" and found this,

"What is Gravity - We don't really know. We can define what it is as a field of influence because we know how it operates in the universe. Some scientists think that it is made up of particles called gravitons which travel at the speed of light. However, if we are to be honest, we do not know what gravity "is" in any fundamental way – we only know how it behaves."

I'm sure if I were to ask Gabriella, she would be able to explain this in the next section. She's a mathematical genius after all.

"Newton's "law" of gravity is a mathematical description of the way bodies are observed to attract one another. The gravitational equation says that the force of gravity is proportional to the product of the two masses (m_1 and m_2), and inversely proportional to the square of the distance (r) between their centers of mass. Mathematically speaking."

Newton's Law means absolutely nothing to me. But what I do know is that Gabriella must learn to control her newfound capabilities if she wishes to have a normal and free life.

Continuing my research, I looked up "telepathy" since she's already shown her acquired control in this area.

Te·lep·a·thy, communication from one mind to another by extrasensory means: It is the purported vicarious transmission of information from one person's mind to another without using any known human sensory channels or physical interaction.

Did she have anything to do with leading Leo's men away from us on the freeway? Did they give up pursuing us because they were unable to determine if Gabriella was in the SUV … or … were they unable to recognize they were driving right beside us? If the latter is true … how can that even be possible?

I plan for Gabriella and me to stay in our room all day to practice her newfound ability. I want her to feel free and succeed as she attempts as often as needed to gain control of her power in an encouraging, safe, nonjudgmental environment. I'm prepared for however long it takes for Gabriella to feel secure in taking charge.

I've instructed Jenna to knock when leaving our food by the door and not to disturb us unless there's an emergency. Outside of delivering our food, no one should remain on the second floor. Dominic, Giorgio, Matteo, and Angelo will oversee the ranch and household while I am otherwise occupied with Gabriella.

Our self-sequestered day begins this morning. I've made sure we have everything we need and are prepared for whatever might occur. I instructed the staff to ignore any bumps, thumps, or crashes they might hear, explaining we may be moving the furniture, and adding that Gabriella wants to redecorate our room.

That remark resulted in some puzzled looks. But my staff have been with me long enough to know not to question me. I had to tell them something to prepare for and minimize the possibility of alarm. I'm prepared for anything … I think.

Gabriella is anxious to have an uninterrupted day to explore her abilities in complete privacy without fear of being seen by anyone other than me.

I leave our bed, walk to the door, open it, and roll the breakfast cart just inside our room, closing and locking the door behind me. I hurry back to bed, kiss Gabriella, and ask,

"Do you think you can guide our breakfast cart to us, without touching it of course?"

Gabriella concentrates on the cart and it starts to roll toward us. It stops as Gabriella looks at me and grabs my hand.

"Gabriella, you're doing great. Go ahead, continue, and bring it to us."

She takes a deep breath and looks at the cart once again. It begins to roll toward us then it bumps softly against my side of the bed.

"Gabriella, when you moved the cart did you have any negative reaction? Do you have a headache or a ringing in your ears, … or any discomfort of any kind?"

"No, nothing. I don't feel any differently than if I had gotten up and physically pushed it."

"Great! Let's enjoy our breakfast while it's still warm. Then we'll continue."

After finishing our breakfast, we load the cart with our plates and silverware. I motion for Gabriella to send the cart back to the door. She does but fails to stop the forward motion of the cart before it hits the door with a jolt. That action causes a plate and cup to fall off the cart shattering on the floor.

Gabriella is devastated, feeling responsible for destroying a porcelain plate and cup. I have a tough time convincing her it's all right. I explained that we have extra replacement sets and many more place settings than we use. *Anticipating future accidents, I'll instruct*

Jenna to serve our meals on paper plates and cups to avoid Gabriella's distress.

We undress and head for the shower. I've asked Gabriella to lift the luffa sponges, body wash, and shampoo using her thoughts, not her hands. She successfully moves each item from the shelf into my hands perfectly. She's delighted as she then takes each item from me, setting them back on the shelf. She decides to show off, mentally lifting the towel off the rack and draping it around my shoulders.

She's excited that she successfully controlled and moved each article with the precision she meticulously meant to accomplish. I applaud her, giving her a hug and a kiss as we dry off. She starts to move my razor when I tell her I'm not shaving this morning. I don't want her to try her talent on razor blades just yet. I want to stay away from sharp things for now. *Humorously, I'm thinking of my self-preservation!*

I've set my sights on heavier and bulkier items for Gabriella to try. I'm not sure if the weight of items she can move fits into the equation of her capability or not. I ask if she can lift the bench at the foot of the bed. She does so effortlessly. As it hovers above the floor, she turns to me and asks me where I want her to put it.

"Gabriella, do you realize you're no longer looking at the bench? You're looking at and speaking to me while continuing to control the bench."

"It feels so natural, Anthony. There is nothing strange or special about lifting an item and talking with you at the same time."

She sets the bench down at the foot of the bed in its original place. Looking around the room she says,

"It will scratch the floor if I slide the armoire across the hardwood, so I'll lift it first and move it to the other wall … okay."

Gabriella lifts the armoire about 10 inches off the floor and successfully guides it as it floats to the other side of the room. She continues to lift every article of furniture in the room. She moves two bedside tables at the same time. She proceeds to lift the bed and bench, sliding the carpet out from under the bed, sliding the carpet back in place, and then set down the bench and bed … with me on it.

For her last feat, Gabriella removes the mirror from the dresser and sets it against the wall. She then lifts one side of the dresser to a vertical position, balancing it precariously with its side on the floor. As a drawer starts to open, it is closed before its contents can spill out.

She loses control momentarily when she looks for my approval and the dresser starts to tip over. Preparing myself for a dresser malfunction, Gabriella quickly turns the dresser right side up and places it gently on the floor, rehanging the mirror behind it. Being quite pleased with herself, she takes a bow.

I'm in a state of amazement and wonder. My kitten is indeed a one-of-a-kind miracle and she's mine. I jump off the bed to hug and kiss my wonderful wife.

"Anthony let's go to the library. I've already lifted and moved everything in our bedroom and bath. I need something new and challenging."

I agree, so we head downstairs to the library. I close the sliding doors and secure the latch as Gabriella turns and looks at the top shelf of the floor-to-ceiling bookcase. She slowly walks from one side of the room to the other. She looks up and concentrates on a particular book.

Gabriella moves the rolling ladder out of her way, then from the top shelf, pulls out and brings down a single book with a gold binding. She carefully directs it to my hand, ever mindful that these books are first-edition classics. Shaking my head in wonderment, I'm amazed at the skill she has shown in such a short time.

"Exceptional, Gabriella, but can you return it without damaging it or the others surrounding it?" I place the book on the coffee table.

Feeling insecure, she says, "Maybe you should return it, Anthony."

"Gabriella, we're doing this so you can build confidence in using your skills. You need to put the book back exactly as you removed it."

"Anthony, this isn't a porcelain plate or cup that's replaceable. It's a one-of-a-kind treasure that can't be replaced. I shouldn't have done this."

"Gabriella, I insist you return the book to its place."

She takes the book in hand and places her foot on the first step of the ladder preparing to climb to the top.

"No! Not like that. We'll be staying in this room until you do as I say. Return the book now."

Gabriella steps down from the ladder. She holds the book out letting go as it floats in front of her. She slowly directs it to the top shelf hovering just outside the space it came from. Painstakingly, Gabriella centers the book and eases the book in its place without any problems.

Her expression of relief makes me smile when I give her a hug and kiss. As I congratulate her success, Gabriella notices the large book on the coffee table. She studies the book as it opens with her thoughts and the pages begin to turn one at a time. She stops at a page titled "Magic and the Wonders of the Universe," a fitting chapter, especially for our activities today.

CHAPTER 22

Gabriella

Sitting down on the sofa, I carefully scan the room. I anxiously look to find another object to practice my skill when everything becomes a blur. It's as if a fog fills the room, and I can barely make out what is right in front of me. As I try to focus my eyes, I feel a sense of panic because I can't recognize what I am seeing.

I'm still in the library, but my eyes are looking into someone else's room, and I can't identify the decor. I reach out to something on a desk thinking I'm much closer than I am. I can't see my hand as I extend it in front of me. I can hear Anthony calling my name, but he sounds so far away. His voice is muffled as if he's in a tunnel.

I can see and smell the smoke from a cigar, but I can't see who's smoking it. I look carefully around the room to see if I recognize anything. It's an elaborately adorned room with elegant floor-to-ceiling windows, framed oil paintings, and a gilded mirror.

I can see the reflection in the mirror of someone sitting in a leather high-back chair. I can't quite make out who the person is but I'm straining to see what the person is holding. I stand and take a step forward to get closer to the mirror when I topple over.

Anthony is holding me, calling my name, asking me if I'm all right. He shakes me until my eyes come out of the haze I was experiencing. I can see Anthony clearly now and the library I never left.

"Gabriella, what happened? Where did you think you were? You tripped over the coffee table when you stood and attempted to walk through it. I knew you were in some sort of a trance and caught you just in time. Otherwise, that could have been a nasty fall."

"I don't know what happened. I've never experienced anything like it before. I was looking into a room that I had never seen before and saw someone's reflection in a mirror. But I couldn't tell whether they were male or female."

"Did you hear anything or smell anything?"

"Yes! I smelled the scent of cigar smoke. Anthony, I feel sick. I think I'm going to ..."

Anthony

Gabriella's eyes suddenly rolled up under her eyelids as she collapsed into my arms. Her natural color has disappeared, and she feels warm to the touch. After laying her on the sofa I call her name hoping she can somehow hear me. Concerned and not sure what to do, I am just about to call the doctor when she opens her eyes.

"Hi! I'm guessing there's a reason I'm lying on the sofa, and you're hovering over me with that concerned expression on your face. Did I break something?"

"No! but you physically reacted to whatever just happened to you. You said you felt sick and then passed out cold."

"Was I out for very long?"

"Not really. It couldn't have been more than five minutes. I'm concerned because this is the only time you had a bad reaction."

"Anthony, this was different. This wasn't me practicing my skills. This was something much deeper. I connected with someone. I just don't know if they connected with me or if I connected with them."

"Does it make a difference?"

"Yes, I believe it does. If they connect with me then they are in control of what I experience and what I see. If I connect with them then I'm in control. Anthony, I'm not sure about what just happened."

"Do you think it was your father?"

"Yes, I do. I've been thinking of him … a lot lately. I've been exploring and practicing these newfound skills and that has brought certain strange feelings to the surface. I'm determined not to communicate with him on any level. But I didn't consider that he can do what I can do. He's my father, and if he uses his power he can and will be able to control me."

"Then you need to stay on top of this. Practice makes perfect. The more you practice the stronger your confidence will be. The stronger you become, the better you'll be able to protect yourself against him."

"Oh, Anthony, I wish my mother were alive. I think she would have liked you."

"Thank you, kitten. I wish I could have met her too. Come on, let's have some lunch then we can get back to it. You can't stop now. You must fight him. You can't let him win."

Jenna steps in from the kitchen serving us our lunch. She tells me the mail was delivered early this morning and is sitting on my desk as usual. Thanking her, I turn to Gabriella and ask where she wants to continue practicing.

"Anthony, I think I'd like to return to the library."

"Are you sure?"

"Yes, I'd like to try something."

"Okay. Do you think you'll be all right for a while? I want to check the mail then I'll be in."

"Yes, I think I'll be fine. I'm just going to practice everything I've done so far."

"Be sure and close the doors. We can't be too careful at this point."

Gabriella makes her way to the library as I go toward my office. Taking my seat behind my desk, I sort through the mail when I come across a letter from Holbrook & Son addressed to Gabriella. Without hesitation, I rip open the envelope. Enclosed is a check made out to Ella Vitale for $1,400.00. That is a substantial amount of money for 4 days of work. I'm impressed.

I unfold the letter and begin reading the following.

Dear Ella,

Until we received your letter, we had no way to send you your pay for the time you spent with us. Please find enclosed a check in the amount of $1,400.00. You were a valued employee.

Thank you for the return of your employee badge. It is much appreciated. I was extremely worried about the abrupt way you were forced to leave with a man you seemed frightened of. I'm happy to hear that you seem to be all right and hopefully doing well. If you ever need anything don't hesitate to call me.

Sincerely,

Jake Holbrook

I read the letter three times. Jake most definitely has a thing for Gabriella. He's telling a married woman if she ever needs anything all she has to do is call him. I angrily crumple the letter. But … thinking better of it, I smooth the letter out as much as possible, returning it to what's left of the envelope and placing it in my drawer.

I'm not going to tell her about the letter, but I'll deposit the check through my cell phone app. That way I can keep the original check after depositing the funds in her account. Knowing Gabriella, she may want to frame the check, memorializing her first paycheck.

I'll wait to see if she notices the inflated amount in her account, then I'll consider telling her where it came from. Since she can't go anywhere off the ranch, her capability to shop for anything is slim to none. It will most likely take some time for her to notice the extra money even if she should make online purchases.

Finally finishing up other business I make a few calls then walk to the library. As I slide the library doors open, I stand in the doorway and look around. At first glance, I can't see Gabriella and think she has left the room.

It is jarring and unsettling when my eyes finally catch sight of her. She is almost luminescent as it appears that she has blended into the bookcase. A ghostly presence would be a better description of what I am looking at. How can that be?

I can only slightly make out the outline of Gabriella's body. It's almost as if she's invisible. I can see the books in the bookcase through her. If I hadn't known that was Gabriella, I would have shot her. I'm going to need a very stiff drink after this.

I step inside the library, closing and locking the door behind me. Being as quiet as I can be, I realize this is dangerous. If any other member of the household catches a glimpse of what I am looking at, Gabriella would most assuredly be dead. My staff tends to shoot first and ask questions later.

I step forward slowly calling her name and telling her I'm in the middle of the room facing her. I find when she's in these trances, she's not always aware of my presence. She walks from the bookcase toward me, returning to her normal self with each step.

Controlling my reaction to cover up my shock at what I witnessed, I reach out to her, wrapping my arms around her protectively telling her she's magnificent. However, my heart hasn't stopped pounding with the fright I experienced.

She wraps her arms around me as she begins to tremble slightly. Holding her affectionately in my arms, I encouraged her to tell me all about what she had just accomplished.

"Gabriella, tell me how you did this. Please don't leave anything out and start from the beginning."

"Anthony, I don't know how I could manage this without you. You've been my strength through all of this. I don't think I could go on without you by my side."

"I'm right here. I'm not going anywhere. I told you we would go through this together. Come, let's sit down on the sofa."

"Anthony, as I was pacing back and forth in front of the bookcase, I was thinking about how I may have been responsible for leading my father's men away from us on the freeway that day. I'm going to attempt to explain how I was able to achieve a shield for us."

As we get comfortable on the sofa, she snuggles into me wrapping her arms around my waist as I put my arm around her shoulders. She begins:

"I projected an image of the two cars driving in front of us to the occupants of the two cars driving beside us. My father's men thought they were driving beside two different cars. I made our larger SUVs appear to be smaller cars to them. Thinking they had lost us, they drove away."

I kiss her on the forehead, "That's remarkable, Gabriella."

"I need you to understand. When you saw me just now, I had not changed. My physical body had not changed." You were seeing me as I projected an image to you."

"But I didn't see you at all when I first opened the library doors. It wasn't until I looked around the room that I spotted you."

"That's because I was waiting for you and projected my thoughts to you the second you opened the doors."

"But I could see right through you. I could even see the books in the bookcase through you. You looked like the invisible man, or woman, ah … person. Do I dare say it? You appeared to be an apparition, a ghost. And I don't believe in ghosts."

"I projected my thoughts to you. You were seeing exactly what I wanted you to see. If you had touched me while you were under my control, you would have realized I was a whole and solid person. Have you ever heard the term 'shapeshifter'?"

"Yes. A supernatural folklore of one that seems able to change form or identity at will, a mythical figure that can assume different forms of animals. I have a few men that come from a region where these tales are believed."

"They're not folklore and they're not supernatural. They aren't shifting their bodies from one form to another. They are projecting their thoughts of illusion to another person, camouflaging, and protecting themselves from those who would harm them."

"How do you know that?"

"Because my mother told me years ago that there is a group of my people who broke away thousands of years ago to live on the land, in obscurity, away from human society."

"Anthony, would you like me to demonstrate on my legs?"

I answer with hesitation "Yes, Gabriella please demonstrate."

I watch in amazement as Gabriella's legs seem to become invisible and I can see the sofa cushion where her legs should be.

"Anthony, touch my legs. Feel your way where my legs should be."

As I place my hand over her leg, I don't know what to say. I can feel Gabriella's leg under my hand, but my eyes are telling me her legs are invisible. I only see the sofa cushion.

"Gabriella, this is remarkable. Whatever you do, promise me you won't practice this where any of my people can see it. Depending on who it is, they would shoot you on sight."

"I promise. I'll be certain no one is around and I'm alone. In the meantime," … I reach into my pocket to retrieve part of my tooth,

"Anthony, I have a serious problem with a tooth I believe was damaged when I was struck in the face. It had been tender, but I thought it was recovering. It must have been cracked because a piece of the tooth broke off when I bit down on a slice of apple during lunch."

CHAPTER 23

Anthony

"Let me see it."

Gabriella reaches out with a portion of her tooth sitting on the palm of her hand. She smiles her beautiful smile and there just behind her lower eye tooth is a noticeably broken tooth. *I'd like to beat the man responsible all over again.*

Shaking my head I say, "I'll take you to see Wayne today. Why didn't you tell me about your tooth sooner?"

"It didn't bother me after the first day I was hit, and it only acted up occasionally. My tooth didn't hurt when the piece cracked off. But it's been throbbing a little now. That may be the reason I wasn't completely invisible, and you were able to see me. I couldn't concentrate with a throbbing tooth."

I kiss Gabriella and walk to my office. Wayne and I go way back to our high school years. As best buddies we were inseparable. We excelled in everything sports and were the popular jocks. All the girls wanted us, and the guys wanted to be us. We were idolized as we were not only the best athletes, but we were also the best-looking guys in school.

We only got better with age and after graduation, Wayne went to Georgetown University School of Dentistry, located in Washington, D.C. I pursued a business degree that eventually led me to the darker more lucrative side of business.

I went on to become the leader of a syndicate with a ranch and racehorses, a dinner club, and other assets. Wayne went on to become the renowned Dr. Wayne Riggert, D.D.S. the most famous dentist in the country practicing in Beverly Hills. With our thick hair and our pearly whites, we are greatly admired by the ladies, a nuisance we put up with.

Aside from general dentistry, Wayne is best known for his cosmetic skills. He pursues the latest techniques and equipment and actively stays on top of his game. Wayne's patients are well-known actors, politicians, and even a few dignitaries he made friends with while in D.C. Additionally, he travels to third-world countries offering his talent free of charge to impoverished people who would otherwise have no dental care of any kind.

It's remarkable as I realize how much we were alike and how we took such different paths in life. Our life choices led to where we both are today. We've remained friends over the years regardless of my reputation. I send him additional business as my men require treatment from time to time. I'm grateful he accepts the clientele, though our office visits tend to be later in the evening.

Making the call I tell his receptionist, "This is Anthony Vitale. What time can I bring my wife in today?"

His receptionist knows not to comment or question my calls as she announces to Wayne that I'm on hold.

It doesn't take long for him to answer. "Anthony! When did you get married and why wasn't I invited?"

"It's a long story and we'll catch up when I bring Gabriella in. What time can you take her?"

"I'll be free in an hour. What's the problem?"

"Her tooth must have been fractured when she sustained a hit in the face a while ago. Half the tooth broke off when she bit into a slice of apple this afternoon."

"I'll need to take a full set of X-rays to see if her jaw and other teeth are impacted. We can talk while my assistant sets it up."

"Thanks, Wayne. We're on our way."

Making one last call to Matteo, I ask him to set up Gabriella's new laptop and place it on her desk then bring one of the gift-wrapped boxes from the ranch house and set it on the dining table in the mansion. I instruct him to make sure both are in their place by the time Gabriella and I return.

As we exit the ranch and drive onto the main road, Gabriella seems depressed and has a sad look on her face.

"What is it, Gabriella? Are you worried about your tooth and how it's going to look?"

"Yes, a little. I've always taken special care of my teeth and to think someone else did this to me is very upsetting."

"I promise it will look and feel exactly as it did. You'll soon forget it ever happened."

"It's not just the tooth Anthony. It's also about the changes I'm experiencing and how it affects you. And what you might think of me now that you can see what I can do. Do you consider me an alien?"

"Gabriella, someone else with a closed mind might consider you an alien. I am not one of those people. How can you reason I would think any less of you regardless of what you can or cannot do? You are a unique, talented, and beautiful young woman. I knew I had to make you mine the minute I laid eyes on you. Gabriella, my love for you will never waiver."

"Even if I find there are more surprises to come?"

"I'm counting on it. I'll be by your side no matter what comes."

I hug Gabriella and kiss her temple. Entwining our fingers, I bring her hand to my lips, then rest our hands on my thigh. There isn't another woman like her, and I'm concerned I can't fully protect her from her father. I must prepare somehow to fight against his capabilities as they are assuredly the same, if not stronger, than Gabriella's.

We arrive at Wayne's office and as we enter an empty waiting room it's obvious Wayne is prepared for our arrival. Dominic and Giorgio take their positions as we're greeted by Wayne and his wife Whitney. We hug each other with a pat on the shoulder when I introduce Gabriella.

Showing her embarrassment, Gabriella covers her mouth with her hand as she says, "It's nice to meet you. Thank you for seeing me on such short notice."

Wayne winks at me saying, "It's my honor." Extending his hand he says, "Gabriella come with me please and we'll get started."

I follow close behind as we enter the examining room. Gabriella is seated in the chair as Whitney drapes Gabriella with a lead apron shielding her against radiation. As I was leaving, Whitney, who sensed Gabriella's anxiety, assured her I would return as soon as she finished taking the X-rays.

Whitney positions the first of several photo cards into Gabriella's mouth and sets the machine on the outside of her jaw. She then takes each radiograph required for Gabriella's treatment.

The monitor displays all the images taken of Gabriella's teeth as Wayne and I return to the room. Wayne examines each photo carefully, and announces,

"There is only one tooth to be cared for. No other teeth were impacted and there is no injury to the jawbone."

Gabriella takes a deep breath of relief upon hearing the news. She noticeably relaxes as Wayne allows me to stay. Knowing I tend to hover, he insists I sit on the opposite side of the room while he performs his magic. He's particular that way.

Wayne, completing the treatment for Gabriella's tooth, sets a temporary crown in place that is an exact match to her teeth.

Wayne says, "The porcelain crown will be ready in a week. I'll call you when it arrives."

Gabriella looks at Wayne's work when he gives her a handheld mirror. Wayne says,

"If you feel any rough spots, I can smooth it out since this is a temporary crown."

Gabriella answers, "No, Dr, Riggert, it's perfect. Thank you so much," giving both Wayne and me a big smile of gratitude.

161

Gabriella's smile is as perfect as it always was. There isn't a hint that one of her teeth has a crown. Wayne is an artist in his profession, and I compliment him on his work as Gabriella and I are quite happy with the results.

On our way back to the ranch, Gabriella couldn't stop looking at her new tooth. She keeps trying to see if there is a slight difference but is unsuccessful and finally puts her compact away. She kisses me and thanks me, promising to show me her appreciation later.

Entering the mansion, we make our way to the dining room. I'm feeling hungry and can smell the meal that will be served shortly. My stomach begins to growl, and I think I'm salivating as we take our seats at the table.

Gabriella's eyes are as wide as saucers as she looks at the wrapped package in front of her. This one is larger than the ones previously presented to her. She looks at me with affection as she asks,

"Could this be a gift commemorating my broken tooth?"

I respond, "That and the accumulation of extra stress you've experienced of late. You have handled yourself well and I appreciate the strength and courage you've demonstrated through trying times."

"Thank you, Anthony. But I believe you deserve a gift for standing by me as we travel on this journey together. I'm sure you didn't sign up for any of this and it hasn't been easy for you either."

"I wouldn't have it any other way, Gabriella. Now open your gift."

CHAPTER 24

Gabriella

With a smile on my face, I take off the bow and unwrap the paper. Lifting the top of the box and pushing aside the tissue paper, I find a beautiful porcelain horse figurine on its back legs and a card. It's from a horse breeder with an appointment time and date to select my horse.

I excitedly stand, turn, and step to Anthony as I lift my leg over his, straddling him in his chair. Placing my hands around his neck I lean in and kiss him gently on his left cheek then his right, kissing first one eyelid then the other, then his nose. I brush my mouth softly across his lips nipping his bottom lip, sucking it into my mouth sensually as I gently shift and rotate my hips while sitting on his lap. He responds exactly as I expected as he grabs me tightly around the waist lifting his hips, ensuring I can feel his arousal.

Jenna must have known we were otherwise occupied with each other as she knocked on her side of the kitchen door before entering. We both laugh as Jenna pretends, she's embarrassed by putting one hand up to the side of her face shielding her view from us while serving our dinner. I reluctantly go back to my chair showing Jenna the horse figurine and the card.

Jenna admires the figurine and congratulates me on the horse that will soon be a new addition to the ranch. Jenna briefly shares a look with Anthony, filling our glasses, and then returns to the kitchen. I can't take my eyes off the figurine and card as I'm eating. Anthony watches me intently as he reaches under the table to stroke my thigh with a gleam in his eyes requiring my absolute attention.

I turn to look at him as he rises from his chair. He slowly unzips his pants with his eyes locked on mine. I look anxiously toward the door and then back at him with concern someone will come in. Anthony, with a serious expression on his face, shakes his head assuring me no one will come in.

That look shared with Jenna was as good as a 'Do Not Disturb Sign'. This is one of those occasions where the fear of being caught in the act only adds to the excitement of the circumstances.

After taking my hand and pulling me up to a standing position, Anthony pushes porcelain plates, cups, and silverware out of the way clearing a wide area on the table. He lifts me and sits me on the table laying me on my back and climbing on the table after me.

Anthony grabs both my wrists in his hand, holding them like a vise above my head firmly against the table. I bite my bottom lip unaccustomed to this aggressive behavior. Looking rather surprised and a bit frightened I look into his eyes.

Anthony looks at me and says, "Do you trust me?"

I answer, "Yes, I trust you with my life."

"Do you love me, Gabriella?"

"Yes, Anthony, I love you with all my heart."

As he looks into my eyes, Anthony pushes my blouse up pulling my bra down, exposing my breasts. He leans down still holding my wrists above my head and places his lips on my nipple. His other hand cups, caresses, and manipulates my other breast. Anthony slides his hand from my breast to my stomach then lifts my skirt to my waist. I let out a shriek when without warning he rips my panties to shreds before he begins to slowly caress, stroke, and fondle my sex.

My body begins to take me to a hypersexual state. Anthony leads me into an increased sexual desire which involves out-of-control feelings and urges that cause high-frequency sexual behavior, literally lifting my body to an elevated state.

My sexual behavior is controlled by a chemical in my brain resulting in hypersexuality that causes me to levitate. I'm not sure if I'll ever be able to control it. But I'm not sure if I should want to. Only time will tell.

As Anthony continues to kiss, touch, caress, and fondle me, I begin to rise. I can feel the tingling throughout my body. When Anthony inserts his girth into me it brings my desire to an overwhelming high as we drift above the table in a haze of sexual pleasure.

My hands are now free to wrap around Anthony's neck as his arms are wrapped tightly around my body. He drifts in the same state I'm feeling as I have bonded with him completely. He feels everything I feel becoming one, attached to each other, in a mating ritual that is ageless.

We float in a sea of bliss, with my head still spinning as I consider what I just experienced. My senses are overloaded because I feel anxious, we could be discovered while in the dining room. Then I felt alarmed as Anthony restrained my wrists with his hand then I panicked when he shredded my panties. Finally, I felt thrilled when he led me through a sexual release knowing nothing else could ever reach the height I had just achieved.

After we've lingered long enough to recover from our lovemaking, Anthony helps me to my feet. As I straighten my clothing, he kisses me tenderly and then hands me my shredded panties. I examine the carnage as he gives me that innocent expression as if asking, "What?"

Not wanting the staff to see the evidence of our sexual activities, I'll dispose of what's left of my panties in the waste basket in our room. I grab the box holding the horse figurine and make my way to my office with Anthony by my side.

I drift in thought as I remember I had no interest in Anthony when we first met. He is the head of the mafia, and I was concerned he had recognized me. I was more frightened of him than attracted to his good looks and charm.

There was no indication Anthony would later pursue me or that he would make marriage part of his condition to save me from my father's plan. Though I find I was unsuccessful in escaping the mafia, I'm happy he came back for me and that we are now mated for life. There is no telling where I would be now if he hadn't.

We enter my office so I can place my porcelain horse figurine in the glass case. It is majestic and masterfully sculpted and glazed with a highly polished shine. This isn't just a run-of-the-mill porcelain figurine. This is special and created by a talented artist. This is a one-of-a-kind collector's piece. Anthony admires its placement in the case.

"Do you like it?"

"Anthony it's beautiful and I will treasure it forever." I put it in the case to keep it safe and protected.

These are moments reserved for only the two of us. The mafia don would never show interest in figurines or other collectibles and would deny it till his dying day. It's a matter of life and death that Anthony shows only the side of him that represents his dominance, aggressiveness, and brutal alpha male behavior for others to see. Sensitivity promotes weakness not tolerated in the mafia.

That's one of the reasons I wanted to escape the mafia. Besides the criminal aspect, the brutality, and the killing, you must always remain alert for self-preservation. It's exhausting! You never truly know who's a friend and who is not. You can never voice your true opinion, guarding against insulting another and those who would use your words against you.

I worry about my father interfering in our life. I know his desire is to bring me to his side to join our powers against his enemies. Joining forces with him is a frightening aspect, but I realize sooner or later I will have to face him.

I'm not sure what he'll do if I continue to refuse his attempts for my compliance. I can't explain it, but I feel his presence. He's like an all-consuming dark cloud squeezing the light out of my life. He has always been the cold to my warmth.

Anthony hugs me, looks at my desk, and says, "I'm going to my office. You should try out your new laptop" then retires to finish business matters that require his attention.

I was surprised as I hadn't noticed the brand-new laptop sitting closed and unceremonious on my desk without the usual gift-giving fanfare. I run down the hall to catch him to thank him for the surprise. As he turns, I wrap my arms around his neck kissing him with extreme glee and thanking him profusely for the new laptop.

"Anthony, I just can't thank you enough for everything you do for me. Thank you. You're spoiling me."

"I like spoiling you. It makes me happy to see you so happy."

Anthony gives me a quick kiss on the forehead then turns me around and pats my bottom as he says, "Be on your way kid; it's time to go to work." Returning to my office with a smile on my face, I sit behind my desk and open my laptop. It even smells new. It's beautiful and I'm so thankful for everything I have.

Opening the invoices that were placed neatly beside the laptop, I bring up the program for the Vitale Ranch and begin inputting expenses. I presume the reason Anthony didn't make a big deal about the laptop is because it's required for my job. I love it anyway and consider it a gift.

It takes only a few minutes to record all the expenditures. After sending Anthony an email with a copy of the updates in an attachment, I searched for what's installed on my new computer. It seems I have everything I need and then some. Noticing I have a message from Anthony, I open it and read,

Anthony: "Thanks for the update. It seems you're doing well on your new computer. Glad you like it."

Me: "I love it, it's great! Thank you 😊"

I'm thinking about how fast the week has gone by as I'm getting ready to go to the dentist for my permanent crown. Anthony has finally opened his office door when the men pile out of his meeting. We greet each other with a kiss and continue to the SUV, along with Dominic and Giorgio who are our constant escorts.

We arrive at Dr. Riggert's office greeted by Whitney as we enter the waiting room. I'm led to the examination room as Anthony goes to Dr. Riggert's office. As I'm waiting, I can hear Anthony and Dr. Riggert's voices. They seem agitated with each other, and I'm concerned. I stand and start to go to the door, but Giorgio blocks my view. I catch a glimpse of Anthony closing the office door, but I can still hear their angry voices.

I ask Giorgio what's happening. He shakes his head and tells me I should return to the chair. Being troubled by his response, I choose to stand with my arms crossed over my chest as we stare at each other.

Dr. Riggert and Anthony finally exit the office with intense looks on their faces.

"Is there a problem, Anthony? Is everything okay?" as I look at both Anthony and Dr. Riggert.

"Gabriella, please be seated so we can complete this process."

Anthony gives me a look that tells me not to ask any more questions and to do as he asks. I sit in the chair as Whitney lays me back and Dr. Riggert takes his seat next to me. He looks flushed and upset. I become concerned because Anthony is standing next to me hovering over us. Something I know Dr. Riggert wouldn't normally allow.

I open my mouth and Dr. Riggert proceeds to remove the temporary crown and thoroughly cleans the area of what's left of my tooth. He looks at the porcelain crown in his hand and then up at Anthony. The expression on his face conveys the question, "Are you sure about this?" Anthony nods once.

Dr. Riggert cements the crown in place. He tells Whitney to take the X-ray, turning the monitor away from my view. Everyone steps out of the room when Whitney drapes me with the lead apron. She

169

inserts the photo card in my mouth, places the machine on the outside of my jaw, and takes the X-ray.

Whitney removes the lead apron from me while I watch both Anthony and Dr. Riggert return to the room huddling together as they examine the X-ray. Can it get any more obvious that something is amiss, and I've been left out of the loop? Anthony takes my hand and helps me up.

Dr. Riggert says, "Be sure and let me know if you have any problems with that crown. It should last you a lifetime." I respond,

"Thank you, Dr. Riggert. I appreciate your care."

Anthony and Dr. Riggert seem to have put their disagreement aside as they shake hands and we leave.

While we're riding in the SUV, I pull my compact out of my purse, open it, and look at my porcelain crown. It's perfect and it looks and feels exactly like my tooth as if it had never been damaged. I continue, though, to be concerned about what caused Anthony and Dr. Riggert's disagreement, leading to their heated discussion.

After admiring my new tooth, I close my compact, drop it back into my purse, and look out the window. I know if I ask what the disagreement is about, I won't get an answer. I'll only be left with more questions.

CHAPTER 25

Anthony

Gabriella looks at me then turns away. She is going to say something and then thinks better of it. She's concerned about the dispute between Wayne and me. It is business and she will just have to get used to the fact that she's not part of my business decisions just as she is not invited to attend my business meetings. The less she knows the safer it will be for her as my wife.

"Anthony, can we stop at the bookstore?"

"It's not safe. Maybe another time when we have more men with us. I rather be safe than sorry. We've already taken the risk just being at Wayne's office."

She looks out the window as we pass by the bookstore, taking in and exhaling a deep breath. She says nothing more the entire trip home.

When we enter the mansion, Gabriella goes directly toward her office as she continues her silent treatment. I don't like it. She's being insolent.

"Gabriella, stop your sulking. It doesn't suit you one bit."

She turns, and if looks could kill, I should be dead. She's defying me. She needs to learn I won't put up with that kind of behavior.

"Gabriella, you better change your attitude and quickly. I promise you won't like my response."

She looks at me softening her angry expression, changing into a questioning expression. She sucks her lower lip into her mouth, lowers her head, and starts to turn as I grab her by the arm.

"Gabriella, there are things in my world that I keep from you for a reason. Shall I tell you the worst? Should I tell you if you were abducted, torture would be used on you to learn what you know."

Gabriella reflects shock in her eyes as her mouth opens in horror. She bites her bottom lip and says,

"Oh my gawd, Anthony, but I don't know anything about your mafia businesses or …"

"You know a lot more than you realize just living under the same roof as me. Keeping as much as possible from you hopefully guarantees your survival if an event like I described should occur."

I let that bit of information sink in when I say,

"So, … are we good?"

She nods saying, "Yes, Anthony, I'm sorry … I let my frustration get the better of me."

I bend down and look into her beautiful eyes. "Is there something else you'd like to say?"

Smiling with a gleam in her eyes she says, "I love you?" as a question, kissing me on my cheek. I kiss her back on her lips with more determination and desire.

"Anthony, do you mind if I do some shopping online?"

"What are you shopping for?"

"I want to look at what books are available at the bookstore."

"Gabriella, I have an entire library full of books. Surely there is something in that collection that interests you."

"Do you have any books on hobbies?"

"Hobbies? No, I don't think I do. What kind of hobbies are you interested in?"

"I'm not sure. That's why I want to see what's available."

I look at her with amusement, responding, "Yes, have fun. If you order anything it will have to be sent to our security office. Let me handle that detail when you're ready to order."

Gabriella continues to her office as I walk to mine. I feel this quiet is like a storm before it erupts somewhere. Leo hasn't left any notes or messages of late, and I know he hasn't given up his plans for Gabriella. He's sure to do his best to accomplish his goal. Waiting for the shoe to drop is causing me irritation.

My Gabriella is bored. The ranch and horse accounting isn't enough to keep her occupied. After she transferred everything to the new program, the business accounting almost ran itself with her at the helm.

I'm holding back her introduction to the Club accounting. Our business dealings with our purchase of alcohol and beef are questionable at best. I rather she didn't know all our restaurant business relations just yet.

I wonder if I can interest her in taking law courses. It would be to my advantage to have legal counsel assisting my consigliere, my counselor. She might even be interested in going to law school and taking the bar exam. I wonder how she would feel about becoming an attorney and practicing law. *That's wishful thinking but I might bring that up some time.*

An hour passes and Gabriella sends me her orders in an email. She's ordered two books on Hobbies for the 21st Century. One book includes a plethora of different hobbies ranging from the least difficult to the most difficult using a wide range of materials.

The second book explains how to create pottery and other items with clay. This pictures a potter's wheel with hands molding clay into a bowl. This looks interesting. These books are for beginners and experienced hobbyists. In addition, she orders a pair of high-cut lace panties. I smile as I add two more pairs and the matching bras. She's very conservative and doesn't spend money as one would expect. I added the address for our security office and paid the amount listed using my card.

I am about to check in on Gabriella when I get another call. I was surprised when I recognized the number. It's Deirdre.

"Hello, Deirdre, I thought we agreed you wouldn't call me. You were only permitted to contact me through my man and only for an emergency."

"Anthony, I've been hurt. I'm at the club. Please, I think I need a doctor but don't want to answer questions from hospital personnel. Can you help me?"

"Did Ronan hurt you? I told you what I would do if he laid a hand on you again."

"Please, Anthony, can you come?"

The club is closed to the public tonight. I'm sure this was planned by Ronan. "I'll be there in half an hour. Put Harold on."

"Harold, secure the club. No one else gets in. How does Deirdre look?"

"Boss, she looks like she's been roughed up pretty good. I've already secured the club. No one is getting in. We're in your office."

"Call the doctor. Have him meet me there and don't leave Deirdre in my office alone. I'm on my way."

After grabbing my gun, I put on my bulletproof vest, throw on my jacket, and yell out,

"Gabriella, I'm going out. I'll be back when I can."

Gabriella runs out of her office to me. "Where are you going?"

"There's a problem that requires my attention."

"Anthony, you're wearing your vest. What's happening."

"We'll talk when I get back. Matteo and Angelo will stay with you. The rest of the staff are on guard. I must leave."

She grabs hold of me as if she'll never let me go. I have to pull away from her. When I turn, she watches me with a fearful expression on her face as I leave with Dominic and Giorgio at my side.

As we pull around to the back of the club, we pay attention to areas where problems could manifest themselves. We look carefully in the direction of nooks and corners that cause shadows in the dark. There are no suspicious vehicles, and nothing seems out of the ordinary as we park and enter the club with no difficulties.

I enter the elevator taking me to my second-floor office. Continuing, I can see Deirdre lying on the office sofa covered with a blanket. Her condition catches me completely off guard. There's no way she arrived here on her own. Ronan dumped her here. He set this up and is counting on my visit. I won't disappoint him.

The doctor arrives and steps out of the elevator as I turn and nod.

"Come in doc. Deirdre needs your attention." We step aside, giving him access to Deirdre.

Dominic, Giorgio, Harold, and I leave the office, closing the door behind us. We're met by my men who have assembled and are waiting for a briefing. I always have six men guarding the club and I call Matteo to send six more to assist in my plan to attack Ronan.

When the doctor completes his examination, he gives me an update on Deirdre's injuries.

"Anthony, she's in bad shape. She has a concussion, a broken wrist, and a cracked rib, but I need to take X-rays because there could be internal injuries. Who would do such a thing?"

"Take her to our infirmary. You can take the X-rays there and will have all the necessary meds and products at your disposal. I'll have someone assist you and stay with her until she can be moved."

I instruct Harold to carry Deirdre to the doctor's car and I'll have someone meet them at the infirmary.

As I approach the sofa to tell Deirdre I'll take care of her, she grabs my hand and shakes her head.

"Anthony don't go after him. He did this to get you where he wants you so he can kill you. Don't go, please. He's working with Leo Farina."

She might have a point. I knew he set this up and planned for my attack. What I didn't know is he's working with Leo. He has the upper hand, and I will lose if I walk into an ambush without a strategy. I decided to set my rage aside to plan my retaliation.

It hit me suddenly that Leo set this in play, not Ronan. Ronan must have told Leo about my past relationship with Deirdre. He knew I would go to her aid, leaving Gabriella's side. I make a call to my men to drive back to the ranch immediately announcing, "The ranch could be under attack."

I shout at the men assembled in front of me, "Everyone to the ranch now."

We escort Harold who is carrying Deirdre and are just about to exit when the door opens, and we are met head-on with a barrage of bullets. Taking shelter within the doorway, behind dumpsters, and crates lined up against the wall, we return gunfire.

Caught off guard, I'm not expecting to be ambushed at both the club and the ranch simultaneously. I underestimated Leo. I should have been more prepared for his actions against me. I can't let him take Gabriella.

We've taken down three of Leo's men and we seem to be at a standoff. It's unreasonably quiet and there has been no exchange of bullets for at least five minutes. Dominic throws a brick in the alley attempting to draw gunfire, but no one fires. I step out from behind a crate to attract attention, but no one seems to be left to fire at me. I shout at my men, "Quick get to the ranch." Leo sent just enough men to keep us occupied while he was attacking the ranch.

CHAPTER 26

Anthony

The doctor and Harold continue to the infirmary with Deirdre as I jump into our SUV. I make a call to Matteo, anxiously waiting for him to pick-up. It rings four times before he finally answers. He doesn't need to tell me they're under attack as I can hear the nonstop gunfire.

"Matteo we're on our way. Is Gabriella protected?"

"She's in the saferoom. We've lost two men, and we need assistance if we're going to keep them from breaching the mansion. I was able to count twelve of them."

"I called our men back to the ranch and we should be there in fifteen. Can you hold them off till then?"

"We don't have a choice. Everyone is engaged in protecting the home front. But hurry!"

Unexpectedly, I hear an explosion and call out Matteo's name. When there is no answer, I tell Dominic to drive faster,

"I don't care if you ram every vehicle that gets in our way, Dominic. Just get us there."

The men I previously called to the club are returning to the ranch and are just ahead of us. We reach the ranch barreling through what is left of the demolished front gate. Racing toward the mansion, we can see smoke coming from the ranch house, but it looks like that fire has been extinguished. All of us exited our vehicles with guns blazing. Our attackers are trapped between us, so they are being fired upon from both the front and now their back.

There is no longer an entrance to the mansion. Just a gaping hole. The explosion I heard while talking with Matteo seems to have hit one of the vans that brought these bums onto my property. Our arrival, none too soon, gives our men some time to reload and reposition themselves to our advantage. I'm taking no hostages. This is war.

It takes about another fifteen minutes of constant firing, but we finally hit the last man. I run into the mansion and quickly reach the safe room. I open the door only a crack calling out to Gabriella, letting her know it's me before I enter.

I talk to her constantly as I step into the room, closing the door behind me. I can't see her, but I think I feel movement to my right side. Reaching out not sure where she is, I feel what I think is her arm.

"Gabriella, it's me, Anthony. Can you hear me? It's safe now. It's over."

She grasps hold of my hand. Gabriella has perfected control over what I can see because I can't make out a ripple or an outline of her. To my eyes, she doesn't exist in this room. The only reason I know she is beside me is because she's holding my hand. Gabriella slowly comes back into view as she releases my mind from her control.

I hold her and look her over to make sure she isn't hurt then hug her tightly in my arms. We exit the safe room and as we make our way toward the front foyer, I ask where Matteo is. My men point to him laid out on the sofa, bloodied and bruised, but alive. Angelo explains,

"One of our men gained control over the drone with the grenade. He dropped it on one of their vans, but they must have had explosives on board because it blew out the front of the mansion. It gave us some time, but unfortunately, Matteo and two others were impacted by the explosion."

I look around at the damage holding tightly onto Gabriella. Two of my men have succumbed to their injuries and everyone else is suffering wounds large and small. I make a call to the doctor telling him he's required at the ranch as soon as he leaves the infirmary.

Gabriella lets go of my hand and attempts to make the men with the most serious injuries comfortable. I don't like it when she turns her attention to other men. Jenna, Angie, and Michelle are by Gabriella's side as all three women tend to the men the best they can.

Gabriella goes to each injured man, one after the other. She systematically lays her hand on each man's forehead expressing her concern as she takes notice of each injury. *What is she doing?* I watch carefully as her eyes close and she concentrates on each injured man. Every man she touches seems to react more comfortably with less pain while waiting for the doctor's arrival.

I'm both amazed and concerned. I don't want anyone to know Gabriella is special or different. I can see she's exercising her power, but her power for what? … To heal! I can't allow these men to know what she's capable of. Gabriella carefully reduces the pain of each man's injury and each man seems to rest more comfortably. Hopefully that can be explained away. Matteo is still unconscious as Gabriella asks,

"Anthony, please have Dominic and Giorgio carry Matteo to the guest room." She whispers to me, "I can't do what's needed with an audience."

We follow behind as Matteo is carried up the stairs and placed on the bed in the guest room. As I excuse Dominic and Giorgio, I catch sight of their silent glance at each other. I know they suspect something's up. Hopefully, they don't suspect Gabriella is different in any way.

"Anthony, all kinds of thoughts came to me while I was locked in the safe room. It was as if everything I am and would ever be, was revealed to me all at once. I can't explain it, but I know I have the power to heal. I can't expose myself, so I only started the healing process for our men to make them more comfortable."

"Gabriella, how are we going to explain Matteo's recovery after everyone has witnessed his injuries?"

"Because his injuries are more serious, make sure he stays in this room for at least three days. Everyone would expect his convalescence to take that long for him to get better and feel like himself again anyway."

"Okay, Gabriella, show me what you can do."

Gabriella lays one of her hands on Matteo's forehead and one on his chest over his heart. Her hands begin to glow ever so slightly at first. The light radiating from her hands becomes stronger, exhibiting a luminous golden color. The light from her hands seems to dissolve within Matteo. As I watch in utter amazement, Matteo's entire body appears to be glowing slightly. When Matteo takes a deep breath and opens his eyes, he doesn't seem to recognize us.

Gabriella softly speaks to Matteo as she says, "Go to sleep and rest Matteo. You'll feel much better when you wake."

Matteo closes his eyes once more and appears to be sleeping more comfortably as his chest rises normally with each breath he takes. The hairs on the back of my neck rise when I think about what I just witnessed. My woman is a miracle worker. She's capable of doing things that no one ever dreamed possible.

I have a sense that there is something I can't quite put my finger on between Matteo and Gabriella that bothers me. I feel a strange pull or attraction between them that doesn't quite reflect the same behavior or acceptable socialization that occurs normally between people who typically work together. It's more than that and yet I've never seen any action by either one of them that would lead me to believe they are enamored with each other.

I'm going to bring this up for discussion with Gabriella, but I don't want her to think that she has done something wrong. And yet I need her assurance that what I'm sensing is inaccurate or something I'm imagining because I'm jealous. I want to be the center of Gabriella's affection and loyalty. I don't want anyone else sharing in that space.

The doctor calls asking if he can bring Dierdre to the mansion. The infirmary is a provisional ER for my men with no one available to care for her while she is recovering. I reluctantly tell him he can. Now I need to tell Gabriella we'll be caring for an unexpected guest for a couple of days.

I'm not sure how to tell Gabriella about my past relationship with Dierdre. However, I don't know if I can trust Dierdre not to tell Gabriella, making herself sound more important in that relationship than she was. I'll talk with Gabriella before Dierdre arrives.

My able-bodied men have started repairs of the destroyed entrance. Sheets of plywood and studs are being erected to close in and secure the mansion. I've contacted my construction crew to schedule the rebuilding of the front entry. The massive columns and the double doors will have to be re-engineered from scratch. The front windows and trim will need to be replaced.

The damage to the main gate, the guardhouse, and the ranch house is not as extensive as the mansion. But it will require the same time to repair all the damage. On a positive note, everything but the main gate is still standing and the stable and the horses were not touched.

I asked Gabriella to come to my office. When she appears, I ask her to close the door behind her.

"Come in, Gabriella. Make yourself comfortable," as I motion to the chair closest to me.

She sits and looks questioningly at me as if she's figuring out an answer to a non-existent question when I begin.

"Gabriella, a situation arose that requires my involvement." Clearing my throat and thinking how best to tell her, I continue with,

"Dierdre Dupre is injured and needs a place to recover. Your father conspired with the man responsible."

Gabriella looks at me with a slight frown and then asks,

"She was hurt purposely! Why would my father plan such a thing?"

"Her injuries are a result of your father using her as a guinea pig to draw me away from the ranch tonight. The man currently seeing Dierdre told your father that she and I had dated once. He agreed to rough her up at your father's request, then dumped her at my club."

"He beat her?"

"Yes. I went to the club to see about her injuries. When we attempted to leave, we were attacked simultaneously as the ranch was also being attacked."

"Were you able to take her to the hospital?"

"No, our doctor took her to my infirmary to take X-rays. But she can't stay there. The doctor asked if he could bring her here."

"How … How long will she be staying?"

"It shouldn't be more than three days at most. Do you think you can handle an unexpected guest?"

"I … of course. Anthony, when were you together? … Was your relationship serious?"

"Gabriella, I took her out three times two years ago. Even though I was clear I wasn't interested in a relationship she wanted much more. I recognized her talent, and I was instrumental in helping to launch her career. I care about her well-being but that's all. It never went further for me."

"Does she know that? She seemed to be more than acknowledging you at the club during her act. It made me uncomfortable watching her serenading you. Does she know we're married?"

"That smoldering persona on stage is part of her act. She directs that attention to all the men in the audience. And yes, she knows we're married."

"I'll do my best to make her feel comfortable while she's here."

"Thank you, kitten. I knew I could count on you."

CHAPTER 27

Gabriella

I'm concerned my father goes to such an extent to bait Anthony by having Deirdre beaten. He uses the knowledge Deirdre dated Anthony, his only connection to what he wants. I'm convinced that if he requests such a brutal action to lead Anthony away from the ranch, he's prepared to do anything or hurt anyone to accomplish his goal of getting to me.

My father knows I'm heavily guarded with or without Anthony's physical presence. His attempt to take me by attacking the ranch fails but I know he'll try again with a different strategy. I must stay calm and keep my mind clear. I can't allow him to read my thoughts.

Turning my thoughts to my next task, I direct Jenna to prepare the guest room for Dierdre at the end of the hall. I don't want Dierdre next to Matteo's room. If Anthony should need to speak with Matteo, we need to guard against any discussions being overheard making sure there is complete privacy. A guard will be posted in the hall as long as Dierdre is a guest.

I peek into the room being prepared for Dierdre. Entering to assist Jenna, I help change the bedding, fluff the pillows, and place an extra blanket at the foot of the bed. A pitcher of iced water and glass is on a tray and ready for use on the bedside table. All guest rooms have an adjoining en suite and a phone with a call button that connects to the kitchen. Everything is ready for Dierdre and her comfort while she recovers.

Jenna and I check in on Matteo making sure his door is left open. Matteo is awake and needs help to get to the bathroom. Jenna calls the kitchen and requests a guard to come to help Matteo. Angelo appears in a matter of seconds. He helps Matteo out of bed while Jenna and I change the bedding and lay out Matteo's bedclothes.

I knock telling Angelo through the bathroom door that the bed and clean clothes are ready for Matteo. Angelo responds,

"I'll stay with Matteo for a while and help him shower."

"Thank you I'll have the doctor check on Matteo as soon as he arrives."

We leave, closing the bedroom door behind us. I ask Jenna to ensure Matteo rests comfortably and his needs are tended to while convalescing. She promises she will care for him.

Anthony meets us in the hall as we are leaving Matteo's room and asks,

"Gabriella, is everything ready for Dierdre?"

"Yes. The room at the end of the hall is ready for her arrival."

"Good. Is Angelo with Matteo now?" I nod and respond, "Yes."

Choosing my words carefully considering Jenna's presence, I let Anthony know Matteo is recovering as expected. I think to myself *"We'll have to confine him to his room because keeping his rapid recovery hidden from the staff will be difficult. Matteo will experience a burst of energy that will cause him to feel like a brand-new person with a brand-new body."*

We make our way to the side entrance while the front entrance of the mansion is boarded up. Having just arrived, the doctor, Harold, and Dierdre entered. Dierdre is being carried by Harold and he asks where he should take her. Dierdre is heavily medicated to reduce her pain and is not aware of where she is or the people surrounding her.

Jenna asks Harold and the doctor to follow her as she leads the way. Harold's actions are protective of Dierdre while he carries her with care, showing his concern. He follows closely behind Jenna, careful not to jostle Dierdre while making his way up the stairs. I ask,

"Anthony, do you want me to help Jenna attend to Dierdre as she gets settled?"

"No. Jenna and the doctor can take care of her for now, and Harold can rejoin the other able-bodied men to help secure the ranch."

I ask the doctor to attend to Matteo before he looks at anyone else. Matteo doesn't need his attention, but the doctor's exam and prescribed medication will lead to the normal assumption of Matteo's recovery. A recovery that will be attributed solely to the doctor's care and not my intervention.

The ranch is secure and those requiring care are being attended to. It's been a long and stressful evening. Undressed and ready to enter the shower, I wait for the water to warm up. Comforting arms are wrapped around me when I feel Anthony's soft lips on my neck and shoulders.

Together we step under the warm water as it spills over us relaxing our nerve-rattled bodies. Anthony reaches for the shampoo pouring some in his palm. Placing his hand on my head he begins to wash my hair, kneading my scalp with his strong fingers. Soothing me, he brings his fingers through the long strands of my hair as the water rinses away the shampoo.

He massages my shoulders and then slides his hands down and over my body with his traveling fingers touching, exploring, and coaxing me into a state of yearning. We indulge ourselves in our passionate desire to seek comfort and sexual healing in each other. Anthony guides my arms around his neck while lifting my legs around his waist. With my legs wrapped tightly around him, I feel his shaft penetrate me moving within me as deeply as humanly possible.

Laying my head back with my eyes closed I am rising, bringing Anthony with me as we build to a crescendo nearing the finale of pure unadulterated bliss. Surrendering completely to our desires we have succumbed to the pleasures of our bonded love.

Exhaustion finds us both, and we're thankful this evening is finally at an end. We retire to our bed wrapped in each other's arms. I'm grateful we survived the attack. Though there is much damage and death because of my father's actions, we are safe. What is damaged can be repaired or rebuilt, but I grieve the loss of life.

I'm sad for the families of the two men we lost. They were close to my age and cut down at the prime of their lives. Some would argue it's meaningless to grieve their death because they knew the risks when they became members of the mafia. Though I know Anthony will provide for their loved ones, I continue to feel sorrow and mourn their loss of life. Closing my eyes I finally drift into sleep.

My mind and body enjoy a deep slumber until my sleep is interrupted by a dark foreboding. I feel like I am physically being pulled into a blackness totally void of any light. I am drifting but I can't tell if I am moving or if I am stationary. I find myself looking into the same room I experienced when I was in the library.

I gaze into the gilded mirror when once again I see someone sitting in a chair holding something. Something that now seems to be a picture frame. I can finally make out who's in the chair. It's my father … and he's looking straight at me. He turns the frame in his hands to face me, never shifting his gaze from my eyes. When I can see who's in the picture, I'm frozen with fear.

It's a picture of me and Julia when we were younger. He points and taps on Julia's image with a menacing look on his face. He is threatening to harm Julia without saying a single word. As I start to scream in horror, he releases my mind, and I find myself in bed with Anthony, drenched from head to toe with perspiration.

Startled, I feel as though I am still under my father's control. Shaking, I sit up and turn on the table lamp, looking around our room and making sure everything is in its place. My eyes search for anything out of the ordinary, but nothing seems different. Trying to settle my nerves, I attribute my panic to my nightmare and the threat my father makes against Julia. *Oh no, does he know she helped me escape?*

If he was seriously threatening to harm Julia, he wouldn't have used an old photo to frighten me. He's fishing for my reaction. He doesn't have her in his control. He needs help reading my thoughts by observing my reaction. He may not be as strong as I first thought.

But I do believe he's capable of doing harm. That may be why he needs me. Is he testing me trying to determine how much power I'm capable of? He must know I'll resist all his attempts to control me. If I'm a threat, will he try to eliminate me?

Turning out the light, I sink back into the bed next to Anthony. Reaching out, Anthony places his arm around me pulling me tightly against him. His affection makes me feel safe, protected, and most of all loved. With my hand covering his I finally relax, feeling myself begin to drift back into a deep sleep.

Waking in an empty bed I linger a while feeling Anthony's absence. I dress and can hear the sounds and activity of the men talking, hammering, hustling, and bustling through the mansion.

When I go down the stairs, I can see everyone is hard at work repairing the damage to the mansion due to the attack. In the dining room, I observe it's every man for himself. Jenna has set the food out in potluck style so the men can take turns in shifts, getting breakfast, eating, and then back to work.

Jenna has set out a breakfast fit for a king. There are waffles, eggs, bacon, sausage, potatoes, biscuits and gravy, fruit and melon, coffee, and hot cocoa. No one can ever say Anthony doesn't treat his men well. Jenna, Michelle, and Angie spoil the men with their food as well.

Jenna greets me telling me that breakfast is served to Matteo and Dierdre. Matteo seems well, needing no help. Michelle, however, says Dierdre is weak and needs her assistance.

"Gabriella, Michelle tells me Dierdre asks if her suitcase containing her clothes can be brought from her apartment to the mansion. Dierdre had been expecting to leave for a vacation when she was attacked."

"I'll ask Anthony, but he may be hesitant to agree to bring her things on site. I'll let you know."

While filling my plate I ask, "Has Anthony eaten?"

"Not yet. He took his coffee to his office waiting for you."

"Hand me the serving tray, please. I'll take our breakfast to his office. It'll be more peaceful in there."

Not sure what Anthony is hungry for, I fill both our plates with a sampling of everything and place them on the tray. I add a carafe of coffee and head to his office. Balancing the tray on my hip I knock twice then open the door. Anthony looks up from his computer with a smile on his face and a sexy "Good morning."

"Hi, I thought you might want to share breakfast in your office. There's a flurry of activity going on early this morning."

"Yes. It is chaotic and quite noisy. Not the best atmosphere for dining and even less for trying to talk to one another. Thank you."

Setting the tray on his desk, I pull a chair close to Anthony making myself comfortable. I refill his coffee cup, drape a napkin across my lap, and tell him,

"Dierdre asks if someone can bring her suitcase to the mansion. Her clothes were packed for a vacation when she was unexpectedly beaten without warning. I suspect she wants a change of clothes."

"I'm not sure that will be wise Gabriella."

"We can inspect every piece of clothing ensuring there is nothing in the suitcase dangerous if it makes it more acceptable."

"Gabriella, I still don't like the idea."

"Okay." I smile, not showing further interest either way continuing to eat my breakfast.

Anthony takes a sip of his coffee, studies me, and then says,

"Gabriella, ... while I'm not in favor of Dierdre's request, I'll give it some thought and let you know later today."

"Thank, you Anthony."

I'm learning with our little conversations to judge Anthony's attitude and the do's and don'ts of asking his permission for different issues. Depending on his mood and how the request is made his emotional reaction is usually positive. Good to know!

I try not to smile outwardly but I really don't care one way or another if Dierdre gets her suitcase. Some might say I have my husband wrapped around my little finger. I'm not sure about that but I do seem to win more than I lose. It's a give-and-take dance between us.

I never take Anthony for granted and make sure he's aware that I would never usurp his authority or show disrespect in front of his men or in private. He is the Don and is always in charge.

CHAPTER 28

Anthony

Gabriella's books and lingerie have arrived. Opening the package and inspecting the items within, I'm quite satisfied with my choices for her delicate underwear. I smile as I think this should make up for the panties I destroyed.

Setting the lingerie aside, I glance at the book <u>Hobbies for the 21st Century</u>, which looks like a good resource. The second book is <u>Creating with Clay</u>. She's selected a hobby I'm sure she'll have fun with. It will be interesting to see how she does with it.

Leaving my office, I'm surprised by Matteo as he rounds the corner.

"Matteo, I don't think it's wise for you to be up so soon. Your body needs time to heal."

"I feel fantastic. I just completed a hundred push-ups and I think I could do a hundred more. I'm fine."

"I want you to return to your room. Please join me and we'll talk."

"But Don Vitale, I'm fine really, better than fine."

Placing my hand on his arm, and directing him to the staircase, I lead him as we ascend the stairs. I strongly convey my physical message that further discussion is not recommended. He responds with a look of concern trying to understand why I'm forcing him back to his room.

"Don Vitale, look at me I'm in top physical shape ready to go to work."

I look out for any of the staff while making our way to his room. Once we enter, I close the door behind us. "Sit down, Matteo. I want to explain."

Matteo has the look of a hurt child who has been reprimanded. I'm not sure I can pull this off, and I'm thinking quickly of an explanation without sounding ridiculous.

"Matteo, you have been hurt by the impact of the explosion. You are lucky you don't have internal bleeding from the shock wave that nearly killed you. The doctor said you would feel as though you are fully recovered, but if you strain your body too soon you could relapse doing permanent harm to yourself."

Matteo caught me by surprise, and I'm not ready to have this discussion with him. I didn't have time to come up with a good-sounding excuse for him to stay in his room for another day or two. I hope I don't sound like an idiot. I believe he can take me on. He's energized and his muscles look like he's been pumping iron.

"Well, I can't stay in this room with nothing to do. Boss … What are those books under your arm?"

"These? These are books Gabriella ordered. She's looking for a hobby and wants to take a closer look at suggestions she might find interesting. It's something she thought she might attempt."

"Don Vitale, can I look through them?"

"That's right! I've heard you have quite a talent for woodworking. I haven't seen your work, but I've heard it's impressive. What have you made?"

"I work with my hands during my downtime. I just finished a storage bench that sits at the foot of my bed. It has an upholstered seat and two wide large drawers to store bedding and pillows. It's made of burl wood rubbed to a highly polished shine. It matches my headboard made from the same burl wood. I'll start the bedside tables next."

"I'd like to see your work sometime soon, Matteo."

Handing both books to Matteo I say,

"You can look through the books until lunch. I want to give them to Gabriella this afternoon. I'll have Angelo bring in a TV for your entertainment later. In the meantime, you'll stay in your room today and rest. Agreed."

Letting out a deep breath Matteo responds without enthusiasm, "Agreed. Thank you."

That was close. It's debatable but I hope he bought it. I just can't have everyone who saw Gabriella touch him to see how fully recovered he is in a single day. It will bring too many questions to everyone's mind. It will be difficult enough to explain away his recovery when he comes bounding down the stairs tomorrow. I won't be able to keep him down another day.

I observe Matteo as he takes the books in hand and makes himself comfortable. Taking a closer look, trying not to stare, I notice his muscles seem larger and more defined if that's even possible. Lately, I've learned anything is possible. I'll make it up to him, but for now, I don't want others to see he's fully recovered yet.

I don't want Gabriella assisting Matteo. It wouldn't matter if the entire staff were with her while attending to his needs. She will not care for Matteo. I still can't place my finger on it, but they seem to mesh too well together. It's an easy, natural sort of thing between them and I don't like it. It almost seems like affection when Gabriella lays her hands on Matteo.

I realize I've become even more possessive of her. Gabriella is my obsession and my weakness, and I struggle to put this feeling in perspective. I can't weaken my position as the head of this family through my insecurities. I need to find balance and control my instincts concerning Gabriella. That's easier said than done.

I trust her with my life, and I know she feels the same about me. Her uniqueness as a person makes her a miracle on a planet full of ordinary beings. She should be worshipped but instead must hide her abilities to ensure her safety and existence. I wonder if our children will inherit their mother's unusual abilities. I'll worry about that later.

I'm heading to Gabriella's office to tell her my decision. I'm allowing Dierdre's suitcase on the premises on condition that every article of clothing is scrutinized. The suitcase will be thoroughly searched, also ensuring it isn't sporting hidden compartments.

I wouldn't put it past Leo to try to plant something in my home. I'll send Harold and Angelo to retrieve the suitcase with strict orders that they complete their search before they deliver it to the guardhouse. I want it searched again. I can't be too careful and I'm not taking any chances.

Harold seems to have taken an interest in Dierdre's well-being. I didn't notice that before. I'm not sure if that's something new or if his interest in her has grown over time. Things change for a man when a woman is involved.

When I enter Gabriella's office I concentrate on her beautiful face. Nearing her desk, I look at how she has decorated her office. Framed photographs and mementos of us adorn her room. Taking a seat beside her, I give her the package with her lingerie, explaining,

"Matteo surprised me when he left his room ready to take on the world. I let him borrow your books till lunch so he would have something to occupy his time until his TV arrives. Gabriella, he's not only completely recovered but his physical appearance has noticeably improved."

"Do you think he'll stay in his room one more day?"

"No! Not without my insistence but then there really must be an explanation that would make sense. There is no rational explanation why he would have to remain in his room for another day."

"Anthony, I think people will soon forget his injuries once they see him and accept his recovery."

Gabriella opens the package removing the panties and matching bras I've chosen for her. Smiling, she admires each set and thanks me with a hug and a kiss.

"Anthony, let Matteo look through the books as long as he wants. I'll look at them when he's done.

"Okay, I'll let him know."

"Anthony, have you made a decision about Dierdre's suitcase?"

"I was about to tell you; that I'm going to have Harold and Angelo retrieve the suitcase. She'll have it this evening. You can tell her if you wish."

"I'm sure she'll be grateful. That's very thoughtful and accommodating of you, Anthony. I'll let her know."

I make my way to the foyer and look at the progress being made in restoring the mansion to its former glory. It's coming along nicely. At this rate of repair, it shouldn't take too much longer. A third of the windows have been replaced, the double doors are being milled, and the columns are being assembled.

The best thing about having my own construction company is there is no interruption in work with complete commitment to my project alone. Material availability and overtime are never an issue.

Harold and Angelo are on their way to retrieve Dierdre's suitcase. My instructions are clear. They are to carefully check her apartment for anything that shouldn't be there. It's not likely but there could be a trap or ambush of some sort. I anticipate anything can happen and probably will when dealing with Ronan and Leo. I try to prepare my men for the unknown and unexpected.

I turn my focus to a positive subject. We have an appointment at the breeder's ranch on Saturday to select Gabriella's horse. I have my eye on a thoroughbred, a three-year-old filly, but ultimately it will be Gabriella's choice.

I'll insist she rides Sweet Georgia today and tomorrow to get the feel for riding before she's seated on the new horse. I'll take her on an easy stroll around the stable, ranch, workshop, and guardhouse. It will help her become familiar with leading a horse by the reins.

I'll leave the rest of Gabriella's lessons to Carlo and Angelo. She's going to be a busy girl with shooting practice and riding lessons as well as her accounting job. I'll keep her too busy to be bored. She won't have time for a hobby.

Harold

In Dierdre's apartment, there's an overturned chair, a broken coffee table, and broken items scattered across the living room floor. I can see her suitcase by the door. She didn't have a chance. Ronan set her up, so she suspected nothing, catching her completely by surprise when he attacked her.

Angelo is looking through the apartment while I start emptying Dierdre's purse. I find nothing out of the ordinary, only the usual things ladies carry with them. With nothing of concern in the purse, I empty the suitcase.

Angelo returns to the living room when the contents of the suitcase are now in a pile on the floor. While I'm checking each garment of clothing, Angelo is examining the suitcase for any hidden compartments.

Angelo takes his knife, cutting through the lining until there is nothing covering the interior of the suitcase. Certain there are no hidden compartments, we haphazardly refold the clothing and throw everything back in the suitcase. We know full well it will go through a second examination.

We take one last look around the apartment, leaving everything as it is. With our task complete we take the purse and suitcase to the guardhouse for its final inspection and continue on our way to the mansion.

CHAPTER 29

Gabriella

Dierdre's suitcase and purse are brought to the mansion after a thorough examination of the contents. Jenna starts to retrieve the case and purse but Harold, who is closer, reaches for them offering to deliver them to Dierdre.

I tell him "I'll go with you, Harold. I need to greet Dierdre in person, and this is my first opportunity to extend our welcome."

Harold's expression tells me he isn't thrilled I'm going with him. I guess he wants a moment alone with Dierdre and my tag along prevents a private conversation between them. I'm sure he'll have other opportunities to speak with her.

When we enter Dierdre's room, she's sitting up with her back against the headboard, sipping from a glass of water. She looks at Harold first, then me with a smile.

"Good morning, Dierdre. How are you feeling this morning?"

"I feel better, and I think I could even get out of bed and sit for a while."

I ask, "Harold, will you bring the upholstered chair …" But before I can finish, he is already in motion moving the chair close to the bed.

Once the chair is next to the bed, Harold helps Dierdre into it. He then brings the suitcase and purse, setting them down within her reach.

Dierdre thanks Harold, then, "Gabriella, thank you, and please thank Anthony for everything he's doing for me. I appreciate this very much. I don't know what I would do without your help."

"We want you to rest and recover Dierdre. You have nothing to worry about under Anthony's protection. You are safe here."

I reach the door when I say, "We'll let you rest Dierdre. If you need anything just press the button on the phone marked K. The kitchen staff will take care of your needs."

Harold lingers facing Dierdre while grinding his teeth. He acts like he's going to say something to her, but apparently decides against it. He turns and follows me out of her room.

"Harold, I'm sure Anthony won't mind if you visit a while with Dierdre."

"Thank you, but I'll wait until I'm off duty. I want to make sure the boss is okay with it."

"I'm sure he will be. Just be patient. It will all work out."

I'm delighted with the thought that Dierdre and Harold might be a couple. I was struggling with my feelings about having her here in the house. I hope it works out for both of them. Everyone deserves a chance at happiness.

Later I overhear Anthony ask Harold if he wants to rotate his responsibilities from Club Vitale to the mansion while Dierdre is here. Harold's response is a quick "Yes." Anthony recognizes their possible relationship and gives Harold the option for the rotation.

It must be hard for men in the mafia trying to balance their duty and their desires for female companionship. It seems most of their relationships are the one-night only kind. Very few of them have steady relationships or families and that's understandable.

I wonder how different it might be if I married someone … like Jake. *Oh no, I feel so guilty, I thought of Jake. It just popped into my mind out of the blue.* I must be stressed because of everything happening. This kind of day dreaming will get me into trouble.

I'm bonded to Anthony for life. There's no changing that. But to be honest … I did spend four days with Jake compared to only four hours with Anthony before my wedding. I justify my thinking of Jake because it's impossible to think of anyone else. Jake is the only other man I know besides Anthony.

I shake my head and put on a new attitude. I need to keep in mind who's at fault for all of this. My father. He's the one to blame for making my life miserable. There is no bright future without Anthony. In fact, there's no future at all without Anthony. I owe him my life.

Day two of the mansion reconstruction and I start the morning early. Matteo unexpectedly rushes past me as I'm leaving my office. I greet him with delight seeing he's in such great shape.

I smile with humor as Matteo stops and glances toward Anthony's office door, anxious to continue on his way. He's attempting to leave the house without Anthony seeing him. I respond with a chuckle,

"Where are you going in such a rush?"

"To the workshop. They need my help with the exterior window framing."

"I'm sure they'll be happy you're well enough to help. Have a good day, Matteo. I'm pleased to see you are feeling well again. Have you had breakfast?"

"Yes, yes, and thank you again, Mrs. Vitale."

And not a minute too soon, Matteo rushes out of the mansion just as Anthony opens his door.

"Who were you talking to, Gabriella?"

"Matteo. He's on his way to the workshop to help with the window framing. He looks great!"

Anthony lets out an exasperated exhale and says, "Well, I guess it's too late to send him back to his room. Especially now that everyone's seen him."

"It will be fine Anthony. Everyone misses him and they're happy to see he's well again."

It's Saturday and I'm excited like a child on Christmas morning. Today is the day I select my horse. Banding my hair in a ponytail, I dress in jeans, tennis shoes, a T-shirt, and a lightweight jacket. Casual dressing is necessary in case I fall off the horse. I laugh to myself at the thought.

I've been practicing on Sweet Georgia for two days at Anthony's side. Riding, no, walking at a snail's pace around the ranch. It was fun but the horses were kept from galloping. They were barely allowed to trot. I think the horses were also disappointed with the slow stroll Anthony insists we take.

When I feel more secure handling a horse, my horse and I will prance and gallop, and we'll be racing all over these grounds. My horse's mane with blow in the wind and the only time you'll see us stroll is when we're exhausted after winning every pretend race I can think of.

Settled in the SUV and pulling the horse trailer behind us, we're on our way to the breeder's ranch. Butterflies surge in my stomach when we turn on the road that leads us closer to our destination. This is horse country and excitement thrills through every muscle in my body. This is a dream come true.

I check my pocket holding the plastic bag of apple slices. I'm giving the horses I see today a little treat. I want them to like me while I'm making such an important decision.

Giorgio backs the SUV and horse trailer toward the stable and parks. A man and woman waiting for us greet us and lead us toward the fenced pen. Anthony introduces me to the breeders, Dwayne, and Sally Easton. While they lead us to the pen, they give us a verbal history of the horses they're showing us today. They will provide documented proof of their lineage when a decision is made.

The three fillies we're being shown today are all three years old. The first beautiful filly is black. She gallops around the pen as her handler coaches her with a training-lead. She is, as are the others, the offspring of well-known racehorses that make them enthusiastically sought after.

Dwayne and Sally tell us that they haven't accepted any offers yet but have received bids on all three horses. They are holding out until we make our selection, giving us the first choice. I had no idea Anthony had such an influence and no doubt he'll pay a premium price.

If she becomes my horse, I will name her, 'Greek Goddess – Aphrodite:' The goddess of love, beauty, and desire known for her irresistible charm and allure.

I reach into my pocket pulling out a couple slices of apple. When she is brought to me, I introduce myself and hold out the apple slices to her. She takes the slices from me and allows me to pet her behind her ear. I tell her how beautiful she is and how happy I am to meet her. She greets me with a nod of her head and a scratch of her hoof. When she is taken away the next filly is brought to the pen.

This beauty is pure white except for her mane and tail which have threads of dark hair running through them casting a gray color. Her white coat doesn't deviate in color anywhere, which causes her mane and tail to stand out. She's the picture of perfection. She shows her talent as she prances for us while being led around the pen. I would name her 'Guinevere–the Fair One': Synonymous with King Arthur who pulled the sword from the stone. She is brought to me, and I offer her apple slices greeting her with affection and a pet. She responds to me with a nod and a scratch of her hoof and whinnies in acknowledgment of my admiration.

The third filly is a horse with the most beautiful British tan coat. She is elegant perfection in every way. Her name should be 'Lady Royal-Nobility': All Royal daughters are styled "Lady" as a forename. She is every bit royalty from the tip of her nose to the tips of her hoofs. She takes the apple slices from my hand as she looks fondly into my eyes scratching the ground with her hoof and gives me a nod.

All three fillies are wonderful. I know horses are a business for Anthony, but I can't choose a horse based on its ability to race and win. I know nothing about selecting a horse based on racing ability.

I touch Anthony's arm and ask, "What happens if I choose the wrong horse?"

My choice is personal because my horse will be my companion who I'll bond with. She will be a dependable friend and protect me while I ride her. In return, I will protect her. She will also be a winner and as well-known as any horse who comes before her.

"There is no wrong horse, Gabriella. I made sure you were shown horses that are completely equal in their lineage and anticipated capabilities. Have you made your decision?"

"Yes Anthony, I believe I have. I choose Guinevere–the Fair One, the white horse. It is a hard decision because I want all three. But I wouldn't be able to give all three the attention they deserve."

"What made you decide on her?"

"When I touched her head, she communicated with me. We seem to connect in a way that feels like we're kindred spirits. I have a feeling we're being reunited from a different time and a different place."

"That's good enough for me Kitten. It's certain she'll stand out in a crowd. Let's sign the contract."

"I want to talk with her first. I want to make sure she wants to come home with me. Can they bring her back?"

Humoring Gabriella, I say, "What if she doesn't want to go with us?"

"Then I'll have no other choice but to select another horse."

Anthony shakes his head with a smile motioning to Sally asking her to bring back the white horse for a second look.

When the horse is brought to me, I bring my forehead to her face just above her nose. I'm talking to her through our senses, informing her I've chosen her to be my horse. I explained she would not be expected to race unless she decided she wanted to and that my attention would be on her and only her. I tell her she will have open pastures to explore and home with four other horses to make friends with. I explain I've chosen the name Guinevere–the Fair one for her. Finally, I asked if she would like to come home with me.

She nods and rears up on her back legs to let me know she is in favor of me being her owner. I smile and kiss her on the nose. Turning to Anthony, I nod.

"Yes, Guinevere agrees. She is very much in favor of going home with us."

Sally shakes her head and has a puzzled expression on her face, rolling her eyes with humor and remarks, "This is the first time I'm aware that the horse decides who she's going home with. She must like what you had to offer." Smiling, Sally lets out a chuckle and says, "Come into my office and I'll have you on your way asap."

Anthony whispers to me, "She wouldn't be laughing if she only knew Guinevere understood every word."

I shush Anthony as we follow Sally and Dwayne to the office.

I sign my name to the bill of sale, then I'm led out of the office to have my picture taken with Guinevere. It will be posted in the Breeder's Catalog. I give Guinevere the last of my apple slices as she is loaded into our horse trailer with no problem.

I talk to her when I come around to the trailer window assuring her that I'm coming with her while I climb into the SUV. What a wonderful day this is. I have my very own horse. I snuggle into

207

Anthony's arms thanking him with a hug and a kiss for a once-in-a-lifetime gift.

CHAPTER 30

Gabriella

With Anthony's help, I bring Guinevere into our stable and introduce her to, Quicksilver Sweet Georgia Brown, Prancing Beauty, and American Queen. I'm pleased the horses show enthusiasm for their introduction to Guinevere. She's the youngest and it's important that she feels safe and accepted. I know the horses will be protective of her.

Walking beside Guinevere, holding her reins loosely, I'm giving her a tour of the grounds. I'm happy when Anthony joins me, taking his place on her other side. I want Guinevere to become acquainted with her new sprawling home and to be comfortable with Anthony and me as her owners.

"You've made a good decision in your choice, Gabriella. Guinevere is a fine filly and will serve us well."

"Anthony, I want to order a white leather saddle with white stirrups, over girth, fender, bridle, and reins. The only leather touching her should be white ... all white. And ... I'm against putting a bit in her mouth."

"Gabriella, you're not being practical. The bit is an aid—a way for the rider to communicate effectively with their equine partner. The Snaffle Bit we use consists of two parts – the mouthpiece and the bit rings which the bridle and reins attach to.

"I don't believe it's necessary. The bridle and the reins can be made to connect without the mouthpiece."

"Gabriella, the bit is needed for control, to direct the horse's movement, right, left, slowing, and stopping her. It does not hurt the horse.

"Have you ever put a bit in your mouth, Anthony, and left it in your mouth all day? It must be uncomfortable and possibly hurt."

"Gabriella, the bit applies pressure to the horse's mouth and tongue, yes, but it doesn't necessarily cause harm. When used correctly and with care, bits will not hurt the horse."

"If Guinevere is truly my horse, then I should have a say in how she is treated, trained, and ridden. Please trust me and allow me to train her with Carlo and Angelo's help. She will allow me to control her without a bit. Of that, I can promise."

Anthony looks at Guinevere patting her on her back then studies me intently. He's quiet, then asks, "Will Guinevere allow anyone else to control her without a bit?'

"I'm not sure. But then I should be the only one riding her, shouldn't I?"

"Not necessarily. This has the potential to be problematic, Gabriella. Did you forget, our jockey will be riding Guinevere in races? Gabriella, your request requires some thought."

Anthony can't see my expression when I lower my head. He doesn't see the huge smile on my face since he is walking on the other side of Guinevere. Hopefully, he'll honor my request and try my way.

Carlo and Angelo take Guinevere's reins, leading her to her stall. Anthony approaches a utility cart when I ask if we can walk to the mansion instead of riding. He agrees so we walk together, continuing our discussion.

Anthony looks into my eyes with a soft smile on his face when he asks,

"Gabriella, since you're determined to have only white leather on Guinevere how do you intend to ride her until your saddle arrives?"

Looking into Anthony's eyes reflecting a smile of my own, "I'll ride her bareback."

"Absolutely not. You're just learning to ride. You'll have no control, nothing to hold on to, and no stirrups to balance yourself."

"Well, I won't be riding bareback for long, and only with Carlo and Angelo's oversight. How long will it take to get her white saddle?"

"Gabriella, with no stirrups just how do you intend to mount her?"

"I'm counting on Carlo or Angelo to hoist me up like they do with our jockey. That way you can rest assured that either Carlo or Angelo will always be in charge when I ride Guinevere bareback."

"Gabriella, you're one who loves pushing things to the edge of reason."

"I thought you liked the way I challenge you."

"Hmm, it can be debatable at times."

Nearing the mansion, we see Dierdre sitting on the wrap-around porch with Harold sitting next to her. She's recovering nicely. It's nice to see her feeling better and getting a little sunshine. They smile and wave then we wave back. We're still far enough away that Anthony can't be heard telling me,

"You've given me a lot to think about. I'll consider your request and get back to you with my decision, Kitten."

I may have gone too far asking to ride Guinevere bareback, but it isn't impossible. I'd like to try it even if I find I'm unsuccessful. The problem is Anthony's overprotectiveness. He's concerned I'll get hurt. It's like riding a bike. You must count on falling off and scraping your knees occasionally. Of course, falling off a horse is not the same as falling off a bike.

We no sooner step up on the porch than Dominic drives up in the SUV. He motions to Anthony.

"I'll catch up with you later Gabriella."

Anthony walks to the driver's side of the SUV. He bends down to the open window and listens intently to what Dominic is telling him. Dominic gets out of the SUV as he and Anthony step up on the porch asking Harold to join them. They're met by Giorgio and Matteo who follow. I watch them enter Anthony's office, closing the door behind them.

I know from experience that whatever the news is, it's serious. I hope it isn't more of my father's attempts to capture me. I hope none of Anthony's businesses have been damaged and our men are not harmed. I hate being left out like this.

Anthony

Sitting at my desk and pouring myself a drink I motion to the others to help themselves. I rarely offer liquor to the men during a meeting. But this news deserves a celebration of sorts. Once everyone is settled, I ask Dominic to tell us what he's learned. Clearing his throat he begins,

"A decomposing body was found by the river yesterday morning. The corpse was not only shot four times but he was also beaten so badly that facial recognition was impossible. He was identified this morning by his teeth. It's Ronan. He was discovered by a man fishing in the area. The body came to the surface after being snagged on the fisherman's hook."

I glance at Harold as his eyes meet mine. He shows his stoic expression and gives no indication that he's surprised by the news of Ronan's death. I say,

"This is one less person we need to worry about. But … I hope one of my men isn't responsible. I gave no approval for this. As it stands, it's a non-sanctioned hit: A serious breach of the rules. Get the word out that if one of my men acted on a personal grudge without my consent, there would be no second chances. His punishment will be an example to others who would act against the rules."

I excuse the men but when Harold stands, I ask him to remain, motioning for him to sit back down. When the others leave, I ask,

"Harold, you left the night you brought Dierdre to the mansion. Where did you go?"

"I went to my apartment to pick up a change of clothes."

"Did you go anywhere else before you returned?"

"Yes. I stopped at Club Blackjack to pick up my winnings. I didn't know Ronan was there. He attacked me before I could get the drop on him. I got the better of him, but he kept trying to get back up, so I shot him four times. It was self-defense."

"Why didn't you tell me when you returned to the mansion?"

213

"Under the circumstances, I couldn't help but think you wouldn't believe that our meeting was purely coincidental. I knew you wouldn't be happy because I deprived you of the satisfaction of taking him out yourself."

"Do you think I'm happy now?"

"No sir. But I'm not sorry I killed him. I'm prepared to take whatever punishment you hand out."

I sit there staring at Harold with my arms folded across my chest. He's been a loyal soldier, and he didn't have a choice if what he tells me is true. But he should have acknowledged what went down the minute he arrived at the mansion. I've decided on a punishment.

"Harold, for your punishment you will not take credit for the hit. No one must know it was one of my men. If you reveal your actions in this matter, you will be dealt with harshly and made an example of. Do you understand?"

"Yes sir, Don Vitale, thank you."

"You're excused, Harold. And Harold ... no more coincidences."

"Yes sir.

"And ... if there should be another coincidence, you are to tell me immediately ... understood?

"Yes sir.

I pour myself a second glass and sit back in my chair. I must admit that I am disappointed I wasn't the one to end Ronan. He's a man known to turn on you so quickly you'll never see it coming. His reputation was a warning to others. Anyone stupid enough not to heed the warning is dead.

I hope I don't regret my decision to go light on Harold. Under the circumstances of Ronan beating Dierdre, I was wise to show restraint and not immediately retaliate against him. Reacting to Ronan's action without a plan would not have been advisable. Being proactive and waiting for the right opportunity, even an accidental opportunity, proves to be our best defense. Ultimately it led to Ronan's demise.

Moving on to my next item of business, I make my call to the saddle maker and submit my order for Gabriella's white saddle. I want the softest and most expensive leather available. I give her height, weight, and measurements to ensure a perfect fit for her riding pleasure. I expect no less than perfection in her one-of-a-kind handmade saddle that I'll pay the price for.

Guinevere is a beautiful horse and comes from a strong and successful lineage. She has the making of a great winner herself. I have no doubt with Carlo as her trainer, Angelo as her handler, and Gabriella's ability to communicate and bond with her, she'll become the horse of the century.

CHAPTER 31

Anthony

Dierdre stops by my office soon after my meeting ends. She thanked me for my hospitality and for the care she received as my guest. She says she feels well enough to return to her apartment and tells me of her plans to leave tomorrow morning. I agree with her wishes.

That's when I motion for her to sit to tell her about Ronan. She surprises me because her response to the news isn't what I anticipate. I expected her to feel relief knowing he could never harm her again. Instead, her initial reaction is grief stricken,

"Oh my god how? When?"

She tries to cover up her initial reaction, changing her physical response with a deep sigh controlling her voice and putting on a calmer demeanor and saying,

"Oh, Anthony, I'm so glad that chapter of my life is over."

Her attempt to fool me is unsuccessful. She's a good actress, but she can't hide the fact that she cares for him more than she's willing to admit to me. I will never understand women who put up with abusive partners. The news obviously upset her when she said,

"I'm feeling tired Anthony. I think I'll go to my room and take a nap if you don't mind."

"Of course, I don't mind. You rest Dierdre, as long as you wish."

Later that night...

Gabriella

Anthony tells me about Ronan's body being discovered and that Dierdre has been in her room all afternoon. It seems she's taking the news harder than expected. I wasn't quite sure how I should respond or if I should say anything at all to Dierdre.

It seems to me that condolences are in order under the circumstances. But then Ronan's the reason she's here, … recovering from his abuse.

I see Harold coming my way and ask him, "Harold, have you seen Dierdre?" He responds,

"She sent me a text asking me to take her home tonight. I'm on my way to get her suitcase and escort her to the SUV I parked outside the side door."

"That's odd Anthony told me she had planned on leaving tomorrow morning."

"Gabriella, she's probably in a hurry to get comfortable in her own space."

"I'll go up and tell her you're ready. That way I can wish her well. Give us a little time, Harold. She may want to talk."

I make my way to Dierdre's room and knock lightly on the door. Dierdre opens the door smiling broadly and asks me to come in, closing the door behind me and saying,

"Gabriella, what an unexpected pleasure."

Stepping into the bedroom, I see her suitcase, next to the bed, wide open on the floor. Her clothes are piled in a clump inside.

"Dierdre, do you need help packing?"

She replies, "I wasn't expecting to see you, Gabriella. How nice of you to see me off. Just a moment, I have something for you."

Bending over, reaching for, and fiddling with something in her suitcase, she quickly turns to face me. It isn't until she grabs me by the arm that I recognize what she's holding in her other hand.

"Gabriella, your unexpected appearance guarantees my success after all."

She's too quick; I can't react before she injects me in the shoulder with a syringe.

My thoughts as I feel the drug take effect is, that *they didn't search her, only her suitcase*, as I sink into darkness.

Harold

I am just about ready to go up to Dierdre's room to see what's taking her so long when she appears, pulling the suitcase behind her. I take hold of the handle to maneuver it down the porch steps when I notice the suitcase is much heavier than it should be.

I remark, "What do you have in this suitcase?" As I lift it into the back of the SUV.

When I take a closer look at the suitcase, I see a clump of blond hair sticking out between the teeth of the zipper. Immediately, I reach for my gun tucked into my waistband at my back when I realize it's gone. Dierdre took it from me when I was turned, placing the suitcase in the SUV. I'm looking at my own gun pointed at me.

"Dierdre, hand me the gun. There is no way you're getting away with Gabriella stuffed in your suitcase."

"Ahh … but I think I can."

I should have known better. I let down my guard with Dierdre. Looking at each other we're frozen for a second when I lunge at her to take the gun. She fires … twice.

Anthony

The sound of gunfire has everyone running toward the side entrance. Jenna is first on the scene as she was in the laundry room when the gun was fired. She steps out the door and sees the SUV screech away toward the back expanse of the ranch.

She didn't notice Harold on the ground at first until she stepped closer to the edge of the porch. Jenna screams, sounding the alarm and shouting, "Help! Harold's, been shot!"

It's then that my alarm, tracking Gabriella goes off. I follow the little blue dot on my cell phone traveling quickly toward the back forty-acre expanse of the ranch. Everyone is on alert waiting for my command as I let out a roar of frustration and fear for Gabriella. I'm sure I was heard miles away.

Matteo is at Harold's side when Harold says, "Gabriella is in the suitcase. Dierdre played me." Then passes out. Matteo looks at Jenna telling her to call the doctor and take care of him.

I'm out of my mind with my failure to recognize that Dierdre's beating was a planned ruse. I should have known it was Leo's only way to get to Gabriella. I let it happen. I let Dierdre in, then brought her suitcase in as well, the very object used to kidnap Gabriella. I didn't expect Dierdre to betray me like this.

Giorgio, Dominic, and Matteo are waiting for me to jump into our SUV while others are in vehicles ready to race after Dierdre. Matteo signals them to chase after her. She must be expecting to meet up with help because there's nowhere to go once, she reaches the foothills.

Racing after Dierdre and fast approaching the foothills, we can see the parked SUV Dierdre drove off in. A man dressed in black clothing is lifting the suitcase into the helicopter with Dierdre climbing in close behind. He stands in the open doorway holding on looking out at us, daring us to shoot, as the helicopter ascends above us.

I exit our vehicle and run toward the empty area the helicopter took off from, the dirt and dust still twirling with the action of the blades of the chopper, as it turns and flies above the mountainous region.

We didn't make it in time. I want to release my outrage, to voice my frustration at the top of my lungs as I watch the blue dot travel across the screen of my cell phone.

"Matteo communicates with our tech team telling them to keep an active connection with Gabriella's tracker. We need to know where they're taking her."

Matteo put his hand on my shoulder and said,

"Don, the first thing they'll do is scan her, looking for a tracker."

"They won't find it. It's in her mouth hidden in the crown of her tooth. Matteo, you'll be in charge here while I take my team to get her."

"No, Don Vitale, I can't stay behind. I must go with you. She's not strong enough yet to fight him alone."

"I quickly turn and look at Matteo questioning his comment. What do you mean Gabriella's not strong enough to fight … who?" *Does he know?*

"Leo Farina … Our father."

Matteo's statement is a shock to my system and his words nearly cause me to black out. Matteo says,

"Gabriella and I are brother and sister. Different mothers, same father. Gabriella and Leo don't know about me."

I anxiously look around to make sure no one is near us to overhear Matteo. "Don't say any more Matteo. We need to go to my office to finish this discussion."

I'm reeling from Matteo's words. It suddenly makes sense. I recognized the connection between Gabriella and Matteo early on. In my effort to protect what's mine, I've mistaken the type of connection they share. It isn't an attraction between a man and a woman. It's a natural connection between siblings.

Matteo follows me into my office. The tech team is still tracking Gabriella and giving me updates as they inform me, she's still in the Los Angeles area. We sit and I ask Matteo,

"Please start from the beginning. I want to know everything." Matteo begins with,

"My mother was raped by Leo Farina. After the rape he wanted her to stay in a bungalow on his property so he could take advantage of her whenever he wanted. Once Leo left the bungalow to go to his big house, my mother ran away and went to her family home for help.

When my mother realized she was pregnant, my grandparents helped her move from Nuevo Laredo, Mexico to California. Due to

221

Leo's wealth and influence, my grandparents would not have been able to protect her if he found out they were hiding her. Leo never found out about my birth.

I inherited Leo's extraordinary capabilities. I was blessed with extra protection in that Leo was never able to sense my aura to connect with me. I was born with a sort of natural blocking mechanism. It keeps me safe and unrecognizable from him and others like us.

I can identify people like me. I'm able to read their minds; they just can't read mine. The minute I saw Gabriella, I recognized her as my sibling. I was concerned at first for Gabriella until I saw how you love and protect her. You are helping her to develop her abilities and I respect you for standing by her.

She has gained a lot with your help, but she hasn't matured completely yet and has more growing to do before she can stand against Leo. It will take both of us working together to stop him."

"Matteo, I wish you had confided in me sooner."

"I have been hiding my identity my entire life. I'm not only protecting who I am, but now I find I must also protect Gabriella's identity."

"How can you help her?"

"I need to find a way to connect with her that doesn't tip Leo off. I can't connect with her yet. Currently, she is still under the influence of the drug she was given. Has she jumped successfully yet?"

"Jumped? Jumped where? Matteo, I'm not sure what you mean when you ask me if she's jumped,"

"Anthony, the dictionary vaguely explains it under the heading **Transmigrate or Transmigrating; for one to go from one state of existence or place to another."**

"I'm still not sure what you mean." Recognizing my confusion, Matteo explains further,

"It's when a person can transport their physical being from one place or area to another place or area."

"Is that possible?"

"Yes, it is. We call it jumping. Picture Gabriella sitting in front of you when she disappears suddenly. She ends up outside in your stable. She's just jumped from one place to another.

We are capable of teleporting short distances, from one side of the room to another, or a few blocks away. We can only teleport ourselves and a very limited amount of mass, up to what we are wearing and carrying.

However, we can only jump one way and it takes an incredible amount of power to accomplish this act. It's only used during extraordinary life-threatening circumstances. We're left powerless and unable to defend ourselves during the time it takes to recover after jumping."

"No, I don't believe she can jump or even know that it's a possibility."

I understand how incredibly unique Gabriella and Matteo are and how important it is to keep their identities hidden. I start to ask Matteo about his heritage when I receive a text from my tech team. They informed me Gabriella is in a compound located near the coast.

CHAPTER 32

Anthony

I'm deep in thought as to how much I need Matteo's help. Not only for this moment in time but as part of Gabriella's and my life. It will mean the world to Gabriella to have a brother who has the same power she has. He can guide her as she continues to evolve into her true nature.

Matteo will provide a unique layer of protection for Gabriella that I can't provide. In return, Matteo will enjoy the protection provided by me and this syndicate for life. The decision I'm making isn't taken lightly.

Standing, I walk around my desk and stop in front of Matteo. He stands to face me. I reach my hand out to him, and he responds by reaching out to grasp my hand. I tell him,

"We'll have the blood bonding ceremony later. But now Matteo, the gripping of our hands signifies a life bond between the two of us that can only be broken when one of us dies. We are bound together as one … as brothers … and by our loyalty to protect each other and Gabriella. Betrayal will result in death. Do you agree to my terms?"

Matteo nods and says, "I accept our bond … brother."

I grab his shoulder, squeezing slightly symbolizing our bonded brotherhood.

"We have much to do as we prepare for war on Leo's territory. We're at a disadvantage but hopefully with your unique insight,

Matteo, we may be able to make ourselves equal in strategy against him and his men."

Making a call, I press the numbers to connect with Cooper Black, head of the Shadow Stalkers. He owes me a favor.

"Cooper, I need a few of your men to help retrieve my kidnapped wife from her overbearing father, Leo Farina. It won't be a social call…"

His voice is mischievous as he says, "Ahh, I owe Leo a surprise party. How many men do you need?"

"How many men can you spare?"

"I can give up twenty-five. We're enjoying a comfortable peace for now. But I'll need to borrow from you once I breach my business agreement with Leo." He lifts the corner of his lips in a sinister smile.

I smile as I say, "Thank you. Agreed. Can you send them to my ranch as soon as possible? I'll get back to you with the information when we have our plan cemented in place. I can tell you we're headed to a compound Leo's commandeered near the coastline."

I end the call with Cooper when I think to myself, Gabriella didn't even get to ride her horse. And I'm thinking of what the proper punishment should be for Dierdre. It will be severe. I would end her, but I don't hurt women. Someone other than me will administer the penalty.

The doctor just announced Harold has been taken to our ER next to the arms vault and is being prepared for surgery while I prepare to wage war. There's no telling what kind of chokehold Leo will have on Gabriella before I can reach her.

I call for my entire unit to meet in the great hall. We can't delay and we need to plan our strategy for attack. We assemble and wait for Cooper's men to arrive while Jenna, Michelle, and Angie prepare food and drink for the men.

Unexpectedly, Cooper arrives accompanying his men. I appreciate his involvement and extend my welcome as we shake hands. Cooper says,

"Peace is nice but very boring. I find I need an outlet and will be happy to participate in your war." I respond with, "Thank you for your help."

Cooper's men join my men, introducing each other and assembling in the great hall. I start with,

"You're here to prepare for the planning of the attack on Leo Farina. For those of you who don't know, Leo Farina and Dierdre Dupre are responsible for kidnapping my wife, Gabriella. Our plan is to get her back alive and unharmed."

Now that I'm aware of who and what Matteo is, I continue with my plan for my bonded brother. There is no better choice for what I'm about to do.

"Before our tech team takes over this meeting, I have an announcement." I'm about to surprise Matteo with my news.

"Matteo, will you rise please?" As Matteo stands, I look out over the men assembled and say,

"I have appointed Matteo as my second in command. As an underboss, you will show him the same respect you show me. His words are as good as mine in all matters. You may congratulate him."

Matteo is indeed surprised as the men congratulate him with pats on the back and shaking hands. After a few minutes, I raise my voice telling the men to settle down. "This meeting is now in order."

My tech team is prepared with drawn diagrams and maps projected on the wall. We are given the plan to divide us into five teams. Ten men for each team, for a total of fifty men. An example is given of how each team is made up of certain members leading each team for their specific talents.

Blueprints of the interior layout are presented, and our tech points out and identifies different rooms and open areas of the compound. The room thought to be where Gabriella is being held, per her tracker, is a specific point of conversation and planning.

We move the meeting into the dining room to make use of the large table. Cooper, Matteo, and I are bent over the table spread out with blueprints, maps, and hand-drawn diagrams. We make use of salt and pepper shakers, cups, and glasses as props to identify the compound and surrounding areas.

We create a strategy using every bit of information we have, and together we agree on the best plan of attack. We also agree on a plan B in case our plan A fails. Our snipers will be our eyes on roofs above, directing us on the ground.

Every man assembled is part of the planning as they ask questions, make suggestions, and offer ideas. These men have all contributed to creating a strong strategy. Together, energized and determined, we've forged a formidable army.

Cooper's men brought their own weaponry and ammunition with them. We make a check list of what they have and what's missing if anything. Once we know what's needed, we retire to the workshop, to the underground arms vault. My men have their favorite revolvers, ammunition, and knives.

To our snipers, we hand off Heckler & Koch high-power rifles. To everyone else, we distribute submachine guns, a rocket launcher, hatchets, grenades, stun blasts, smoke bombs, and fixed blade tactical knives.

For those needing a second gun, we offer a choice of .38 Caliber or .357 Magnum Caliber, four-inch and two-inch revolvers; Glock 9mm, Glock.40 Caliber, and Glock.45 Caliber, and Heckler and Koch pistols.

In preparation for fire power from above, three of my men are attaching guns and grenades to all the drones they'll be controlling. They'll be our eyes where we can't see.

The location of the compound is only an hour away. This is one of the multiple locations Leo has at his disposal. I didn't know Leo was silently encroaching on the LA region. My region. It's news to Cooper also. Leo's been very careful to cover any activity that would alert our scouts.

He hasn't made a move on our territory or products. The only thing he's shown his aggression toward is his attempt to take Gabriella. I assume he's waiting until he has everything in place before he goes after a share of our business. Hopefully, he hasn't grown strong enough to take control of our territory.

My only concern at this moment is getting Gabriella back, safe and sound. Then I'll concentrate on what needs to be done to defeat Leo. It is most definitely understood by everyone concerned that there is no longer an alliance between the Farina and Vitale syndicates. It was a weak union, to begin with.

We pack up and get in our SUVs, Vans, Hummers, and bullet-proof vehicles. The stream of cars driving through side-streets and finally the freeway looks like a funeral procession. Only we're not driving slowly. At this speed, we should reach the compound in forty minutes.

Matteo is attempting to connect with Gabriella and signals with a nod of his head. To keep others from overhearing our conversation, Matteo types out a text sending it to me. The message,

Matteo: "Anthony, think of nothing but Gabriella and tell her you're coming to get her."

No problem. Gabriella is all I can think about. I close my eyes and feel my heart pound in my chest as I try as hard as I can to communicate with her, thinking of the words in my mind,

"Gabriella, my love. I'm on my way to get you, I'm coming, Kitten,"

Anthony: "Matteo, can you tell if she felt me, or heard me at all."

Matteo: "She's still under the influence of the drug but she did hear you. Your love for her is strong."

Anthony: "Can she communicate with us? Can you see where she is?"

Matteo: "She can't communicate until the drug completely wears off. She can't project herself until it does."

It pains me to want to know more, but I need to be content that Gabriella heard me. That'll have to be enough for now. I can't allow my impatience to jeopardize revealing Gabriella and Matteo's secret.

Looking ahead we can see that there's a problem on the road. One minute we're speeding down the freeway making excellent headway and the next minute everything comes to a screeching halt. Up above we watch an accident in the making as an 18-wheeler big rig swerves to miss hitting a car then jackknives, falling over on its side and blocking all three lanes.

We approach the overturned truck, get out of our vehicles, and help the driver who seems to be unharmed. Assessing the problem, we carefully measure the space between the overturned cab and the drop off the shoulder of the freeway. We determine we have barely enough room to negotiate our way through.

I've instructed the driver of the big rig to uncouple his cargo containers from the cab. He asks that someone spot him in case he needs help getting back out. Matteo and I climbed onto the cab with the truck driver. We hold on to his ankles as he makes his way back into the overturned cab.

Carefully the truck driver maneuvers himself between the steering wheel, the controls, and the seat of the cab. He stretches his arm out, reaching for, and barely touching, the controls. When he's able to pull a lever, the sound of compressed air being released can be heard.

The cab is successfully uncoupled from the cargo container. After helping the truck driver back out, I pat him on the back and give him a wad of cash.

Matteo motions for our Hummer to come ahead creeping slowly pulling up close enough so that the hummer is touching the cab of the truck. The Hummer is given more gas, and with no one the wiser,

Matteo's sleight of hand assists in moving the cab aside. The cab of the truck is out of the way, just enough to give us the room we need to get through.

We get back in our vehicles and slowly drive through the area barely wide enough to make it without falling off the shoulder. Once we're on our way again we push the pedal to the metal going well over the speed limit trying to make up for the time we lost.

My anxiety is at its highest. I can't remember ever feeling this way even with my experience with life and death hand-to-hand combat. I know Leo won't hurt Gabriella physically, but he can take advantage of her in other ways. Ways that no other human can ever conceive. Ways that can influence her for the rest of her life.

CHAPTER 33

Gabriella

My head feels like it will explode. This throbbing pain in my temple is more than I can tolerate. I can still feel the path the drug took as it coursed through my blood stream. It affected every nerve ending in my body. It was powerful enough to paralyze me temporarily until my body slowly recovered from its effect.

I'm able to lift my arms and wiggle my fingers. Breathing is a little easier. I can bend my legs but can't quite lift them above the bed I'm lying on. I can move my feet and toes, so I guess this is progress.

While I'm slowly recovering, I remember that Anthony spoke to me. I thought, at first, he was standing near me, his voice was so clear. It was like I was hearing him through a different wave. I know I didn't contact him; he was the one contacting me. But something helped him get through to me. How? What? Dare I say ... Who? Who helped him?

I become angry and shocked when I think that Dierdre is to blame for this. I extended my welcome to her. I was in favor of Anthony permitting her suitcase on the premises so she could have a change of clothes. We opened our home to her. But she was just looking for a way in.

How can Dierdre do this after all Anthony has done for her and her career? Does Harold know? He must. Was he part of this? My gosh, I hope not, but I know he likes her. No, Harold wouldn't betray Anthony and the family like this... At least I don't think he would.

My circulation is returning to my legs, feet, and toes, allowing me to sit up feeling more mobile and physically stable. Sliding off the bed, balancing myself despite a slight wobble, I straighten myself to a strong stance. My headache is much better now but I wish I had some water.

I look around the room to see if there's a bathroom. Cautiously walking toward a door, I turn the handle. Proceeding to the sink and turning on the water I drink until I'm satisfied. Cupping my hands and filling them with cold water I splash my face. The water against my skin feels good.

I'm feeling better but realize I'm still under the influence of the drug. Raising my arm, I try but I'm unable to bring the towel from the towel rack to me. I find it necessary to bend forward and grab the towel with my hand.

After drying my face and hands I try to use my thoughts to put the towel back on the towel rack but fail. I let it rest where it falls on the marble sink top. *What kind of drug did they use on me?*

I make my way back to the bed resting on the edge of the mattress and look around, not recognizing anything in this room. I tense up as I sense someone nearing when the bedroom door is opened. I am surprised to see Bennet, a man who was my guard throughout my school years.

"Hello, Ella. I'm here to escort you to your father. He's anxious to speak with you."

"Bennet, do you realize those are the most words you've ever spoken to me?"

"Hmm, you might be right. Follow me please."

I half expected a different reaction from him; however, true to form, he is who he is. Bennet has always been considered a man of few words. He was my guard the entire time I was enrolled in boarding school. But now I consider him to be a big jerk.

Bennet seems to share the same indifference where I'm concerned as my father does. They are like two peas in a rotting pod. If my opinion seems a bit jaded, it's because at this moment in time, it is. My experiences influence my thoughts.

I stand and walk toward Bennet when he turns, expecting me to follow. Walking closely behind him, with my hands hanging at my sides, I raise the fingertips of my right hand, and point at the doorknobs on the doors I pass. They turn as I mean them to. *Success, yes, the drug has worn off.*

Bennet stops abruptly, looking back at me. He looks down the hall, then back to me. I mimic him when I turn and look down the hall and then back to him. He gives me the stink eye when he says,

"Keep your hands to yourself, Ella. No funny business."

"What are you talking about? I haven't touched a thing."

Bennet has a questioning look on his face when he turns and proceeds down the hall as I follow close behind him. I can't keep the smile from forming on my lips.

We descend a staircase with elaborately scrolled wrought-iron-balusters topped off with a highly polished wooden handrail. The stairs are carpeted with a black scroll design against a white background matching the design within the balusters.

I'm concerned when I look down at the design of the carpet because it has a mesmerizing effect. I can't let my eyes linger on the design too long because it causes me to feel lightheaded and dizzy; it's disorienting. This isn't a mistake in decor design. It was purposefully thought out because the design of this carpet has a function.

At the end of the staircase, we turn to the left making our way across the foyer to stand in front of massive double doors. Elaborately carved figures of warriors at battle are portrayed on both doors. The stunningly intricate figures are disturbingly life-like, and the scene seems to be taken right out of an old-world history book.

Bennet knocks on the door and we're asked to enter. Surprisingly, the heavy doors open with ease as we enter a large sitting room. My father sits in a high-back leather chair behind a large desk fit for a king. All he needs is a crown to complete the scene.

"Ella, finally you are where you belong. Please … take a seat."

When I sit, I can't help but look at the life-size lion statues seated on either side of the fireplace hearth. They are ferocious looking and sculpted to perfection. Each hair of their fur and mane and the meticulously molded sharp teeth and claws create the illusion they've been frozen in time. If I didn't know they weren't real, I'd fear being too close to them.

I look back at my father and respond, "You've never cared about my whereabouts before. What's changed?"

"Ahh, but that's where you're wrong, my dear. I have always cared about your whereabouts."

I look up at the tall ceiling and see a painted fresco representing the Andromeda and the Orion Nebula Galaxies. A large globe hangs in the place of a chandelier. It is spectacular; however, this misplaced exhibit should be in a planetarium somewhere, not in this room.

My father seems satisfied that I've noticed the special touches exhibited in his domain. Everything meant to be seen as artistic flare has a purpose and should be regarded with caution.

"It's a shame you weren't concerned with my comfort as well. The very first thing I did as a free woman was select my own footwear. It was liberating."

"There was a reason I made you wear uncomfortable shoes."

"Really? … Do tell."

"You see, my dear when you are uncomfortable somewhere on your person, you are unable to concentrate one hundred percent. Discomfort renders your capability to move things or complete other tasks with your mind unpredictable. It holds you back from developing to your full capacity."

It's true. I think back to when my tooth began to throb after it broke off while I attempted to disappear into the library. I was unable to concentrate, and Anthony could see the outline of my body.

"So, what you're saying is that you need me to strengthen your power, but you have diminished mine from evolving in the process."

"I was holding you back from developing your skills too soon. You needed my guidance during the process. I couldn't be with you at that point in time. I didn't want you to discover your talents without the control necessary to keep your capabilities a secret."

"I'm no longer your concern. I'm bonded to my husband and finally free to develop normally as intended by my nature."

"You're forgetting my blood runs through your veins. My power is much stronger than yours will ever be. You're either with me or against me, and we can do this the easy way or the hard way."

236

"I think it's quite clear, father, that I am not with you. I am my own free person, and I will live my life as I choose. I am not only married but our marriage is based on love. Not as a slave used as payment for a debt. I'm under Anthony's protection and he will not allow you to have control over my life."

Smiling with a chuckle he responds, "That's an endearing little speech Ella, but where is your husband and his protection? Because it looks like you're in my territory now and under my control."

"Is this how you treated my mother? By controlling her? How did you break her bond? Did you treat her like a slave in a loveless marriage like you planned for me?"

"What we had in the beginning was good. It just ended badly. I take the blame for that because I was young and arrogant and felt entitled to take what I wanted. And I took everything I wanted. I still do."

He looks at me with … *is that regret?*

"My attempt to marry you to Vincent Amato was for you to inherit his fortune as his widow when he died of … natural causes."

"Was that before I was to be raped or after?"

"I planned for Vincent to drink his glass of "special" champagne and then keel over with a heart attack before a roll in the wedding bed. You were never meant to submit to him or be attacked by him."

"When were you going to inform me of your plan?"

"I planned to tell you the day before the wedding."

"How was his champagne going to be different from mine?"

"I arranged for a nicotine tablet to be dissolved in his glass before being served. It would have caused a heart attack by interacting with his blood pressure medicine."

"Then you were expecting me to be an accessory to his death. If an autopsy were performed, I'd be arrested for murder. Just how is that to my advantage?"

"You're looking at this all wrong. Nicotine is undetectable once in the system. The cause of death would have been recorded as a heart attack."

"I still would have been an accessory to murder. I would not want anything as a result of your actions. Besides, I'm sure his family would contest the transfer of his estate to me."

"Ella, you underestimate me. There would have been no problem to transfer the estate to you."

"I wouldn't accept it."

"Then it would have come to me" … *as originally intended.*

There's a knock on the door. When the door opens a servant rolls in a tray. She plates an assortment of fruit, cheeses, and finger food and sets it on the table in front of me.

"Ah, great timing. Let's take a break and eat our meal. Ella, you'll need your strength so eat up."

CHAPTER 34

Gabriella

My father opens a manila folder taking out a picture of a man standing on the steps of a large building, possibly a courthouse.

"Ella, I would like for you to try to communicate with this man."

"What! You can't be serious. I've never seen him before. I have no idea who he is or where he is. What makes you think you can perform such an act?"

"Because it's been done."

I look at my father through skeptical eyes.

"I find that hard to believe."

"When I was a young boy, I was a test subject being studied by one of our government entities experimenting with ... shall we say ... long-distance communications with the enemy. There were three of us being trained in this technique. Of course, only certain people, people like us, qualified for the course."

"How did the government know about you?"

"Our Democracy isn't as free as we've been led to believe. The information withheld from the American people is vast all in the name of National Security. Especially where Extraterrestrials are concerned, which is top secret. In fact, all governments around the world act the same when it comes to government secrets."

"Then the government knows who you are. How is it you're not locked away somewhere or dead?"

"An incident caused the death of the test subjects and researchers alike. I was able to escape the blast through an air vent that led out of the facility. There was a cover up. The bodies were incinerated, and proof of the study was destroyed. The experiment was disbanded, and my identity was wiped out with the rest of the evidence."

I'm stunned to learn how my father intends to use his power as he connects to mine. With this power comes great responsibility. No wonder we're not trusted to live freely among the inhabitants of this world. The possibility of death, destruction, and war is likely for those who would use their power, like my father, to take control and govern.

"Now come to me. We need to touch physically. You need to concentrate on this photograph as we try to connect with this man."

I shake my head and stay seated. "No! I won't even try such a thing."

My father glares at me as he uses his mind to glide my chair across the room with me in it. When the chair rests next to his, he grabs my hand.

"I hoped for your cooperation, so we could do this differently. I'm counting on you seeing the error of your way as we progress."

I try to yank my hand out of his and struggle to stand, but it's as if I'm strapped to the chair. I try to fight against him mentally and physically with everything I have, but it's no use.

It's the breeze I'm aware of first whirling at my feet. I watch a linen napkin spin as it begins to rise and float upward toward the ceiling. My eyes follow the napkin to the fresco of the galaxies pictured above.

The ceiling starts to expand with movement. I believe I'm hallucinating when I watch the galaxies come alive as they turn, expand, and twirl. The colors merge in elaborate designs. The globe spins on its orbit as stars begin to shoot across the ceiling leaving colorful trails of light in their wake.

I barely have a grip on what I'm seeing when it appears there is a black hole forming in the middle of both galaxies. It's sucking items into its darkness. I watch as it claims cups, saucers, plates, and cutlery into its depth. It's getting stronger as the coffee table starts to shake.

I close my eyes as I bend my head down, touch my chin to my chest, and hold my breath. Repeating over and over to myself *"It's an illusion, it's not happening"* when it stops. I open my eyes to see cloth napkins fall back to the ground and the cups, saucers, and plates drop and shatter on the floor.

The galaxies are once again only paintings on the ceiling and the black hole is no longer visible. My father is staring at me with a smile on his face.

"What a pleasant surprise, Ella. Your powers are coming along well. I didn't expect you to take control so completely. Nicely done."

I need to calm myself and step away from my father for a while. "Father, I need to go to the lady's room to freshen up if you expect me to be a hundred percent."

He presses a button on a control box and Bennet enters the room.

"Bennet, escort Ella to the bathroom, and don't linger unnecessarily."

Bennet nods.

"And Ella, don't misbehave and don't dawdle."

Bennet escorts me out of the great room across the foyer to the other side. The elaborate bathroom is adorned with the same luxurious decorator items found throughout this estate. Gold fixtures, gilded mirrors, and marble finishes. The ceiling, however, is disturbing causing any occupant not to linger.

A painting on the ceiling is an illustration of a winged, horned man with nothing on but a loin cloth and carrying a double-sided sword. While he is quite beautiful and built like a Greek god, he is not an angel. His eyes are strangely lifelike, and he projects a darkness that warns of danger. His eyes seem to follow me, and it becomes impossible to relax under the glare of such a terrifying portrait.

There is no window, however, there is a vent in the ceiling. The opening though, is too small for a person to climb through. With no other way out of this room besides the door, I quickly do my business and wash and dry my hands. I look back up at the portrait of the winged man, and feel a chill, as though he's invading my privacy.

I hurry out of the bathroom and rush past Bennet as he sprints to get in front of me to lead me back to my father. I slow down rolling my eyes crossing my arms across my chest and allowing Bennet to lead the way.

I'm unable to hide my resentment as I return to my chair. There has got to be a way for me to discourage my father from his pursuit of combining our power for his personal use.

The problem is, that I'm not strong enough yet to fight against him successfully. Though I succeeded in passing his test with the black hole, I lacked the experience and the endurance required to stop him.

He again takes my hand and holds the photograph in front of both of us.

"Concentrate, Ella. His name is Phillip, and he is one of us. I want him to know we are acting as one to communicate with him. He is currently in London in an art gallery. See if you can see through his eyes."

"Since I've never done this before, just what am I looking for?"

"Ella, this is only an exercise to test our combined capability, nothing more. He will most likely be admiring the paintings exhibited in the museum. Just look through his eyes."

"What will you be doing while I'm looking through this man's eyes?" I don't trust a word my father says and am determined to do nothing more than look through the man's eyes. If that's even possible.

I shake out my shoulders, loosen my tense neck, and take a deep breath. I stare at the photograph with an intense glare and think about the man I'm about to contact. I feel my father as he invades my thoughts. I try to push him out as he tightens his grip on my hand.

Concentrating on my objective, I feel myself drifting as I look at the paintings hanging on the wall of an art gallery. I'm surprised I'm successful. I'm astonished as I appreciate one lovely painting after another.

My line of vision shifts to the people in the gallery. Men and women are strolling from painting to painting viewing the art exhibit. A couple is resting on a bench in the middle of the room. A gallery guard is standing at a doorway entrance watching the people as they pass by. I watch intently as we walk into another section of the gallery.

I see two men in suits nod in my direction. This isn't just a stroll through an art gallery. There is something else at play here. The men in dark suits look as if they are surveying the gallery, planning something illicit. It's obvious that Phillip and the men know each other, as Phillip nods in response. Their meeting is no accident.

One of the men holding a large briefcase is intently looking at the guard, while the guard watches the entrance and doorways. The other man is studying a second guard as he reaches into his pocket. They're here to rob the gallery!

I'm overcome with panic. I've invaded the mind of a criminal with an ulterior motive. He's not merely admiring works of art. His motive here is art theft. This is wrong, I won't be a part of this. I try to disconnect from the man named Phillip, but my father is in control. He won't let me. I'm determined not to be part of this exercise. This is why I tried to escape the mafia.

I close my eyes tight and thrash my head against the upholstered high back chair again and again until I have disconnected from Phillip. I'm surprised I'm able to free myself. I'm in a haze and things aren't quite crystal clear yet. I manage to set my vision on one of the lions on the fireplace hearth.

My father is cursing. "You interrupted my plan. You shouldn't have been able to disconnect." He glares at me with contempt. He's upset I was able to free myself from Phillip and his control. He tells me, "I've chosen a Rembrandt, a debt Phillip owes me. You've spoiled the perfect opportunity."

"But you can duplicate that art in every way in a second. Why steal it?"

"Because I want the real thing, not a duplicate."

My father continues to reprimand me but I'm not listening. He's nothing more than a buzz in my ear when I focus my attention beyond him on the lion on the hearth. I slowly raise my chin, and when I do, the lion's head lifts as well.

Quickly glancing at my father, I check to see if he's aware of my action, but he's too deep in his reproach, attempting to convince me to cooperate, and spewing ultimatums.

I bring the back of my hand to my mouth pretending I'm wiping my lips. The lion lifts his front leg and licks his paw. I shake my head as if clearing my thoughts. The lion mimics my action and shakes his mane vigorously. He's alive! He just opened his eyes, and stared into mine!

I glance at my father once again, ensuring he's still unaware of what I'm doing. Looking at the lion gives me confidence that I'm able to do things I haven't tried yet. I'm stronger than I first thought. My continued resistance to my father's control has brought my defenses to the forefront, and I find myself in a self-protective mode.

The frescos, carvings, balusters, and other components in this mansion are here for a reason. To protect the master and can conceivably do bodily harm to those who would threaten him. If he can control these elements, then so can I.

The lion crosses over to the other side rubbing against the Lioness, licking her face, then nuzzling her before resting beside her. I assume they are mates. I disconnect from the lion letting him return to his previous state where he remains next to his mate... for now.

A knock brings my attention to the massive doors. I hadn't noticed until now that the warriors were carved on both sides of the double doors. They capture my attention when my father responds with "Come!" Dierdre enters with Bennet close behind.

CHAPTER 35

Anthony

We're on the Pacific Coast Highway approaching backed-up traffic that has come to a crawl. A boulder has rolled down the mountain side and fallen on the freeway blocking one lane of the two-lane highway. I can't believe it. First the big rig accident and now this.

Matteo and I get out of our vehicle to see what we're up against. Traffic is being directed by an LA County crew leading one car at a time from one direction then the other. That just won't do. Our vehicles need to proceed continuously as a convoy around the boulder, not held back one at a time.

Bribery is one way to face this dilemma. I explain my intent to Matteo as he makes his way to one of the county workers and I approach the other. It seems the exchange of money is always the deciding factor in getting things done our way.

Matteo and I return to our vehicle as the crew member directing us holds the 'SLOW' sign, and the other crew member pointing in the opposite direction of traffic holds the 'STOP' sign.

The drivers in their stopped vehicles honk their horns and raise their fingers gesturing their frustration as we continue to pass in front of them. If they only knew to whom they were showing such blatant disrespect. I try not to let it bother me, given the circumstances, and ignore the anger of the motorists as we pass by.

It's another tight squeeze maneuvering around the boulder. Matteo was unable to give us more room by shifting the blockage aside as he did with the cab of the truck. It would have been witnessed by too many. It took longer than anticipated for all of us to make it around the boulder. When the final vehicle of our convoy is clear, we pick up speed and continue to our destination.

I ask Matteo if he's sensing Gabriella and her condition. He tells me,

"Think hard and tell her we're on our way, but it will be a while. Tell her traffic has hampered our ability to get there sooner. Communicate as much information to her as possible. It will make her more comfortable and put her at ease the more she hears from you."

I raise my hands to my temples with my head lowered thinking of nothing but Gabriella. I visualize her beautiful face while I think of the words, I want her to hear. I repeat Matteo's words and end with "Hold on, Gabriella, I love you, and can hardly wait to hold you in my arms."

Looking at Matteo when I finish my attempted telepathy he nods and smiles. "You're getting better at this. I only had to lead your voice this time. She hears you loud and clear."

"She does? I was hoping she could hear" but before I finished my thought, I sensed Gabriella. "I'm okay, Anthony. I love you and can hardly wait to be in your arms."

Matteo says, "Anthony, she's holding back because she doesn't want Leo to know you can communicate with her."

CHAPTER 36

Gabriella

Dierdre looks at me with a smirk on her face reflecting pride in her success in deceiving Anthony and me so completely. She walks toward my father and makes herself comfortable on his lap. I couldn't hide my astonishment at the sight. My father and Dierdre? How is that possible?

It angers me that while I'm sensing Anthony, Dierdre is studying me as she smugly sits on my father's lap. I never thought my father was a good man, nor do I have much respect for him, but I never for once thought of him as a fool. I considered him too intelligent to be manipulated by someone like the woman sitting on his lap. Frankly, I can't see him manipulated by any woman.

He pushes Dierdre off his lap telling her, "Leave us. Ella and I have personal matters to discuss."

I don't know why but I feel the urge to snicker at her, giving her the same smirk she gave me. It causes the reaction I expect. With an indignant expression on her face, she purses her lips and turns a brilliant shade of red. Feeling very satisfied with myself I sit up and look as regal as I can.

Dierdre stands straightening her skirt, turns around flipping her hair over her shoulder, and walks to the door. Bennet following her opens the door and leaves the room behind her.

I smile to myself because with people coming and going in this room no one seems to notice the lion I left snuggled next to his mate on the fireplace hearth. My frivolous behavior gives me pleasure every time I look in that direction. I'm not changing a thing. I'm just waiting for my father to notice.

"Father, … How did you become acquainted with Dierdre Dupre? I know you're not part of the music business. In fact, I don't recall ever hearing any music being played at all, ever. Not at home or in the car."

"I researched your new husband and found he had dated Dierdre briefly a year ago. I knew she was upset when it ended. She thought the relationship could be renewed, even after your wedding. He made it perfectly clear it was over between them. He continues to help her with her career as a parting gift, but her popularity is waning. I sent her my business card with a promise of putting her back on top again."

"But you don't know anything about the music industry. And when did you get a business card?"

"Correction, I DIDN'T know anything about the music industry. I DO now. It's all about knowing the right people. The business card was created just for Dierdre's benefit."

"What did you offer her?"

"I made her an offer of a new album rising to number one on the charts in a month. She didn't hesitate to accept. Including the condition to assist in kidnapping you."

"Did you have Ronan beat her so she would call Anthony for help?"

"No. Dierdre was in a car accident that night. She called me with her plan to take advantage of the situation and I accepted."

"What was her plan?"

"She called Ronan asking for his help. He obliged her by adding a few bruises to her face and smashed up a few pieces of her furniture to make it look believable. Then he dropped her off at Anthony's club. Because he'd roughed her up before, everyone assumed he did it again."

I thought to myself even though Ronan was working with the other side, he was a marked man because of that event and was killed because of his involvement. But what about Harold?

"Where does Harold come into all of this?"

"That was not planned. It seems Harold is smitten with Dierdre, … or was. She thought he would go along with her plan to take you. But when he didn't and tried to stop her, she shot him with his own gun."

Oh no! She shot Harold! I don't know if he's dead or alive. His loyalty to Anthony and his attempt to protect me may have killed him. I feel bad that I doubted his loyalty to the family. I need to find out if Harold survived.

CHAPTER 37

Anthony

We're out of heavy traffic and the obstacles that plagued us are finally behind us. We are taking a little-known short cut to our destination. Hopefully, it will be smooth driving from here.

We're on a two-lane highway headed for a one-lane unpaved road that is seldom used. Due to having only one lane of travel, only one turnabout, and only our headlights for lighting it isn't a popular drive for anyone, especially us.

We'll be crossing a single-lane bridge to get over a gorge to the other side. From there the road intersects with the frontage road that runs parallel to the freeway. We'll be able to merge onto the freeway after the quarter-mile mark.

The drive after getting around the boulder has been uneventful and the traffic flow normal as we approach the turn off for the unpaved road. It will be dusty, and the incline will slow us down, but we don't have much further to go before we reach the bridge.

Our convoy is making its way up the incline with little difficulty. The glare from our headlights gives us more than enough lighting. Our continuous flow of cars bears a resemblance to a huge lighted snake winding its way up the road.

We approach the area where the incline finally levels out to flat ground and leads the way to the bridge. My SUV is the lead vehicle as we stop. I look at Matteo in disbelief. "Do you see what I see? This can't be happening Matteo."

Matteo and I get out of the car and walk to the edge of the ledge where the beginning of the bridge should be. But the only thing we see is the bottom of the gorge.

With the flashlight in his hand, Matteo shines his light toward thin air. He directs his light on areas where the bridge should be. He looks at me then shakes his head, and stoops down to pick up a rock.

"Matteo, what are you doing? What's going through that brain of yours?"

"Just watch. If my hunch is right, you should see this rock float. Try to keep your flashlight aimed at it as I throw it."

Matteo throws the rock. It makes a noise consistent with landing on something as it sits in thin air. There is absolutely nothing holding it up. He bends down to retrieve another rock.

"Keep your light pointed to this rock as I throw it as well." Matteo throws the rock higher when it deflects from something invisible and lands in mid-air close to the first rock.

"Matteo, what does that mean?"

"Think, Anthony. Didn't Gabriella show you her powers when she was practicing?"

"Are you telling me the bridge is still there?

"That's exactly what I'm showing you. Only one person could have done this: Leo Farina!"

I'm concerned that Gabriella and Matteo's secret is at stake here. "Matteo, how do we explain this to our men without giving away your identity?"

Matteo thinks while pacing back and forth. "We'll tell them it's mass hypnosis to keep us from passing. After we make it across, I'll remove that portion of memory from their minds. It's the only thing I can think of."

"Mass hypnosis! Do you think these men will buy that?"

"They'll have to. Those who are superstitious will be easier to convince. I can't influence their minds to forget until we're on the other side. Their full attention is required to successfully drive across that bridge. It is either that or kill them all after we reach the other side." Matteo has a smile on his face.

"This is serious. That's not funny Matteo."

"Sorry, Anthony, it just popped in there."

I try not to show my amusement with Matteo's comment. We ask the men to step out of their vehicles and gather when Matteo explains why the men can't see the bridge. To convince them there is a bridge across the gorge he asks them to step forward. Cooper is the first to step on the bridge.

Once the men can feel the bridge under their feet and touch the side barriers with their hands, they look at each other in amazement and nod at Matteo. Although they seem to find this hard to accept, they return to their cars and start their engines.

Matteo instructs the men to follow closely behind our SUV and the car in front of them.

"We'll be driving straight down the middle of the bridge but keep your eyes on the car in front of you. Concentrate! The fact you can't see the bridge will play tricks on you, especially since you can see the gorge below us."

253

I lead our convoy down the middle of the bridge by focusing my attention on a road marker on the other side. With Matteo's assistance, I carefully proceed across the bridge. This is a challenge because I can't see what's holding us up and I'm stunned by how real the gorge below us looks.

It appears as if we're floating on air. It would be easy for our minds to drift and turn the steering wheel to the right or left under these circumstances. If this is a sample of what Leo can do, I'm not sure how we can proceed against his psychological warfare. If it weren't for Matteo, I don't know if we would have a chance against him.

We make it across to the other side and then we pull over and park. Getting out of the SUV we walk to the edge of the bridge motioning our men forward with our flashlights. All have come across except the last car.

Matteo asks, "Who's in that car?"

Cooper says, "That's Emilio. He's one of mine."

Matteo walks toward Emilio holding his flashlight. He looks like he's floating on air since the bridge he's walking on is invisible. Matteo continues forward as he calls out to Emilio coaxing him to let the flashlight guide him across.

Emilio finds enough courage to drive the car forward, but he accidentally loses control, and his foot lands too hard on the gas pedal. There is absolutely nothing I can do but stand there and watch the car lunge toward Matteo. I know Matteo couldn't survive if the kid ran over him or hit him with such force that he fell off the bridge.

Emilio immediately slams on the brakes, looking wide eyed at Matteo who was now standing on the hood of his vehicle. It was as though Matteo knew what was going to happen before it happened.

Matteo had jumped on the hood of the car when the car lunged at him. He stoops down glaring at Emilio through the window and yells, "Put the car in park." Which Emilio did immediately.

Matteo jumps off the hood of the car, opens the driver's side door, and tells Emilio, "Slide over, I'm driving." When Emilio slides to the passenger side, he opens the door. No longer able to control his nerves, Emilio throws up. Sitting back in his seat he turns to Matteo apologizing profusely over and over.

Matteo drives the car across the bridge. He stops the car, looks at Emilio, and says, "I know it was an accident, but you need to hide your fear and learn control under pressure if you're going to survive in this world." Emilio responds, "Yes sir, I'll work on that, and thank you for not shooting me."

Matteo shakes his head, reflecting a smile on his lips as he exits the car.

Matteo, Cooper, and I get the men together which is difficult given the ground space we have available to assemble as a complete group. Matteo has me step behind him as he speaks to the men in a low hypnotic voice. Matteo is becoming more and more difficult to hear and all ears are straining to listen. I no longer hear his words, but I can feel him speaking as I take another step back.

I feel a little woozy. I don't think Matteo meant for me to be part of his mind-altering activity. I understand why Matteo and Gabriella need to protect their identity. It is disarming to know someone exists with such power. It makes you question everything you've ever been taught.

When Matteo finishes, he excuses the men to return to their cars and tells them not to look back. No one did. They follow his instructions to the letter. He doesn't want them to look back at the deep gorge. For all they know, nothing was out of the ordinary when they crossed over a seldom used one-way one-lane bridge.

CHAPTER 38

Gabriella

My father has upped the ante when I find myself in a battle of the wills against him. He's forced himself into my mind and is using me to distort the room we're sitting in. Moving furniture is child's play when compared to what he's doing now.

He's changing the molecular structure of certain items. The physical changes involve alterations in properties such as texture, and shape. Changes of state result in modifying a solid to a liquid or gas. In addition, physical deformation results in cutting, denting, and stretching an item. Chemical changes include temperature fluctuations and color shifts. When the molecular structure of any item is changed, the item cannot be returned to its original state.

It's as if we're in a bad science fiction movie, only this isn't fiction. This is real and happening before my eyes. He turned a wood coffee table into ash, and a porcelain figurine into liquid, He elongated and stretched a metal coat of armor until it became a spear. He changed the cloth drapery into stone and the temperature in the room to freezing. All in the name of power.

I use all the skills I've gained so far to make myself powerful enough to resist his hold on me. My body rises from my chair with my eyes fixed on my father. I've levitated about five feet in the air and holding steady. My father joins me, and we are both weightless and floating off the ground caught in a game of chicken. Neither of us is prepared to give in to the other.

My father, however, plays dirty when he distracts me by tossing memories of my mother at me, one after the other. I'm so distracted I lose my concentration and fall back to my chair with a hard thud. Our merging is disconnected for now, allowing me to rest and take a breather. I feel drained and weakened after that confrontation. I must learn not to let anything distract me or he'll win in the end.

"Gabriella, I'm impressed with your resolve to resist me. You surprise me with the talent you've gained in such a short time."

"Is that a compliment? Is that a reflection of fatherly pride?"

"Gabriella, I was always proud of you. However, I'm one who rarely shows my feelings or emotions. I would say my compliment is better late than never."

"Unfortunately, father your compliment is too little and far too late to influence me on any level. My animosity toward you is clearly understandable."

"I admit I won't win an award for my fatherly skills. I was busy building my empire and there was no time for you in my life. I did make sure you had a first-class education. I kept tabs on you and made sure you were safe by surrounding you with protection."

"Yes, you surrounded me with protection, but there was no show of affection or love in my life. There was no one to look up to or to build a family relationship with. I had no friends, I had no one. I was isolated and alone. You lack the ability to be a father because you lack the ability to love."

"Love is a word to describe a useless emotion that binds one to another. It is neither appreciated nor reciprocated. It only causes the strong to become weak. We cannot afford to weaken our minds with such ridiculous emotions."

"Do you hear yourself? Your frame of thinking has made you more alien than you were intended to be. A man who cannot relate to those who inhabit this world, who has no empathy for any other being is nothing more than a machine dressed in living tissue."

"Hmm, a machine in living tissue. I think I like that observation. As this world evolves, we may find that one day we can incorporate our brain into a vessel that will never grow old or deteriorate. That would mean endless life. Life forever. That suits me just fine."

I shake my head regarding his statement. I think I just realized that no matter how wondrous our race is, it's possible for one to go crazy. His hunger for ultimate power has affected his mind. He has become a danger to the human race. I'm certain when he gains my power, he'll be searching for others until nothing on this planet can stop him.

CHAPTER 39

Anthony

"Matteo, we must warn the men. What they're about to face will most likely hamper their ability to focus. The bridge is just a prelude to what's coming our way in this fight. There is no telling what Leo's prepared to throw at us."

"I can try to prepare them, Anthony. However, you know as well as I they can't conceive what I'm about to tell them until it's right before their eyes."

"Matteo, advanced preparation is always better than no warning at all. At least they'll know some of what to expect. They'll believe it soon enough. Hopefully, they'll be prepared enough to be able to fight without panicking."

"Leo has two armies we're up against. The human side and his mind-altering creations. If I can reach Gabriella sooner than later, together we'll be able to defend ourselves against both and defeat him. The first battle that must be won, though, is to disconnect Leo from Gabriella."

"Then it's important that our plan for you to find Gabriella quickly is successful. The men we brought with us are your back up and protection. When you and Gabriella connect, our men will protect you both, with me standing at your side."

We pulled off at the side of the road onto a sightseeing lookout point. We exit our vehicles for our last gathering to prepare for battle. Matteo lowers his voice as he begins to speak. He is using more than a vocal explanation. He's including a bit of his hypnotic power to help prepare them. I'm relieved he's on our side.

The men are pumped up when they return to their vehicles. This is it, we're on our way to save Gabriella.

We pull into a rest area not far from our destination and park our vehicles, walking the rest of the way until we reach the compound. Separated into our teams, team one quickly scales the six-foot barrier taking out the guards on the wall with the other teams following close behind them. Team two scales the mansion and settles on the roof top. The other teams take their positions around the compound waiting for the signal to attack.

Matteo, me, and Cooper are watching to ensure everyone is in their place. Our drones are whirling above us hunting for the enemy. The team on the roof is ready to invade from their position and has already opened the roof-top maintenance door to let themselves into the second story.

"Matteo, there were only a few guards on the wall. There are no guards monitoring the grounds or on the roof. Something's wrong. This seems too easy."

"That's because he knows we're here. His men must be inside waiting for us."

Gabriella

I felt a little weak and was trying to recover from my father when the guards, Dierdre, and Bennet came rushing into the room exclaiming we were under attack. I can hear the shooting from the second floor and men shouting orders. Suddenly there's a loud explosion and I hear someone yell, "They blew out the front door but they're not rushing in."

I hear Bennet yell to them, "That's because we altered the view. They can't see the damage and can't tell they're successful. Use your men to cover that area and shoot whoever finally comes through that gaping hole."

I stand and run past Bennet while his back is to me and make it to the stairs. Bennet and another guard start to chase me and are close to catching me then suddenly stop. They watch as I take two steps at a time until I too, abruptly stop. The scroll work, both printed on the carpet and the wrought iron baluster, begin to move, swirl, and slither, taking shape into a thousand snakes.

I looked up when Anthony, Matteo, and our men reach the top of the stairs. They watch in shock as the snakes wrap around my legs, slither up to my thighs, and hold me tight in their grip. Anthony and the men jump into action attacking the snakes with the butts of their rifles. When that has no effect, they start shooting the snakes.

Leo's men turn from the damaged doorway to fire on Anthoney, and his team. That's when the rest of our men come rushing through the gaping hole with guns blazing, firing at Leo's guards. Anthony shouts, "It took you long enough!" Someone responds, "We couldn't tell we blasted through until now."

As both sides exchange fire, I'm being held down by snakes who are now wrapped around my arms. I'm trying to concentrate on controlling the snakes when I notice the double doors start to bulge in and out like they're breathing.

The carved figures of the warriors on the door are moving, turning their heads, raising their weapons, then stepping off the door onto the floor. They must be seven feet tall and carry different forms of antique weaponry. Swords, hatchets, spears, chains, and archery. The warriors look around, then react knowing exactly which side they will defend.

Matteo gets close enough to grab my hand as he too is attacked by the snakes slithering around his legs climbing up to his chest. Matteo shoots at the snakes while holding firmly on to me. Anthony and our men shoot as many snakes as possible but more keep appearing.

Matteo says, "Gabriella, close your eyes and drift with me." I'm confused, not sure if what he's asking will work, but I do what he says. I find myself in a haze, and I can see Matteo's light shining through. I know instantly Matteo is just like me. We connect as he pulls me up with him levitating above the snakes.

Anthony and his men hurriedly descend the stairs as the snakes disappear changing back into their original forms: A baluster and a design printed onto a white carpet.

Matteo and I levitate past the stairs touching down to stand on the floor with the battle raging around us. Anthony grabs me with Matteo still holding tight to my hand. "Gabriella, Matteo is here to help you; he's a friend. He will guide you to fight against your father. Trust him like you trust me."

The warriors strike but bullets seem to have little to know impact on them. Matteo yells, "Head shots, shoot them in the head." Suddenly the bathroom door begins to bang furiously from the inside. One of our men starts to open the door as I scream "NO" but it's too late. When the door opens the winged, horned man is alive and flies out the bathroom with his double edge sword. Everyone shoots at him at once.

We stand together united and connected as we concentrate on stopping the warriors. The double doors are open, and Dierdre comes toward us with a gun in her hand. Anthony takes aim when the winged man scoops her up and flies with her toward the sitting room. She's shocked and frightened. Dropping her gun, she screams for help.

It looks as if we have the upper hand as all our men are in the mansion battling with Leo's men and remaining warriors. Matteo and I have been successful in doubling our power as we unite as one. We rushed into the sitting room to face my father together. The winged man is perched on the huge fireplace mantel with Dierdre in his arms as she furiously struggles against his hold, calling for Leo to help her.

My father activates the lions. I mistakenly thought that since I took control of them first, they would be under my control making them my protector. I was wrong. The lions prepare to strike, but their attention is not on my father, their coming for me and Matteo. Together, joined as one, Matteo and I reduce the lions to stone just before they attack. They are again in their original form sitting on the hearth.

"So, you think you can defeat me, with this man's help? Who is he, Gabriella?"

"He's a friend, and yes, between the two of us we can and will defeat you."

"You may have won the battle, but you won't win the war. This changes nothing. You are still my daughter, and you will be at my side again."

Suddenly the air shifts and a whirling sound begins as the galaxies on the ceiling begin to move, swirl, and expand. Stars are shooting across the ceiling when the black hole begins to take shape. At first it takes smaller lightweight items into its darkness. It becomes stronger quickly taking heavier items into its wake. Matteo and I cannot stop it.

The winged man flies off the mantel with Dierdre in its clutches as she screams and kicks crying for Leo's help. My father has an evil smirk on his face when suddenly the pull of the black hole is so strong it pulls the winged man and Dierdre into its darkness before they reach the door.

My father and Bennett follow as they are also pulled into the wake of the black hole. Anthony yells for all of us to run out of the room and out of the mansion as we hold on to each other and anything else that can help us resist the pull of the black hole.

Many of Leo's men have been absorbed into the blackness but all our men successfully leave just in time. When we are a safe distance from the mansion we turn and watch in horror as everything is sucked into the black hole. The mansion itself is pulled inside out. When it's over there is nothing left but an empty lot. There's absolutely nothing to indicate a structure of any kind was ever here.

It's remarkable that any of us got out before it took us. Anthony holds me tightly in his arms kissing me and looking me over for any cuts, scrapes, or bruises. He stops and pulls Matteo's hand to meet mine. All three of us are holding hands when Anthony says,

"Gabriella, it gives me pleasure to introduce you to your brother. I couldn't reveal that while we were in the mansion. Leo doesn't know he has a son, and we want to keep it that way."

I hug Matteo as tightly as I can. I look at him with tears in my eyes and say,

"I have always felt a pull toward you and now I know why. We are bonded as sister and brother. I'm so glad we've found you and that you are now in my life. I have a husband and a brother. Life is good."

Matteo calls the men together for another meeting to ensure certain memories are erased. Anthony and I stand together holding onto each other as we watch Matteo take charge to ensure our secret is still intact.

"Anthony how did all this come about."

"When you were taken, I was going to leave Matteo behind to take care of things at the ranch while I came after you. He revealed himself to me so he could go with me to help defeat Leo. I've made him my blood brother and my underboss. The three of us are bonded for life."

"Thank you, Anthony. I'm so thankful to be your wife. I love you with all my heart."

When Matteo concludes his special meeting, we all walk back to our cars. On the drive home Anthony explains what happened on the freeway with the big rig, the boulder, and finally the bridge. We laughed about Emilio's mishap with the gas pedal and Matteo's jump that landed him on the roof of the car. I guess it wasn't funny then, but it was hilarious when Matteo retold the story.

Dierdre's name came up while we were laughing. Anthony said, "It looks like Dierdre has a new boyfriend."

Matteo says, "Yeah, I think that horned devil has a crush on her."

I add, "Did you see her expression when they were sucked up into the black hole?"

We all laugh so hard my stomach aches. Then I remembered Harold.

"Oh my gosh how is Harold?"

"The doc texted that Harold made it through surgery and is on the mend. Harold feels bad you were kidnapped because he didn't see through Dierdre's deceit in time. He paid for his mistake when she shot him twice in the chest with his own gun. He'll be happy to learn we got you back safe and sound."

"Poor Harold. I hope you weren't hard on him."

"Oh, we wouldn't dream of it." Anthony chuckles,

"At least not until he's up and about." Matteo laughs.

CHAPTER 40

Gabriella

"I can hardly wait to see Guinevere. I hope she hasn't forgotten me, and I hope she doesn't think I've forgotten her. When we get home can we stop at the stable so I can at least tell her goodnight?"

Anthony responds, "Yes, we'll stop at the stable so you can say goodnight to Guinevere."

By the time we reach the ranch, I've fallen asleep. Anthony gently shakes my shoulder telling me we're here. I open my sleepy eyes and reach my hand to Anthony's as he helps me out of the car.

We enter the stable and make our way to Guinevere's stall. I'm excited, as I place my forehead on Guinevere's nose telling her how much I missed her and that we'll go riding in the morning. I kiss Guinevere and pet her behind her ear telling her to sleep tight and not let the bed bug's bite. Matteo and Anthony raise their eyebrows and roll their eyes.

I look at them and say, "What!" You know she understands every word."

In The Morning

I wake up in good spirits excited that I'll be riding my horse today. When I start to get out of bed, it's as if I'm captured in a massive vice. Anthony has his arms wrapped around me holding me tightly against his chest. I also feel his very distinctive arousal poking me in my hip with his leg draped over mine.

As Anthony begins to stir, I'm aware that he has already planned this morning's activities that I'm sure includes bed exercises of the carnal kind. I turn into his arms and seduce him with a passionate kiss and press my hips into his arousal. I smile at my handsome husband with my sexiest smile and pull off my camisole.

He growls and buries his head between my breasts. He nips me with his teeth making me squeal as I try to twist away from him. That's a waste of effort as his hold on me is unbreakable. I reach under the covers and grab onto his stiff rod that begins to grow even larger in my hand.

I'm feeling playful and let a low seductive hum come out of my mouth and say, "Hmmm, come to mama, big boy." I surprise him and he lifts his head to look at me with wide eyes and a smile on his lips. He buries his head in my neck, biting and sucking, pulling my skin into his mouth. He'll leave a hickey if I can't stop him. I'll wear a scarf around my neck for a couple of days.

Anthony surprises me when he lifts his mouth from my neck long enough to say,

"I think I like it when my wife speaks dirty to me."

I didn't really consider what I said to be dirty. Playful, blunt and aggressive, but not dirty. I think I've graduated to dirty bedroom talking and Anthony likes it.

"These need to come off also." Anthony reaches down to remove my panties. "Do you have anything else you'd like to say to me?"

I'm trying to think as he's mauling me but all I can come up with is, "What's taking you so long … daddy?" I can't help but giggle as he freezes and looks at me with a devious smile, then proceeds to tear my panties to shreds.

The giggling comes to an abrupt end, and heavy breathing takes its place when play time is over and intense love making begins. I begin to drift up taking us soaring into our blissful levitated state. Our intimacy reaches an elevated passion. We are consumed with each other as we achieve that ultimate high, climaxing together as one.

As we lay in each other's arms enjoying the afterglow I'm trying to find the energy to make my body move to get up and shower. If I let myself, I could stay in bed all day, but I'm too eager to take Guinevere riding this morning. I ask Anthony,

"Will you go riding with me today? Do you think Matteo would like to join us?"

"Yes, but your white saddle won't be ready until next week sometime. You'll have to choose one of the saddles we already have."

"I thought we agreed I would ride bareback. If it doesn't work out, I'll use a saddle until mine is ready. But I'm definitely firm on no bit for Guinevere. Agreed?"

Anthony doesn't respond right away then says, "Okay, you can try riding bareback but as soon as there's a problem, it's off you come and on to a saddle. Her bridle and rein is already altered with no bit."

I give Anthony a big kiss then off the bed and into the shower I go. Anthony is right behind me. We enjoy our shower which leads to additional love making. You would think we're addicted to each other the way we're acting. I think our experience with my father has given us a newfound appreciation to make the most of every minute of every day. We never know when our lives can take a turn for the unexpected.

Ready for the day, we greet the staff. We're seated in the dining room when Jenna serves us our breakfast. When we finished Anthony tells me to get my holster and gun. I'm concerned and question why he wants me to wear my gun.

"Gabriella, you need to get used to wearing it for your protection. Your father didn't seem to panic when he was being swept away. We have no idea of his condition or where that black hole took him. He could be in another realm or back here somewhere."

I reluctantly go to my office to strap on my holster and check my gun before sliding it into the slot. I come out with a smile on my face and slap Anthony on his butt. Anthony smiles and says,

"What's gotten into you today? Are you experiencing delayed shock from yesterday's trauma?" I smile and kiss his cheek.

We get into a utility cart and drive to the stable. Guinevere is ready for her exercise, and she is led from her stall into the training pen awaiting our arrival. Carlo and Angelo are with Guinevere, and I notice they have placed a saddle on the fence, ready to access, in case it's decided it will be used.

I brought apple slices with me as a treat for Guinevere. Once she has eaten and I have kissed her I stand facing Carlo with such excitement I can barely stand still. Carlo twines his fingers together making a step for me with his hands. I slide my foot into his hands and when he hoists me up with such ease, it feels like I am flying for a second. I lift my other leg to straddle Guinevere, landing firmly on her back.

Once in position Carlo hands me the reins and asks me to lead Guinevere around the pen. He explains he wants me to get the feel of her and the only way to stay seated properly will be through the strength of my legs pressing together against her sides. He suggests I use the saddle.

"Carlo, please give me a chance to try to ride without one. I promise if you feel I'm not balanced and firmly in place I'll agree to the saddle."

Carlo looks at Anthony with concern but Anthony nods to him giving the go ahead to try it my way. Carlo, Angelo, and Anthony climb on the fence sitting on top giving me and Guinevere room to explore the pen.

I give her a little nudge as I jut my hips forward, clicking my tongue and telling her, "Let's go Guiney." She responds well as she takes her first steps to my command, and we start to trot around the pen. I will admit I needed to find my balance when bouncing on her back, but it didn't take long to adjust.

We trotted around the pen with no problem until Carlo instructs me to stop Guinevere in the middle of the pen. He asks me to lead her to the right, then left, then trot until he tells me to stop her. She follows each command perfectly. Carlo tells Anthony to mount up we're going on a tour of the ranch.

I'm so thrilled that Guinevere and I are like old friends and blend comfortably with each other as one. She is so beautiful, and she seems magical to me. Matteo was watching me put Guinevere through her paces and applauded our success. All four men Carlo, Angelo, Matteo and Anthony, mount their horses and we head out to explore the ranch.

What a wonderful feeling to ride a beautiful horse, touring a magnificent ranch on such a sunny day. I can't believe this is happening. I am ecstatic as my eyes fill with joyful tears. Anthony, who's riding close to me, reaches out and hands me his handkerchief. He doesn't say a word because he knows what I'm feeling.

Confident with myself, I direct Guinevere toward the racetrack as the men look at each other and follow. We lead the horses from a trot to a gallop and we enter into a little race. Guinevere is in the lead by a head. These men can't turn away from a challenge as the five of us are side by side racing as if we bet money on it. We're picking up speed when Anthony shouts "Okay, that's enough. We'll play this game again when Gabriella has a saddle on Guinevere."

We all made a moaning sound of disappointment because we had been fully engaged in the thrill of the race I started. Anthony smiles with approval when he shakes his head and compliments me, "You're a natural, Gabriella. You did exceedingly well and I'm proud of you."

We headed back to the stable when we spotted something on the path. Matteo dismounts and walks toward the broken heap of plastic and metal. It's one of our drones. The only way it's recognizable is because a propellor is still intact. It is bent out of shape but identifiable.

Matteo reaches down and picks it up. He says, "This is one of the drones we lost in the black hole. It's still warm." He hands it to Anthony who responds, "Let's take the horses back to the stable and take a look to see if the images the camera captured can be viewed."

The drone is a reminder of yesterday's battle, and the question on everyone's mind is. Is it over or is this a prelude of things yet to come? I had been enjoying myself so much until this discovery. It's discouraging to think that my father could still be lurking somewhere nearby. The stress that had left me reappeared and for good reason. I know my father isn't dead, but I hoped he might be in a different galaxy far, far away.

I take Guinevere to her stall while Anthony and Matteo go to the house to see if the camera captures anything viewable. Eager to groom

Guinevere, I brush her, making contact all over her body with her brush. I talk to her telling her how much fun I had riding her today. Lifting and inspecting each of her hooves, I make sure they are clear of debris. Ensuring she has everything she needs; I kiss her before I leave.

CHAPTER 41

Anthony

Matteo and I enter my office. When I set the drone on my desk I ask, "Matteo, why did this thing land on my property? We were an hour away in the next county over. I would have expected anything surviving that black hole would have landed in the ocean, not my ranch."

"I'm not sure, Anthony, but it's no accident. I'm sure Leo had something to do with this."

Matteo takes out his knife and unscrews the only screw left holding the military grade drone together. The camera falls off, landing on the desktop. The camera is a small detachable box with a 120-degree lens and sensor capable of aerial photography, plus 6X digital zoom which transitions between varying distances, directions, and compositions.

Matteo attaches the camera to a small screen and pushes the button. There is nothing but static. We are about to turn the camera off when a face floats in front of the lens. It's the winged, horned creature that took Dierdre. It passes quickly in front of the lens and then it's gone. Soon after the winged creature appears a man passes in front of the lens. It must have been one of Leo's men. Seeing those two proves they were still alive when their images were captured by the camera. *A worrying realization.*

"Anthony, I think Leo created that black hole to escape. He knew you would go after him with everything in your power to rescue Gabriella. I think it was his plan B in case he was unable to win the battle. He didn't act concerned at all when he was pulled into the black hole. Instead, he was smiling. When he was unable to protect himself against us, he simply activated his escape plan, taking everything with him."

"Matteo, don't your people have some kind of underground organization to take care of someone like Leo? His power-hungry ambition can be the deciding factor against your race. If he becomes a threat to our government, it won't just be our government hunting all of you; it will be all the governments on the planet combined. There wouldn't be any place to hide. It would be nothing less than genocide."

"We've been so programmed to conceal our true identities that we tend to stay on our own away from others like us. Gathering as a group would attract attention and make it easier for the authorities to locate and identify us. If there is some sort of organization like you describe I'm not aware of one."

"I know this is not the time, and I'm not sure if it's even possible because the risks would be great. Would it be possible for us to create such an organization using the Costa Nostra as a model for a hierarchy with security, protection, and strict rules in place to guard against discovery? It wouldn't be a mafia, but the business model and security would be similar."

"Anthony, it would be very difficult to create such an organization. We would need to find others who are well hidden within this society. Information to enable us to locate them is nonexistent. If we found anyone, we would have to convince them of the idea. Written records of individuals joining the organization would be prohibited. The risk of such a record would be too great. We would need to appoint scribes to record and store the information of such an organization in their brains. Nothing could be recorded in writing electronically, or in any hard copy form. Nothing!"

"Matteo, is it possible for someone to keep such records in their minds?"

"You forget, Anthony. Unlike a human, most of us are capable of using one hundred percent of our brains. That's what gives us the power we possess."

"A scribe's identity would be the greatest priority to keep confidential and protected. If such a person was captured it would be the end of the organization and the members if discovered. Every member's identity in the organization would be revealed."

"If what you say is a concern, like gathering as a group, why would you need to meet physically at all? Why couldn't meetings be conducted through thoughts instead? Think about it. You would need to elect the head of the organization, the underboss, scribe, treasurer, protectors, etcetera ..."

"Wait, why would we need a treasurer?"

"Members would pay dues to finance the organization. An account would be set up for the benefit of the members. For instance, a family mourning the death of the head of the household. Funds could be allocated to help with expenses. A member has lost his job. Funds could be used to assist financially until he is again employed. A member needs a new identity. Funds could be used to give him a new one. The list goes on and on and is ultimately decided upon by the Capo or boss, or whatever name you choose for the head of the organization."

Matteo is thinking about the possibility. I can see him in deep thought going over everything I have suggested as he paces back and forth in front of my desk. He stops and faces me when he says, "I'm part of the mafia. It's a decision I made years ago. I'm not sure there would be many like me."

"Why not? You're on the same planet as me. We make our life decisions based on our life experiences. Some of us are thrust into our lifestyle. What makes you think you're the only person within your race to make this type of career decision? Hard times lead us to our destination. Many times, there aren't other options for survival."

"You've given me much to think about Anthony. It would be beneficial if my race had the support you described. I'm not sure it's attainable, but it's something to consider."

"Matteo, I have never heard the name your people go by. What I mean is, that we are known as Humans. What are you known as?"

"We call ourselves **Territhian**. We originated on the planet **Territh** thousands of years ago. Don't repeat it please."

Gabriella knocks twice and then opens the door. "Did the camera capture anything viewable?"

"Yes. We think your father is still alive. We need to locate where he might have landed."

"Do you think my father poses a threat anytime soon? I'm asking because I'd like to invite Ed and Mackenzie Carlton for dinner. Before all the trouble we've had, you said we could entertain them here at the ranch."

I look at Matteo then turn back to Gabriella. "There are some areas of the mansion that still need a touch up after the attack your father led against us. Let's count on another week for those final repairs. I want the mansion to look as it did before the attack."

"Great that gives me more than a week to plan the visit. Do you think they would like to tour the ranch on horseback? I was hoping we could make a day of it. I thought we could ride horses in the afternoon, have dinner, and maybe we could end the evening with a card game ... or something. What do you think?"

"That sounds like a lot Gabriella. I'll ask Ed if he's in favor of riding. If not, we can skip the tour of the ranch and just have dinner and maybe a card game."

"Okay. I'm just eager to visit with Mackenzie again. I like her and hope we can become friends. I hate that my father makes everything so difficult for us. I was hoping he was in another galaxy."

I kiss Gabriella on the forehead telling her, "Gabriella, we'll figure something out for a fun visit. Don't worry. We should be safe for a while. I'll call Ed tomorrow and we'll pick a date and make a plan."

Gabriella

The next day I meet Monte at the shooting range for my weekly practice. I've become comfortable handling my gun and had no idea target practice could be so much fun. I ordered targets that are more than just bull's eyes and circles. Finding a special website, I ordered a batch of what is labeled 'Bad Guys.' It contains a colorful assortment of seedy looking characters holding different threatening weapons of different sizes.

I could tell they would be a hit. It's more fun when you have something a little more realistic to aim at. Anthony commented that the men enjoy the new targets also, and he has decided to make them our permanent shooting targets. After using four ammunition clips and destroying multiple targets, I put my gun back in my holster and walked toward the stable.

My Guinevere is ready and waiting for me. I keep a bag of carrots and apples in the stable now for all the horses to enjoy. This way the treats are always on hand and something the horses expect. When I give Guiney a treat, I'm careful to include all the horses with a treat.

Angelo hoists me up on Guinevere's bareback and we gallop toward the racetrack. Guiney and I are going to enjoy a little pretend race. Since we're the only ones on the track I'll just have to imagine we're in a race competing against the best.

I imagine that I line us up, count down from five, and then we're off. Guinevere and I gallop down the stretch of track and near our first curve when I see something drop from the sky. Slowing to a stop, I led Guiney back to look at what had fallen. It's crumpled rotary blades from one of our drones.

These falling items are a hazard that can strike someone and are dangerous to our horses. They could step on one of these, injuring their hooves. They're also cause for concern for a different reason. Are they a warning of things to come?

I slide off Guinevere and pick up the rotary blade. Now I'm not sure how I'm going to get back on her. I lead Guinevere toward the fence so I can use it as a ladder. That doesn't work out as well as I thought it would. I'm thinking a saddle would be nice at this moment. I ask Guinevere if she thinks she can bow on her front legs, bringing her closer to the ground and allowing me to hop back on. Surprisingly she does. I failed my first attempt but got back on with my second try.

I should have realized our drone was nearby watching every move I made. Anthony's voice can be heard through the speaker, "Nicely done, Gabriella, nicely done. Was that another piece of a drone that was on the track?"

I turn to the drone and hold up the rotary blade, nodding and saying "Yes."

"Go ahead and bring it in so we can take a closer look at it."

I wave at the drone, then head back to the stable. We're trying to race a little more before stopping for the day when Guinevere begins to gallop as if she, too, is pretending she's in a race. We are galloping headfirst into the wind as it rushes past our faces. It's picking up strength when I notice something strange about the wind. It seems to be swirling around us as we race.

What's happening isn't natural. I start to panic when it reminds me of how the wind started before things were lifted into the black hole. Anthony alerts the men I'm in trouble. I wrap my hands tightly into Guinevere's mane as I direct her to go as fast as she can. I'll hold on. I'm afraid if we slow down or stop, we might be lifted into the swirling funnel that's forming around us.

It appears we are in the middle of a tornado with a clear sky and not a single dark cloud to be seen. Thankfully the twister is void of any debris. I can see the men running in our direction with ropes in their hands. Carlo is the closest and his rope lands around Guinevere's neck.

I quickly raise my right arm as Matteo's rope just lands around my shoulders sliding down and settling at my waist like a crossbody strap. I let go of Guinevere's mane and place my right hand into the rope loop so that the rope slides around my waist as I jump off Guinevere.

The wind has picked up in strength, but the men have Guinevere under their control, holding on to her while Matteo has pulled me close

281

to him. We run into the shelter of the stable, but the wind follows us until the stable doors are closed and secured behind us. It sounds like a hundred hands are banging on the doors trying to get in. It's official: We're fighting something supernatural.

Anthony is on the phone with Angelo asking if I'm okay. I've stepped out of Matteo's rope and am looking over Guinevere to make sure she hasn't been harmed. I hug Matteo and thank everyone for their quick thinking. Because of their action, we made it safely into the stable. But the wind is still very active outside.

Suddenly the wind starts to bang against the closed doors at the opposite entrance of the stable. This means my father must be in control and directing the actions of his tornado. Matteo and I go into the empty stall for privacy so we can combine our power to locate our father.

Matteo calls Anthony to tell him our plan. He tells Anthony to keep everyone inside the mansion. It's too dangerous for anyone to be outside until the wind has stopped.

Matteo and I stand face to face, holding hands, with our foreheads touching. We drift into a realm only we can understand. We're searching for our father's image until we locate him. We successfully place a block around his mind, reducing his power and ability to control the tornado.

I imagine his estate in Mexico as Matteo, and I place our father's image within it. We place a block around the estate securing it like a prison. We allow only provisions needed for survival to be allowed in and nothing else. We're aware this is only a temporary solution. Our power will need to be reinforced regularly but it is well worth the effort to hold him for now. Matteo and I stay connected until we are sure we have imprisoned Leo Farina.

The wind has stopped, and the tornado funnel has disappeared. Cautiously looking out the stable door, we find all is calm, and things seem normal again. I decided this would be a good time to get back to the mansion. The stable doors are again open, and everyone seems to be going back to what they were doing as if this is just a natural thing that occurs on the ranch.

CHAPTER 42

Gabriella

The last two weeks passed quickly. We've had no additional items falling from the sky, no more tornados, and our lock on our father seems to be holding as there have been no new threats. The mansion has been totally repaired and brought back to its original glory. You would never know the extensive damage that had been done.

Ed and Mackenzie Carlton have been invited to be our guests this evening. Mackenzie is bringing her sister, Mackayla, who's come for a visit. Because Mackayla is a plus one, I thought Matteo's presence would benefit them both and even things out, eliminating the socially uncomfortable odd person situation.

I urged Anthony to invite Matteo to dinner. As Anthony's underboss and my brother, Matteo should be at all our social events, especially this one. It gives Matteo a chance to meet someone of interest. He's unaware I've planned this little introduction. It's only dinner and enjoyable conversation. Surely, he won't be mad at me. *Will he?*

Ed will be driving the Carlton Z2, the sports car that's the envy of every man on the planet. Anthony's eyes sparkle with desire every time he sees it. I remind him, "You can't drive the Z2 downtown, and most certainly can't park it anywhere safely. The Z2 wasn't made for stop and go traffic and going 200 miles per hour on our freeways would result in getting a speeding ticket or worse."

Anthony responds, "Yeah, but what a way to go!"

When the Carltons arrive, I expect the guys will spend time admiring the car while the girls have a little time to engage in small talk. I want Mackayla to feel comfortable so she can focus on Matteo. It would be nice if Matteo found someone. The ranch, being an hour away from civilization, doesn't offer many opportunities for socializing.

We've been notified by our men at the front gate that the Carltons have just arrived on the property. Anthony, Matteo, and I stand outside to greet them as the car approaches us and parks in front of the mansion.

Anthony steps off the porch to take a closer look at the legendary Z2 and to greet Ed, while I follow and hug Mackenzie. When Mackayla climbs out from the single seat in the back and exits the car Matteo looks as though he's been struck by lightning. He is almost frozen.

While Anthony's eyes were on the Z2, Matteo couldn't take his eyes off Mackayla. When Anthony makes the introductions, he can see the immediate attraction between Matteo and Mackayla. I couldn't be happier or more thrilled for Matteo.

Ed explains, "I'm driving the prototype. The car currently being manufactured will be racing in its debut this year. Anthony, I expect you to be there."

"I wouldn't miss it, Ed. You can count on that."

We escort our guests into the house offering them our hospitality. Our conversation is full of laughter and banter. Matteo and Mackayla are genuinely responsive to each other and can hardly take their eyes off each other.

There's still time before dinner is served when I ask, "Mackenzie and Mackayla would you like to go to the stable and meet my new horse, Guinevere?"

Anthony adds, "I think we would all like to be included, Gabriella."

"Wonderful! Shall we?" As I point to the door. Anthony and I, Ed and Mackenzie, enter one utility cart with Matteo and Mackayla selecting the other. The utility carts seat a maxim of four passengers, and I'm thrilled Mackayla and Matteo will be on their own for the short ride.

When we enter the stable, I can't help but notice Matteo standing close to Mackayla in a protective stance. I smile and I'm excited that their meeting is such a success. It looks like love at first sight, because Mackayla seems just as infatuated as Matteo is.

I reach into the treat bag for the horses and hand everyone a carrot explaining that once Guinevere gets her treat, all the other horses get one also. After introducing Guinevere, and giving her a treat, we continue on to greet, Quicksilver Sweet Georgia Brown, Prancing Beauty, and American Queen, giving them their treats. Everyone is enjoying their interaction with the horses.

When everyone has been able to provide a treat and pet each horse, Anthony looks at his watch and says, "Dinner should be ready, so I suggest we get back before my cook gets impatient."

Heading back to the utility carts, I notice Matteo extending his arm to Mackayla. She folds her arm into his when they walk arm in arm to the cart. I'm encouraged that this has the potential of becoming a relationship. Being friends with Mackenzie and having a relationship between Matteo and Mackayla could lead to a great extended family. That would be a wonderful outcome.

We were on our way back to the mansion when it sounded like something had landed on the top of our cart.

Ed asks, "What was that?"

Anthony replies, "Oh, ... not to worry, ... I must not have secured the visor properly. The strap must have come undone." *NO! Not, tonight of all nights."*

Anthony and I look at each other, concerned at what it could be. We continue to the mansion going faster than when we started. We reach the mansion and Anthony tells everyone to go in. Matteo escorts Mackayla inside, then turns back toward Anthony.

"Anthony, I saw something small land on the top of your utility cart."

"That's what I'm looking for now."

Anthony

I looked on the top of the cart and found the camera of one of the drones that was pulled into the black hole. Shaking my head I handed it to Matteo.

"Matteo, we'll have to wait until our guests leave before we can look at that. I'll tell Ed to park the Z2 under the carport. This is all we need."

Approaching Ed, I tell him, "If the wind should pick up tonight anything could be thrust against the car. It will make me feel easier if you park under the carport."

Matteo and I watch as Ed drives his car under the protection of the carport. Not knowing what more to expect, we stood ready for action just in case, while escorting Ed back to the mansion.

We sit down to dinner attempting to hide the stress that has taken over this night due to the falling camera. If that is the only thing that happens while our guests are here, I will be extremely grateful.

Proceeding with our meal, our guests are relaxed and enjoying themselves. My cooks have outdone themselves with great food, and the conversation is light and amusing. Jenna serves the dessert and sets a steaming carafe of coffee on the table. Gabriella suggested a game of cards when Mackayla gleefully pulled a deck of UNO cards from her purse.

Gabriella says, "I've been meaning to order us a deck of those cards. I'm so glad you brought them." She looks at us hopeful we'll agree to play when Matteo winks at Mackayla and says,

"Count me in. That looks like fun." Ed and I smile and then follow suit, also agreeing to play.

Gabriella

Mackayla hands the deck to Anthony and reads the basic instructions out loud just in case someone has never played before. When the instructions are read Anthony says, "Does everyone understand?" We all agree nodding and answering yes."

Anthony starts the game off by dealing the cards. As the game progresses, we indulge in boisterous laughter and half-hearted complaints when ending up with too many cards and someone else has the winning hand shouting "UNO."

Everyone has had a turn to deal the cards, and everyone has won a hand except Mackayla. We're on our last round, it's Mackayla's turn to deal, and I feel a shift. I look at Matteo and realize he's manipulating the outcome of this hand in Mackayla's favor. It's official, Matteo is smitten. This is so out of character for Matteo. I find it heartwarming.

Matteo has kept himself hidden his entire life and tonight he's allowing himself a small slice of enjoyment and happiness using his power to ensure his love interest wins a hand at UNO. I couldn't be happier.

We've finished the game and it's been an enjoyable evening. The night ended far too soon. We all seem to mesh so well together. Communicating with each other is so easy and natural. Nothing is forced; it's as if we're already a family.

We escort Ed and Mackenzie to the door. We are so busy talking about the next time we get together that I almost missed the fact that Matteo and Mackayla lingered back talking quietly to one another. They've exchanged phones entering their phone numbers in each other's cell phones. This has been a fantastic evening all the way around.

I can tell that Matteo doesn't want Mackayla to go, and Mackayla is hesitating to leave as well. Mackenzie remarks, "It looks like the love bug has bitten your brother and my sister."

"Yes, and they make a beautiful couple."

Mackenzie motions for Mackayla to come. They're waiting for her as she walks with Matteo toward us. Mackenzie says, "It was very nice to meet you, Matteo. We hope to see you again soon."

Ed shakes Anthony's hand and turns to shake Matteo's hand. "Yes, Matteo it was a pleasure to meet you. We'll be getting together soon."

CHAPTER 43

Anthony

Exiting the house while continuing our conversation we gather on the wrap-around porch. Ed and Anthony are just about to place their feet on the step when, without warning and out of nowhere, a double-edged sword falls from the sky striking the ground, standing straight up with its point penetrating deeply into the earth. It missed Ed by a foot. Shock and surprise caught us all off guard when Ed said, "Hell! Where did that come from?" pointing at the sword. "And a huge bird just flew over us."

Ed walks out further to look up attempting to get a better look at what he thinks is a bird. Matteo and I grabbed his arm, pulling him back under the protection of the covered porch. The sword is still vibrating, moving from side to side from the impact.

Mackenzie rushes to be next to Ed when Matteo grabs her arm telling her and Mackayla, "Quickly, go back into the house."

Mackenzie responds, "What's going on? Where did that sword come from?"

Ed says, "What the hell is going on here? Are we being attacked?"

The winged, horned man, flies down wearing nothing but his loin cloth. He perches himself on the porch banister looking at us as we look back at him. We quickly rushed back into the house slamming the door behind us.

Matteo pulls Anthony aside, "Did you notice all the holes in that thing?" There is no blood, just bullet holes. Bullets don't seem to faze it. Did you happen to see what it was before it was activated?"

Anthony replies, "No I didn't, but maybe Gabriella knows."

Anthony motions for Gabriella to come forward. "Gabriella, did you happen to see what that winged man was before he attacked?"

"Yes. He was a painting on the ceiling at our father's mansion."

Matteo says, "I know how we can fight it. Gabriella, keep the Carltons calm. Tell them the truth if you want. I'll take care of their selective memory when this is over."

Matteo sounds the alarm and calls Dominic and Giorgio to go to the workshop, giving them instructions on how to prepare to fight this entity.

"Anthony come with me. We need to get our weapons ready."

I'm unsure of what we can find in the laundry room besides a washer and dryer and laundry items. However, the room has become a temporary holding space for stored tools and things after undergoing construction to repair the damage to the mansion.

"Matteo, what are you looking for in our laundry room that can help fight that thing?"

"Anthony, help me empty these spray bottles of stain remover, fabric softeners, and bug spray."

"What! Matteo, you need to explain now or I'm going to think you've lost it."

"Anthony, that thing was a painting before Leo activated it. Nothing will affect it except, … this."

Matteo holds up two cans of paint remover.

"I informed our men to locate more paint remover and pour it into as many spray bottles as they can find."

"How is this going to work?"

"We'll try to spray his hands and arms first. Then his wings. Once he's totally disabled, we'll continue to spray him until he's just a swirl of paint on the ground." I think the only way he can be revived is if someone recreates him in a painting."

After emptying six spray bottles of their original contents, we pour equal amounts of paint remover into each of them. We check each sprayer to make sure they are working properly. Returning to the living room, we hand Ed, Mackenzie, Mackayla, and Gabriella each a spray bottle. Armed with the two remaining bottles we explain how we plan to protect ourselves against the winged man.

The winged man is actively looking for a way in. He bangs on the door and then flies from window to window knocking as he passes. He seems to become more determined and agitated as his knocking converts into powerful pounding. His actions take on a more frightening and sinister trait. We can see his eyes turn red as he passes by the windows.

He finally breaks through a window leading into the foyer. We were prepared for this as Matteo, Ed, and I stood side by side ready to spray him, but he flew right over our heads straight for the girls who screamed and grabbed onto one another. Thankfully they still have their bottles in their hands while the creature circles above them.

"Gabriella, I don't think he can tell the three of you apart. You all have blond hair!"

Gabriella lifts her bottle and aims it at the thing, but I caution her saying, "Gabriella he's too far away. Don't spray unless you know you can make contact. Don't waste the paint remover; that's all we have." Gabriella lowers her spray bottle keeping her eyes on the thing above her.

Suddenly it dives at the girls, grabbing Mackayla and lifting her high to the ceiling. Matteo runs toward the staircase leading to the second floor trying to get close enough to spray him. He sprays one of his wings, but it's not enough.

When the paint remover isn't effective, Matteo jumps on its back spraying more of the paint remover onto its wing. Finally, Matteo can see the color and the wing start to swirl and begin to dissolve just as he thought it would. The winged man lands on the floor with Mackayla, letting her go. Matteo grabs Mackayla holding her firmly in his arms as she clings to him.

He hurriedly rushes to confine Mackayla, Mackenzie, and Ed in the dining room. He tells Jenna, Michelle, and Angie to join them there. Matteo closes the entrances to the dining room instructing them to lock the doors.

Dominic and Giorgio arrive with their spray bottles of paint remover. Dominic tells Anthony, "Carlo, Angelo, and the men are standing by outside. They'll be ready for him if he escapes and heads their way."

"Good job, we might have enough to take care of him. Let's dissolve this painting once and for all."

The winged man is attempting to fly with only one wing but is unsuccessful. The men surround him continuously spraying him with paint remover. He's cornered and has nowhere to go. He sees Gabriella pointing to her as if he finally recognizes his objective, but it's too late.

The winged man has been reduced to a large swirling puddle of colorful paint. Matteo tells Dominic, "Ask Jenna for rags and dishcloths. We need enough to clean every drop of paint off the floor. Ask her to bring in that empty paint can in the laundry room."

The men take the cloths and wipe up every drop of paint using the last of the paint remover. Matteo has the men deposit the used rags into the empty can when he notices Mackayla has paint on her arm and it looks as if it's moving.

Fearful that he might have underestimated Leo's creation, Matteo points out. "The paint might be as active as the painting."

He takes his handkerchief and vigorously rubs the paint off Mackayla's arm then throws his handkerchief into the can. He says, "Inspect each other carefully. Any paint that might be on your clothing or skin must be removed and destroyed."

He walks out of the mansion placing the can next to the sword still standing where it landed.

"Does someone have a light?"

Giorgio hands him a lighter and Matteo lights the rags on fire. The fire turns into sparks, then a huge puff of smoke, then nothing, taking the sword with it. Matteo places the lid on the can tapping it tightly into place. Everyone looks bewildered that they just fought a painting.

Matteo asks everyone involved in witnessing what occurred to step inside. He wants to explain. Everyone except Gabriella and I sit comfortably in a semi-circle anxiously waiting for Matteo to begin. Matteo's voice becomes lower, softer, and more difficult to hear.

Gabriella

My new saddle arrived a couple of days ago, but I was unable to try it out until this morning. I'm in the stable watching as the white saddle blanket is draped over Guinevere. It has been specifically woven with the softest of yarn and fringed rather than tailored at the ends. Then Angelo places my saddle on top and fastens it onto Guinevere's body. He places her bridle and reins onto her head minus the bit per my instruction.

I ask Guinevere if she's comfortable, and she acknowledges with a scrape of her hoof. Though I have a stirrup to slip my foot into, Angelo hoisted me up with his hands. Lifting my other leg over Guiney, I land comfortably on my brand-new saddle. Having both my feet in the stirrups and holding the reins in my hands, I find it just as joyful as riding bareback.

I'm thinking, as we gallop toward the track, about last night. Once our guests' memories had been primed to forget certain elements of the evening, they left declaring how much they enjoyed themselves. We were then able to view the camera that started last night's ordeal.

The camera captured images of Dierdre, my father, Bennet, and numerous items floating past the lens. My father expressed no special messages or threats. It was a hodgepodge of things representative of floating in a galaxy somewhere, nothing more.

I hope after last night's failed attempt to force me to join him, my father might be thinking of leaving things as they are. Sending that thing for me was a weak attempt to gain control of me. I don't know what he expected but I'm not sure if he planned it or if it was a carryover from his original attempt to capture me. Either way, I'm safe and exactly where I want to be.

It's a beautiful day and Guinevere and I plan to make the most of it. I'm thinking of all the positive things happening in my life. I think about the day I met Anthony, my first job, my wedding, and the good things I've experienced. I think about my newfound brother Matteo, my friendship with Mackenzie, and my beautiful horse.

I'm especially happy to hear that Harold is recovering from his wounds. Thankfully Dierdre is no longer around, and Harold doesn't have to be reminded of her betrayal. My father made good on making her number (1) again, and Dierdre is more popular now than ever, especially since she's missing, and with all the conspiracy theories floating around on her behalf.

Matteo has already called Mackayla this morning making plans to see her. I'm already thinking ahead about how much fun it would be to plan a wedding for my brother. I overheard Matteo and Anthony discussing an organization for the benefit and support of my species. I'm not sure if something like that is possible. But … wouldn't it be fantastic?

I've just motioned to our drone following me; we're on our way to the racetrack. Life is good, and Guinevere and I are going to take advantage of this wonderful day. I looked down to reposition my foot into the stirrup when I noticed a speck of paint on my shoe. I'll have to remember to wipe it off when I go in.

The End … Or Is It!

ABOUT THE AUTHOR

Appreciating various hobbies, Lillie's interest lies in multiple tools, concepts, metals, and materials as she has extensive experience in the use of porcelain slip, 14K wire, glass, acrylic paint, and fabric. When she is not creating some form of art, she's constantly writing thoughts on Post-it notes or notepaper. Lillie's notes eventually take shape as a plot for a story. Always searching for the next challenge, she wrote her first book. As a new author, she's anxious to continue on this journey with her third book, and hopefully, readers will enjoy her stories.

Books by Lillie Timmons

The Don; The Story of Discovery, Deception, and Defiance

Big Trouble in Little Italy

Coincidental Entanglement